PRAISE FC
AND A1

"Dr. Frankenstein has at last perfected his art and hung out his shingle in Hollywood...a hell of a novel."

— STEPHEN COONTS, *NEW YORK TIMES BESTSELLING AUTHOR*

"With a Crichton-like mix of scientific intrigue and pulse-pounding suspense, the Gears deliver a fascinating exploration of the frontiers of science."

— *BOOKLIST* ON *RAISING ABEL*

"Gear writes superbly rolling prose with flair, confidence, wit, an ear for sounds, and an eye for details .... And he has another gift: the ability to teach his readers as he entertains them."

— *ROCKY MOUNTAIN NEWS* ON *THE MORNING RIVER*

"Extraordinary .... Colorfully integrates authentic archaeological and anthropological details with a captivating story replete with romance, intrigue, mayhem, and a nail-biting climax."

— *LIBRARY JOURNAL* ON *PEOPLE OF THE OWL*

GENESIS ATHENA

ALSO BY W. MICHAEL GEAR

Big Horn Legacy

Dark Inheritance

The Foundation

Fracture Event

Long Ride Home

Raising Abel

Flight of the Hawk Series

The Moundville Duology

The Wyoming Chronicles

Saga of a Mountain Sage Series

The Anasazi Mysteries

The Athena Trilogy

GENESIS ATHENA
THE ATHENA TRILOGY PART TWO

W. MICHAEL GEAR

WOLFPACK
PUBLISHING
— EST 2013 —

Genesis Athena
Paperback Edition
Copyright © 2024 (As Revised) W. Michael Gear

Wolfpack Publishing
701 S. Howard Ave. 106-324
Tampa, Florida 33609

wolfpackpublishing.com

Paperback ISBN 978-1-63977-190-5
eBook ISBN 978-1-63977-189-9

GENESIS ATHENA

CHAPTER 1

The water was colder than Nancy Hartlee had anticipated. A chill unlike anything she had ever experienced ate through her, trying to numb her muscles. Above, the night sky seemed remote, cold as the water, and as callous. She swam on, glancing up on occasion to orient herself by the bowl of the Big Dipper. Shivers were picking at the edges of her muscles. The midnight waters had an oily feel. From some vague corner of her mind, she was reminded that ocean swimmers greased their bodies.

Come on, Nancy. It can't be far.

Aboard ship, she'd seen the faint sparkles of lights just after dusk. She hadn't expected to see them from the water, not bobbing on the surface. Not until she got close.

Stroke after stroke, she forced herself forward. A leaden feeling had grown in her legs. Had it been so long since she'd been on the high school swim team?

It seemed a distant memory, as though from a dream life. She maintained the rhythm. Stroke and kick, stroke and kick. This race wasn't to the fast, but to the steady.

She had too much to live for. Not just herself, but the others. They all depended on her. No one had escaped before. It was all up to her. The world had to know what Genesis Athena was all about. No matter what the cost.

It would be so nice to stop, float, and rest for a bit.

Stroke and kick, stroke and kick.

She tried not to think of the black depths below. What did it matter? One hundred fathoms? Or fifty? All it would take in her condition was six feet.

Stroke and kick, stroke and kick.

She maintained her pace, doggedly panting as her muscles began to ache. A desperate fear had knotted in the back of her brain. What if she cramped?

Who would ever know?

No one. Only the black and lonely sea.

Stroke and kick. Stroke and kick.

Blessed God? Where are the lights? Please, just show me the lights!

CHAPTER 2

As the Gulfstream winged eastward with the night, acclaimed Hollywood screen sensation Sheela Marks glanced at her manager, Rex Gerber. He was in the window seat, his head lolled to the side, slack mouth agape. A faint snore was borne on each exhalation. The stubble on his dark cheeks marred the shiny texture of his skin. She could see where the oils in his hair and scalp had smudged the clear plastic of the window. What was it about men that they were at their most hideous when they were asleep in an airplane seat? Their breath seemed to taint the very air, thickening and fouling it with a faint odor.

She unbuckled her seat belt and stood, walking back in the hunched posture necessary to clear the Gulfstream's low cabin. Dot was propped sideways in her seat, a pillow cushioning her hair. Her two makeup and wardrobe women were likewise slumped on their side of the aisle.

Sheela found her private security agent, Lymon Bridges, and his newly hired investigator, Christal

Anaya, sitting across the aisle from each other in the rear. Lymon had the reading lamp on and was scrutinizing papers. Christal was frowning down at her laptop as she periodically tapped the *scroll* key. Sheela hunched down in the aisle between them. "What are you both doing awake?"

"Just double-checking the itinerary." Lymon tapped the papers on his lap. "We're on schedule for an eight thirty am arrival at Teterbough. We'll check into the St. Regis in the city by nine—traffic and security willing. You can nap until three. Makeup and prep until five, when you've got a podcast interview. *CosmoCeleb,* I think. At six thirty, Rex throws them out if they haven't left already. At seven, we leave for the premiere."

"I'm still a little hazy on this," Christal said. "We're flying to New York, checking into the hotel, watching a movie that Sheela didn't even star in, and flying back to LA the same night. Am I the only one who thinks that's a little nuts, or is there something wrong with Zoom presence?"

"Fox is going to be there," Sheela said with a shrug. "I have to smile and hug and schmooze in person. *Jagged Cat's* producers want me sucking up to the Fox bigwigs. The company producing *Jagged Cat* still hasn't locked down the distribution rights. Universal and Paramount are dickering for them, and involving Fox adds heat to the deal." A pause. "Can't do that with a Zoom call."

"Don't they have people to do the selling?" Christal seemed confused. "You're an actress. You're supposed to be playing a character."

"Christal, you seriously don't think that they just pay me to act, do you?"

"Uh…yeah."

"Oh, you dear naive girl." Sheela gave her a sympathetic smile. "This entire trip is targeted on three men who will be at the screening. They run Fox's film and streaming distribution. That means they put the movies into the theaters and on your television. My sole job is to smile and flirt, to snake my arm around their shoulders and bat my eyes suggestively. My people want pictures of me and the Fox management in *Variety, People,* and most of all, going viral on social media. By tomorrow morning, rumors will be floating all over Hollywood that Fox is interested in distributing *Jagged Cat.*"

Sheela managed a dry chuckle. "Next week, I'll be doing the same with Netflix, Apple TV, and Paramount to help sell the streaming rights. That will probably be in LA, but we might have to fly to San Francisco. It's all about whetting appetites."

Christal pursed her lips, frowning. "Just how far will people go?"

Sheela caught the undercurrent. "Christal, these deals can be worth tens of millions of dollars depending on the picture's success. It's just as ripe for abuse as any other deal when people stand to make or lose fortunes."

"I got it. Suddenly a midnight flight sounds perfectly reasonable." She paused, laughing. "Oh, hell!"

"What?" Lymon asked.

"I stood Tony Zell up. I promised him dinner tonight." She pulled out her phone, staring at the dark screen. "Bet when we land, I'll find a thousand frantic messages waiting."

Lymon burst out laughing. "He'll be stewing! That's

hilarious. Do you know when the last time was that a woman stood him up for dinner?"

"Nineteen ninety-six?" Sheela wondered. "Oh, Christal, what a blow to his overinflated ego. He's going to be drooling for you now."

"Lucky me."

"Make room." Sheela motioned Lymon over, aware of Christal's return to introspection. She replaced her phone and was evaluating something, expression pinched.

"What are you thinking?" Sheela asked.

"Brad Pitt was assaulted in New York tonight." Christal tapped her laptop suggestively. "He was getting into a cab when some guy in the crowd outside a club on West Fifty-second shot him in the ass with some kind of dart gun."

"That's a joke, right?"

Lymon, who had moved over to the window seat, slowly shook his head. "No joke."

"Shit!" Sheela dropped into his vacated seat, feeling his body warmth. Reassured by it. "So, they grabbed the guy?"

Christal continued, "Witnesses said he looked Middle Eastern, dark complexion, medium build. When spectators tried to interfere, some kind of stun device was detonated. Probably just like the one that flattened you and Lymon at the St. Regis a while back. In the confusion, he got away."

"The dart is interesting, too," Lymon remarked. "Kind of like a harpoon, it apparently spools out, impales its victim, and is reeled back in."

"So, how's Pitt?"

Christal was pensive. "They took him straight to

the emergency ward. They're running tests now. Trying to see if anything was injected. They've got him on antibiotics and an HIV protocol, just in case."

"It's not an injection." Lymon gave Sheela a meaningful look. "It's another...what? Specimen retrieval? Just like snipping a bit of Manny de Clerk's penis."

Sheela leaned back, closing her eyes. "This doesn't make sense."

"Witchcraft," Lymon muttered as he stared down at his papers.

"Hey," Christal chided softly from her seat.

Sheela glanced back and forth between them. "That's the second time I've heard that brought up. You want to fill me in?"

Lymon rubbed his eyes, then looked at her. She liked the concern in his weary hazel gaze as he said, "How are you on soul possession? Targeted evil? Voodoo dolls and the like?"

"Not very. I don't believe in that sort of thing."

"Neither do we," Christal answered. "It's just something we're tossing around. It has to do with the personal nature of the things being taken." She made a helpless gesture. "It shows how baffled we are, Sheela. Surely, you've heard the stories of witches collecting fingernail clippings, strands of hair, and navel lint. Taking some personal item to do sympathetic magic. It's the only comparison we can find. And it's silly."

"Is it?" Sheela felt a coldness in her breast. "Did Lymon tell you about my freaky fan? The one with the slice-and-dice course for unrequited love? She just knows that when I smile down from the screen, I'm smiling straight at her."

"Must make you feel peculiar."

"Until you've been there, I'm not sure I could ever make you understand. It curdles your soul. In a world full of eight billion people, how many of them have wounded minds? How many were abused as children? How many brain damaged? How many have fried their synapses with drugs? How many have chemical imbalances? How many live for their fantasies, and how many would sell their souls to satisfy their delusions?"

"I've heard figures as high as one to two percent," Christal answered. "More, given the right circumstances."

Sheela barely nodded. "One of the most horrifying moments of my career came after I made my first film, *Joy's Girl*. My character was a young prostitute. I did a scene that was sexually explicit."

"I've seen it. That expression on your face is a heart-stopper. Was he really that attractive?"

"Hey, there were thirty people on set at the time. I hated the guy. The director knew it, so he told me to imagine that my favorite dessert was being dribbled on my face. That's where that look came from."

Christal laughed in delight. "Wow! It worked. The first time I saw that, I thought the screen was going to melt. Every man in the theater walked out weak-kneed."

Sheela shrugged. "That scene was pieced together with bits from four days of brutal shooting. Do the shot, change the lighting, redo the shot, change the camera angle, redo the shot, change the color of the sheets, redo the shot. And on and on. You can only dream of chocolate soufflé for so long. After the first hour, I felt as sexy as bread mold."

She glanced at Lymon, curious about how he was

taking it. "It wasn't until the screening that I finally understood what a good film editor can do. I couldn't believe that was me up there. My manager at the time, Angel, leaned over and said, 'Well, kid, how about it? When this starts streaming, you're going to have a half million men playing it slow motion, over and over, while they slump on their couches and jack off.'"

"Yuck!" Christal gave her a disgusted look.

Sheela arched an eyebrow. "Sometimes, on really bad nights, I try to imagine that...all those men. I can picture them, illuminated in the television's glow, sweaty, hairy, their rumpled pants down around their knees, hands stroking, and their wide eyes fixed obsessively on mine. How are they playing it in their minds? What would they give to turn that momentary fantasy into the real thing?"

Christal swallowed hard and looked away. "Jesus."

Sheela made a gesture of acceptance. "In that instant, they all possess me in one way or another. Maybe my soul, but always my body. So, what's a little witchcraft compared with reality?"

CHAPTER 3

FBI Special Agent Sid Harness strode down the hall, his coat flapping as he entered the New York City medical examiner's office. He was still blinking, wishing desperately for another cup of coffee, and decidedly sleep-deprived. He'd had a whole blessed three hours of somnolence in his own bed, next to Claire's warm body before the phone rang.

He'd left his wife sleeping, taken a quick shower, driven into downtown DC, and parked his car in the long-term lot at Union Station. The morning train had taken him to New York's Penn Station. A cab had carried him to the ME's on the Lower East Side.

Now he hurried down the hall, found the right office, and leaned in the already-open door. He tapped lightly, calling, "Hello? I'm Special Agent Sid Harness for Dr. Helen Lambout."

A middle-aged woman who sat at the desk looked up, peering over the tops of her glasses. Gray streaked her brown hair, and her face had a severe look. A green surgical smock covered a gray dress.

She smiled and nodded. "Yes. DC said so͞ coming up. Come on in. Can I get yo͞ Coffee?"

He grinned at that. "Yeah, I'm running o͞. and nervous energy."

She studied him, apparently noting his swollen eyes and the lethargy that three hours of nodding to Amtrak's version of comfort had left imprinted on his face. "Come on. You'll want to see the lab results, too."

She led him back the way he'd come, down a flight of stairs, and along a hallway lined with examining rooms. They stopped in a small lunchroom with a table, chairs, a snack and pop machine, a microwave, and a stained coffeepot from which she withdrew a cup of something that looked like crankcase drippings.

Lifting the paper cup, she inspected it, peering through her glasses down her nose at the cup. "I don't know how fresh this is." She handed it to him with a shrug. "Creamer and sugar are there. While it's not necessary, any donation to the cause would be appreciated." She indicated a large coffee can marked DONATIONS with a slit in the plastic lid.

Sid fished out a dollar and slipped it through the slot. He tried the coffee, struggled to keep his face straight, and went for creamer and sugar after all.

As he sipped cautiously, he followed Dr. Lambout through double doors and into one of the forensic labs. He'd been in similar rooms before, but each time the surroundings sent a chill up his spine. The autopsy table with its lights, hoses, and drains always hulked like some ghost of the Inquisition. Computer screens displayed X-ray images. This room had a counter that sported a covered microscope, a small centrifuge, and

.ass-fronted cabinets full of test tubes, pipettes, beakers, boxes of rubber gloves, plastic specimen bags, and the other accoutrements of necropsy. Even the air seemed chillier.

Helen Lambout led him to the counter where a manila folder had the letters FBI marked prominently in black felt pen. She propped herself on one of the stools and flipped the cover open, asking, "Do you want to see the body, or are the photos sufficient?"

"The photos will do." He bent to peer at the glossy eight-by-tens. A naked woman lay on the table, eyes half-slitted in death. She looked incredibly pale, the whiteness a result of demise. Outside of being a floater, she appeared to be a typical Caucasoid woman of moderate build. He could see no immediate sign of trauma, no indication of any abnormality except that she was obviously dead. "Got a cause of death?"

"She drowned. Preliminary samples test positive for seawater. When we opened her up, we found no evidence of foul play. We're still looking for the more obscure pharmacology, but we came up negative on the usual: alcohol, marijuana, opioids, meth, and so forth. Internal organs look healthy."

"Stomach contents?" he asked.

"She had steak—beef, we think—at the last meal. Potato and broccoli were ingested about four hours before death. Again, the stomach contents tested negative for alcohol. Her lungs were fine, but deoxygenated from the salt water. We found no lesions on the skin, no evidence of injections or injuries. Vaginal swabs came back negative for semen or spermatozoa."

"Any scars?"

Lambout nodded. "A couple of faint scars around

the hands." She flipped back to a diagram that reproduced them. "And one longitudinal scar on the right thigh."

"From the time she had her femur pinned after a car wreck when she was twelve," Sid finished. "Did the pins match?"

Lambout shuffled through the photos to a photocopy of a radiograph. "This is the shot we took. Attached to it with a paper clip is the fax her physician in California sent to us last night. That, along with the dental records, are pretty conclusive. We won't know on the DNA until next week at the earliest. Dermatoglyphics will be in sometime this afternoon."

"Where did you get a reference sample of her DNA?"

"She left a lot of it. All curated at the California lab." Lambout tapped the folder with a narrow finger. "You want my opinion? I'm ninety-nine point nine percent positive that this is Nancy Hartlee's body."

Sid frowned as he flipped the pages back to show a photocopy of a nautical chart. "So, tell me, Doctor, where has Nancy Hartlee been for the last five years? And just why do you think her body was found floating ten miles out from the beach off Long Island?"

CHAPTER 4

My god, have I ever been this tired? The question rolled around in Christal's head as Lymon walked back and opened the limo door for Sheela. The crowd exploded in applause and whistles as Sheela took Lymon's hand and stepped out into the New York night. Lymon wore a black tux, and Sheela was resplendent in a powder-blue Ungaro gown, her metallic red hair up, with ringlets falling about her pale shoulders.

Flashes of white lit the night, popping in the crowd like bottled lightning let loose. Christal could hear the frantic click of the shutters as she ducked out on Sheela's heels. Christal had outfitted herself in an off-the-rack black Ralph Lauren she'd found on sale during a last-minute panic trip to Bloomingdale's.

Reporters were calling out in a cacophony. "Sheela!" "Ms. Marks!" "Have they found your tampon?" "Sheela! Look this way!" "Sheela! How do you feel about the recent publicity?" "Sheela! Is it true that someone cut off Manuel de Clerk's penis?" "How

do the recent assaults affect your shooting schedule?"
"Sheela! Who are you seeing these days?"

"Remember." Lymon bent close, shouting into Christal's ear. "You have her left. Stay close behind her and keep your eyes open."

She did, forcing herself to concentrate, eyes on the crowd as she and Lymon followed a half pace behind Sheela. Christal wore an earpiece along with a throat mike at her collar. Somehow the fragile-looking velvet ropes held the mob at bay. Ahead of them, Sheela walked up the red carpet to the theater entrance. She was waving, nourishing the feeding horde with her famous smile.

"How does she do it?" Christal wondered as she squinted against the lights, searching for any sign of threat in the press of bodies behind the ropes. She kept the mantra in her head: Attacks come from the third row back. It seemed like a sea of shining faces and glittering eyes. To her, they all looked like predators.

"Sheela's a pro," Lymon answered, his voice barely audible. How the hell had he heard her over the raucous babble?

Once they were checked through the theater's security, the lobby was crowded with black-tie-clad men in sharp tuxedos, women in exotic, expensive, and often revealing evening gowns, and liveried caterers passing through the throng like fish in seaweed with trays of champagne, caviar-heaped crackers, and other goodies. Every wall was covered with huge posters hawking *Night Stalker* and its stars.

Christal picked out faces: Jennifer Lawrence, Bradley Cooper, and someone she thought might be Lady Gaga beneath a garish hat. Halle Berry, clad in something that looked like cellophane, was surrounded by smiling men, some of whom pointed microphones toward her mouth.

The not-so-well-dressed wandered around talking into their cell phones or tapping on the screens. Christal assumed these were the dreaded critics come to pass judgment on the final product. They seemed to move from star to star, talking, taking photos with their phones.

Then Christal fixed on the elegantly dressed men in the rear and off to the side. None of them looked distinctive, but each had a following. The moguls, perhaps?

"Sheela, *darling!*" an elderly woman in silver sequins cried; she flowed forward with an outstretched hand. "How perfectly *ghastly* that someone would do these things!" A throng rushed in on her wake, washing around Sheela.

Taking Lymon's cue, Christal followed him as he split off and walked toward the side of the room.

"From here on out..." Lymon told her as they took a position under one of the huge posters that showed a hard-eyed Halle Berry staring down the sights of a huge silver semiautomatic pistol. "We just try to be unobtrusive."

Christal nodded, aware of the other wallflowers— mostly men, professionally dressed—who stood, watching alertly at the fringes. When their gazes crossed Lymon's, they would give a slight nod, then move on. Some spared Christal a great deal more than just a second glance. She could feel herself being sized up. The rest of the Brethren, she decided.

"How do you determine who's who?" she asked,

indicating the people in the center of the room. Some were obvious sycophants; others seemed to be movers and shakers. Photographers slipped about like coyotes around a flock of sheep.

"Watch how much a person moves," Lymon answered. "The closer a person is to the top of the heap, the less he moves through the crowd. Those guys"—he pointed to a knot off to one side—"are the Fox bigwigs. They've got nothing to prove to anyone. They won't move until the curtain call. Watch Sheela. She'll drift her way over to them without seeming to. Power meeting power."

Christal studied Sheela, having seen her at the Wilshire reception but unaware of the social dynamics. A collection of people had gathered around her, laughing and smiling. Others worked their way through the press to take her hand, give her a slight hug, or that faint kiss of the cheeks that had taken so long to come back in fashion after COVID. New Mexico-raised Christal still found that custom peculiar.

She was considering that when she saw the dark man; he didn't fit. Instead, he stood to one side, his black eyes fixed, gleaming, and focused on Sheela Marks. He remained oblivious to everyone else in the room—even though Sam Elliot stood no more than two paces to his right. He was dressed immaculately in a black silk tuxedo that shimmered in the light like an insect's shell. She pegged him for a rich Arab by his facial features, complexion, and the regal way he held himself.

"Lymon?"

"Hmm?"

"Check out the guy. He's alone, standing five feet to

Sheela's right. He's all by himself, detached, and if my instincts are right, he's not a movie type."

Lymon fixed on the man. "Not a movie type at all. He looks like oil money. A lot of rich oil Arabs invest in films. Hell, give me ten or twenty million worth of discretionary cash and I might, too." A pause. "He's sure holding a bead on Sheela, isn't he?"

"Trouble?"

Lymon gave a faint shake of the head, frowning as he watched the guy watching Sheela. "Probably not. At least, not that kind. You don't get in the door without an invitation." He paused. "Still, I don't like him. That expression on his face isn't right. Hell, he's not even blinking. Just keep an eye on him, okay? He can drool all he wants, just so he doesn't touch."

Christal's gaze kept going back to the hawkish Arab. In her grandmother's quaint vernacular, the guy made her whiskers vibrate. What was that look in his eyes? An almost obsessive gleam. She had seen men at livestock auctions stare at prize animals with that same careful appraisal.

"It's hardly a livestock auction," she muttered, forcing herself to turn her attention elsewhere.

"Pardon?" Lymon asked.

"Nothing."

"A livestock auction? Is that what I heard you say?"

"Yeah. Silly, huh?"

Sheela had managed to drift her cluster of admirers to within several feet of the Fox executives. Then, most artfully, she turned on her heel, seemed surprised, and rushed to greet the first of them. She kissed the man on the cheek, and over the babble of conversation, Christal heard, "...so *glad* to see you!"

The photographers, like hunters from a blind, seemed to pop up from the very carpet, their cameras clicking. Sheela gave a little cry and skipped to her second target.

Christal gaped, even knowing it was an act. Sheela seemed to radiate joy at being in their presence.

"She's good, isn't she?" Lymon asked.

Sheela melted against another of the men, her posture a balance of restraint and provocation. Was that another of her arts? The ability to be both tasteful tease and provocative temptress in the same breath? Was that part of the A-list portfolio?

"So, the trip's a success?" Christal asked.

"She'll work them all night." Was that weariness in Lymon's voice? "After the preem, Sheela will attend the Fox party. By the time she leaves, she'll have dates with each of those guys."

"No way!"

"Yeah, but none of them will happen. There are shooting schedules, conflicting business meetings, and last-minute cancellations, and what do you know? After a month has gone by, it's all forgotten but the goodwill."

Christal shot Lymon a sidelong look, aware of the hardness in his eyes and the muted tones of his voice. Puzzling at it, she was on the verge of revelation when her sixth sense made her glance back at the Arab. A second man had walked up to stand just out of sight behind the Arab's right elbow. Christal couldn't see his face, but he spoke in a confidential voice. The Arab leaned his head slightly to hear better, then nodded, a slight smile on his thin lips.

Christal craned her neck, trying to see the newcomer's face. Something about him haunted her: the way he moved, the set of his shoulders, and the gestures he made.

"Just a minute, Lymon." Christal moved out from the wall and angled behind the group that surrounded Elliot. The Arab and his shadow were moving now, heading toward the door. That walk! Damn it, yes. She *knew* him.

Christal hurried along the wall, paralleling the Arab's course, trying to thread her way through the packed bodies with as much decorum as she could.

The man was still on the Arab's off side. Christal had closed the distance, angling up on the right. She could smell the Arab: a perfumed scent, not unpleasant, but not attractive, either. He was tall, aloof, and walked with a liquid grace. A look of deep satisfaction, as if someone had just used oiled fingers to massage his soul, was betrayed by his lingering smile.

They were nearing the door, the Arab still blocking the view. "Excuse me," Christal called, stepping close.

The tall Arab turned rapturous black eyes on her, unfocused as if she had just interrupted a reverie.

"Oh, sorry," she said with a smile. "I thought you were Antonio Banderas." But her gaze went to the shorter man, who stepped past the Arab to see her. In that instant, their eyes locked and the world stopped.

Christal's heart skipped, then began to pound. He looked just as shocked as she did, those familiar eyes wide and disbelieving. An instant later, a rush of loathing rose to replace the surprise in his face.

"Chris?" he stumbled. "What the hell...?"

"Sorry, Hank," she managed through a clenched jaw. "Your friend here *isn't* the guy I'm looking for."

The Arab had turned confused eyes on Hank, then glanced back at Christal. He smiled then, saying in a whisper-accented voice, "She is a beautiful woman. Spirited. You know her?"

A feather of fear tickled within her as a growing appreciation filled the Arab's eyes. He studied her face, bending slightly to stare at her breasts and the way her dress rode the curve of her waist and hips.

Shit! Mistake! Get the hell out of here!

"Sorry to bother you, Hank. Have a nice night."

She spun on her heel and kept her back straight as she turned, walking back toward the side of the room. She could feel the Arab's hungry eyes; a creepy shiver crossed her skin, and a terrible sickness was spreading in her gut.

For some reason she couldn't comprehend, she joined the periphery of Cooper's group. Maybe it was some primal urge—a search for safety in numbers. The muscles in her legs had gone rubbery. She clamped her jaw tight to keep it from trembling.

Cooper was saying, "What? Sure, I'm typecast. What do I care? If it's a good script…"

Taking a quick glance, she could see Hank Abrams talking rapidly, gesturing with his hands as he walked with the Arab out past the guards at the door. In that last instant, Hank shot a quick look over his shoulder, meeting Christal's gaze. A smothered rage burned there, seething and coiled.

"What's up?" Lymon appeared like magic at her shoulder.

"I haven't got the foggiest idea." She glanced hesitantly at Lymon as he led her away.

"You want to tell me who that guy is?"

"No." She could see the irritation growing behind Lymon's flinty expression. "But I guess I'm going to have to, huh?"

He lifted a wary eyebrow.

She said, "Yeah, later, all right? When I get my guts back."

She was saved when a voice called out, "Ladies and gentlemen, if you will take your seats, you are about to be part of filmmaking history! The premiere screening of *Night Stalker* is just five minutes away!"

A sporadic burst of applause and cheers was followed by people walking toward the doors on either side of the concession stand where harried caterers still poured champagne.

"What now?" Christal asked, taking a deep breath and centering her quivering soul.

"Now we wait." The question was hanging unanswered between them.

"We don't get to see the movie?"

"Sure. Either buy a ticket when it comes to a multiplex near you or rent it from whatever streaming service has picked up distribution rights." He was watching her, the look evaluative. "Meanwhile, come on. I'll introduce you around. Like everything else, personal security is a small world."

Yeah, a world that has Hank Abrams squiring a mysterious Arab—one with a penchant for raping women with his eyes.

CHAPTER 5

Ever since the Gonzales disaster had ended both his marriage and his FBI career, Hank Abrams had hated walking down halls to his supervisor's office. But here he was, once again plodding down a much-plusher hallway.

Verele Security's Manhattan headquarters dominated the entire twenty-second floor of the Flatiron Building where Broadway crossed Fifth Avenue at 23rd Street. It was a successful company. The offices reflected that and were furnished with expensive decor, nice woodwork on the walls, thick carpeting, and occasional pieces of artwork that gave the place just the right cachet.

Once, Hank Abrams had radiated in the attention of his superiors. Now their slightest notice of his existence sent the heebie-jeebies up his backbone. Dear God, why had Verele sent for him? He couldn't be sure, but he was afraid it was because of the very same woman who had ruined his career in the FBI.

An ill feeling had settled on his stomach—heavy

like a carry-out fast-food breakfast. The sensation in his too-tight nerves reminded him of the metallic sense of touching a nine-volt battery to his tongue.

He pushed open the frosted glass door to his boss's office and walked up to the glossy ebony desk where Trina, the secretary, held sway. She looked up, a knockout attractive Black woman of thirty-five who had the most omniscient eyes of anyone—male or female—that Hank had ever known.

"Verele sent for me."

"Gotcha, Hank." She gave a smooth tilt of her head to indicate the door. "He's waiting for you."

"Thanks." Hank took a deep breath, squared his shoulders, and straightened his tie before he pushed the door open and walked into Verele's lair.

He had been here once before when he was hired, but the place still set him back. The white carpeting had to be worth five hundred dollars a square foot. It was like walking on air. Whoever had designed the decor of black walnut, polished cherry, mirrors, and chrome had been a genius. It actually worked, each element complementing the other. Huge floor-to-ceiling windows gave a view up both Broadway and Fifth. Down below, traffic was flowing in slow starts and stops. The lower roofs of Midtown gave way to the upper Manhattan skyline in the hazy distance.

The big desk in the middle of the room was a composite of red cherry wood and chrome, its surface dominated by two computers, a modular communications system, and several telephones. An open laptop rested to one side. In a monstrous chair, upholstered with overstuffed soft maroon leather, sat a very small man.

Verele Yarrow was more than a dwarf and less than short. He stood four foot five inches tall, his head over-sized and nearly bald. Light-blue eyes watched the world from a wide face, and the guy's nose was like a misshapen ball. On this day he was dressed in a bluish silver silk suit.

When Hank had first met him, he'd almost made the mistake of judging Verele by his caricaturish looks. Then the man had spoken, and all doubt had vanished. His speech was precise, articulate, and his intellect cut like a hammer-forged Randall blade.

"Good day, Mr. Abrams," Verele began in his crisply formal way. "I thank you for your prompt arrival."

"Yes, sir." Hank tried to ignore the butterflies in his stomach.

"I would like to thank you for your excellent attention to the Sheik last night. You did very well in your first stint as a detail leader. The evaluation of your performance is excellent for your initial assignment in the hot seat. By the way, I think you've been informed that the Sheik will require your services again this evening."

A faint wave of relief washed through him. "Thank you, sir. Yes. My team picks him up at the Ritz-Carlton at six tonight. I understand that I'm to take him to one of the piers in Brooklyn."

"That is correct. As detail leader, you are to accompany him and his people. Take a small kit with you. Pack light. I'm not sure just how long this detail will take, but plan for several days at a minimum." The light-blue eyes narrowed. "Whatever you see or hear is strictly confidential, do you understand?"

Hank swallowed hard. "Yes, sir." He winced. "Sir, I am an ex-FBI agent. I wouldn't want...I mean—"

"You will not be required to participate in anything illegal, Hank." Verele watched him intently. "Our mandate is the protection and safety of our clients. That is our only responsibility. Beyond that, we do not ask, we do not care. You should not be compromised in your service of the Sheik over the next couple of days." He paused, seeming to look right past Hank's defenses. "Do you have a problem when it comes to not asking and not caring?"

"No, sir."

"Good. Now, about last night. There was a woman?"

The relief was replaced with fear. "Yes, sir. I think I should explain, sir. She approached me. I did nothing to initiate contact."

"I'm sure that is the case. The Sheik reported that she actually approached him." A slight smile bent his broad lips. "Thought he was Antonio Banderas? The Sheik was flattered. He is also very interested in the woman."

"He is?" That caught Hank out of left field.

"You know her."

"Yes, sir." He swallowed hard. "She was at the Bureau when I was."

"We already know a little about her. Now we would like to know more. Tell me about her." The light-blue eyes hardened like marbles. "*All* about her."

Hank winced. "Yes, sir." And the story began to pour out of him.

CHAPTER 6

Christal and Lymon sat at their usual table in the back of Al's Hollywood restaurant. She glanced sidelong at her boss. He was carefully scraping tamales from their corn husks, his fork peeling the steaming *masa* onto his plate. She hovered over a medium-rare buffalo filet with mashed sweet potatoes and wild rice. To drink she had selected a Sierra Nevada Pale Ale; Lymon nursed something called an Alaskan Smoked Porter. The color of it reminded her of the stuff mechanics drained out of engines.

They had only catnapped on the flight back from New York. She had been deposited at her hotel room at the Marriott Residence Inn a little after one yesterday afternoon and would have slept clear through but for an annoying phone call from Tony last night at seven. She'd promised to call him back when her brain functioned again. Then, that morning, she had taken Lymon's call to have lunch at noon. By some not-so-subtle feminine instinct, she knew exactly what he wanted to discuss.

"I think it was a combination of things," she said. "Hank was really on a roll. So was I. It was his first big investigation, and I was the spark plug that gave it combustion. I'd figured out the link that tied the entire Gonzales puzzle together." She glanced at Lymon. "We were both high on success, and it just kind of happened. Hank was handsome, smart, and full of confidence. Like I was telling Sid that night. Hank listened."

"And he was married."

She lifted a weary eyebrow. "Lymon, sometimes that gets lost in the rush, you know? Especially on a long investigation. We were together day in and night out. I knew he wasn't...well, what I'd look for in a man. But he was there."

"You said he was a smart guy."

"Yeah. Really smart. I suspect he'd have eventually busted Gonzales without my input. He's got a good head for organization and detail. He's quick, methodical, and orderly. He ran a good operation. We didn't have many screwups in the field because Hank could keep all the balls in the air and know which one to toss up next."

"Was he the stick-to-it type?"

"More or less. Not really a bulldog, but I had him figured for promotion to special agent in charge within five years. He was a bright-burning candle, and when he looked at you right, those brown eyes would melt you."

"Is that what happened?"

Christal stared at the square of buffalo steak dangling on her fork. "We'd had a few drinks together just before we went on duty." A pause. "Well, maybe I had a few more than I should have. I don't normally do that, but we were flushed with success. That was Tuesday; by Friday, we were going to actually make the arrest. Hank had volunteered to change shifts with one of the other guys whose wife was having a baby. Hank asked if I wanted to take that shift with him. You know, just company. I said yeah."

She chewed thoughtfully as she replayed that night in her head. "We met at a place for a late dinner. It was just past ten. Maybe it was the hour. Maybe it was because I wasn't really going to be on duty—just standing in, you know? But I had a martini. I hate vodka. Then I had another. It was fun, Lymon. We were laughing—both of us on top of the world. It was a celebration."

She attacked the sweet potato. "When we relieved the guys in the van at midnight, we were still giddy. Nothing was happening. Gonzales's place was empty, the house completely dark. One of the guys we worked with had a bad back. He had one of those thin little blue foam pads rolled up on the floor." She sipped her soda. "It just happened. Him and me in the middle of the night. One minute we were sitting next to each other, watching the screens, and the next we were kissing; then we were on that blue mat."

She glanced at Lymon, seeing understanding in his eyes. "Would I have screwed him if I'd been stone-cold sober? Yeah, probably. I was attracted to the guy."

"Did anyone ever figure out how they compromised the van?"

"No. After the photos landed on the director's desk, they searched that van—and I mean thoroughly. They got squat. Whoever had put the camera in had taken it out again. From the resolution, it was a very good camera." She avoided his eyes. "You can see everything. God, how humiliating."

"And then Hank shows up at the *Night Stalker* premiere in New York with an Arab who is fixed on Sheela like a Brittany spaniel on a pheasant." Lymon jabbed halfheartedly at his tamales. "If you'll remember, we were sitting right here when Sid said that Hank had taken a job with Verele Security."

"Escorting mucky-mucks."

"Yeah, mostly the hyper-rich. There's specialization in this business. Multibillionaires have different concerns than actors do. Their biggest fear is either assassination or kidnapping. Sometimes it's corporate espionage. Their security is based on creating a safe buffer zone. Our job at LBA is tougher. We have to ensure personal privacy and bodily safety for very public people. In a lot of ways, their job is easier. They can build walls."

"He'd be good at that."

"Pardon me?"

"Hank Abrams. He'd be good at executive protection. Like I said, he's got a thing for the little stuff. In fact, he's a nut about details. He did things like plot the route we were going to take on an operation. He'd know the nearest hospital, have a list of alternatives, that sort of thing."

"Then he's a natural for executive protection. Good advancing is what it's all about. If you ever get jumped, have to use your cover-and-evacuate skills, it's already too late. You've screwed up."

"You can't always predict all the details."

"You can try." Lymon paused. "I did some checking.

The Arab was Sheik Amud Abdulla. He's a Saudi national who lives in Qatar. He put twenty million into the production company that made *Night Stalker.* The funny thing is, he wasn't going to attend. Then, at the last minute, he flew in."

"And didn't stay for the movie."

"Maybe it's just me, but I thought he was just there to see Sheela."

"Almost like he walked in, got an eyeful, and walked out," she agreed. "I remember you saying he could drool, but not touch."

"You were the one who said it was like a livestock auction. What brought that on?"

"He was looking at her like she was a piece of meat." Christal shivered. "Lymon, I swear, he was looking right through my clothes when I stopped him at the door. He went from dreamy-eyed to rapacious. He was talking to Hank like I wasn't really there."

Lymon took a swig of his porter, pursed his lips, and frowned. "I'm going to mention it to Max. He's all wrapped up with the follow-through for the meetings he had on Wall Street. He used the trip for face time with the people who handle Sheela's investments. I think I ought to give him a heads-up."

"How come?"

"Just in case the good Sheik Abdulla wants to invest in one of Sheela's pictures."

Christal considered that. "You think ten or twenty million worth of investment would come with strings attached?"

He gave her a guarded look. "It happens. Funding for a fuck or two. It's all a weird game, mostly driven by power, by who can control whom. Think of the rush a certain type of man would get knowing that his money gave him control of Sheela Marks, even if just for a night or two. Is that Godlike, or what?"

"Why do people even get involved in this business?"

"Because balancing out the scum, you will always find the ones who want to make movies: the artists and creators. They're the myth makers and storytellers—our tribal shamans. You know, the spiritual dreamers with the glow of universes in their eyes. They spin dreamlike fantasies to make people feel better about themselves. They give visions of hope to a society that is glutted with riches but suffering from a poverty of the soul."

He lifted a lip. "Then you have the parasites. The people in suits. They've figured out ways to make money off of the creators, dreamers, and doers. They're the brokers, lawyers, agents, accountants, and shady producers. In Hollywood, if someone has an MBA, count your fingers after you shake hands. Chances are, a digit or two will be missing."

She sipped her beer. "I know the type. In my part of the world, they're called Anglo bankers. Somehow anyone who ever went to one for a loan ended up thrown off his land."

"Speaking of the sharks, how's Tony?"

"The guy's desperate, I guess. He left a note taped to my room door. I've got seven messages on my cell phone. I'm supposed to call him as soon as I get an off moment."

"Watch him."

She laughed at that. "Hey, he's not a Hank Abrams.

Not even close. How on earth do I take someone who calls me 'babe' seriously?"

"He's one of the biggest agents in Hollywood." Lymon studied her thoughtfully. "With your looks, he's going to offer you a screen test."

"He already has." She shrugged. "It's a ploy to get me into his bed. Maybe you'd better warn him that the last man I was involved with wasn't happy afterward."

"Aren't you just a little curious?"

"About going to bed with Tony? Are you nuts?"

"No. About the screen test."

She smiled. "Maybe, Lymon, when this is all over. Sure. It would be fun. Just for kicks, you know? But I'm not fooling anyone. I'm not even close to Sheela Marks in caliber. Had I been in her place, those Fox executives would have laughed me out of the room, and I'd have blown the deal."

"False modesty doesn't become you." He smiled, changing the subject. "So, now we've added Pitt to the list. Who's next?"

She considered that. "Something's been on my mind. I keep coming back to Genesis Athena."

"I looked at their questionnaire. When I read the questions, they were just questions. Some of them, like the ones about the bathroom, seemed pretty silly."

"So, why does a company pay out as much as they do to support a website full of silly questions?"

"Got me. It's their money."

"I think," she said coolly, "that it's time to take the test, Lymon."

CHAPTER 7

Sheela took a deep breath and held it as she stood on her cue under the burning set lights that illuminated the wrecked kitchen. All eyes fixed on Manuel de Clerk. The tension in the room was palpable, like a ticking bomb. Sheela tensed, pleading, *Come on, Manny, you can do it this time.*

For this scene she wore a short-cropped wig, and her face had been smudged by makeup. Her loose T-shirt was blood smeared and torn to give the slightest glimpse of her right breast. She was standing on a taped X in the ransacked kitchen. The table was turned over, flour had been thrown around, and silverware lay strewn across the countertop behind her. She gripped a rusty hunting knife as though ready to use it.

Across from her Manny de Clerk had stopped on his cue, made the half turn Bernard wanted, but the stern glare he was supposed to give the camera collapsed into a sad convulsion. A sob caught at the bottom of his throat, his mouth puckering.

"Cut!" Bernard called and let loose with a string

of curses. Moans could be heard around the set. Then Bernard came storming out from behind the camera, a fist knotted and shaking as he stomped up to de Clerk, shouting, "Goddamn it! Get it together!"

"You don't understand!" Manny implored. "Dear God, I just see her. Smiling down at me. That knife in her hand!"

"Yeah, Sheela's got a knife. Remember the scene? She's supposed to chase your ass out of the kitchen with it!"

"No, I see that *woman!* She *cut* me!"

Bernard waved his arms. "That's fucking bullshit, Manny. I read the medical report. She nicked your dick. Ninety percent of the babies in this country get circumcised—and it's a hell of a lot more traumatic than what happened to you!"

"I'd say forty-five percent," Sheela offered flatly.

"Huh? What?" Bernard turned on her.

"More than half of those babies are girls, and a moderate percentage of boys aren't circumcised for various cultural reasons." Sheela tossed the knife up, catching it by the blade tip—a trick she'd learned in the filming of *Blood Rage.*

Manny continued to sob.

"What the hell do I have to do?" Bernard shook his head and lifted his hands imploringly to the lights that hung on the overhead scaffolding.

"Call it for today," Sheela said wearily. "Get the man some professional help while we shoot the scenes with me and Gene." She looked across to where de Clerk's double stood off camera. He nodded woodenly as Sheela continued, "Shoot the scenes with de Clerk later.

Spot Manny in later, and if worse comes to worst, use AI."

Bernard granted her a speculative look. "You think that would work?"

She lifted a challenging eyebrow. "I could oversee it, shepherd it through the process—but I'd want your cut of box office."

"What about costs? It'll be a fortune!"

"Bernard, if the rest of us hoof it, we can move ahead of schedule, right? Each day we save is a day's overhead you can move to FX."

De Clerk had wilted to the floor. Bernard's lip was quivering as he physically fought to keep from sneering. "Yeah, right." Turning, he called to his assistant, "Vern, call Manny's agent. Have him take care of this."

Sheela stuck the knife into the wooden countertop and peeled the close-cropped wig off. She tossed it to the costume assistant and pulled out the bobby pins before running her fingers through her hair. She shook it out as she walked off the set, passing the cameras.

Bernard followed behind, saying, "I just don't get it. What's with this guy?"

"He's a wimp," she told him, speaking so the grips and riggers couldn't hear. "I didn't want to do this picture with him, if you'll recall. And I can damn sure tell you I'd never have won that Oscar if he'd been in *Blood Rage* like they'd originally cast him."

"So, why'd you agree this time?" Bernard asked, a sour note in his voice.

"Because, you begged, Bernie. Remember?" She sounded jaded, and she knew it. At the stage door, she paused. "Look, just change the schedule. We'll shoot all of my scenes and those with the rest of the cast. It'll be brutal, but it will put us ahead of schedule. And as for the stuff we've got to do on location, I'm serious: Use a stand-in and fix it in post production."

He hesitated, hanging in the doorway after she'd stepped out. "When it gets out, it could ruin his career."

"As if what he's doing in there isn't already accomplishing just that?" She met Bernard's worried eyes. "See you in the a.m."

She walked to her trailer and climbed the aluminum steps. When she entered, Lymon was kicked back on her couch, his legs up on the small coffee table as he flicked fingers up the screen of his iPhone. Glancing up, he read her expression and asked, "What's wrong?"

"Manny's a basket case. Bernard's panicking." She walked to the refrigerator and pulled out a beer, lifting it so he could see. "You want one?"

Lymon shook his head. "I'm working."

Sheela popped the top and walked over to settle on the couch beside him. She leaned her head back, took a deep breath, and sighed. "God, I'm tired. That's the bad news. The good news is that I used Manny's breakdown as a way of getting the schedule changed. If Bernard does it my way, I'm out of here in two weeks instead of a month."

"Have you ever heard of Sheik Amud Abdulla?"

She gave him a sidelong glance. "Should I have?"

"He was watching you at the *Night Stalker* preem. Christal picked up on it. If he gets in touch with you, let me know, all right?"

"Jealous?"

"Worried. The way he was watching you wasn't normal. I want you to keep your antenna up. Thing number two: Krissy sent an email to your website. She wants you to know that she's having your baby."

Sheela couldn't help herself: She laughed, almost spilling her beer. "Well, at least that's an improvement. She's gone from sharp objects to pregnancy. Did she say just how she was having my child? Seems to me, last time I looked, the equipment was wrong—or am I missing something in the translation?"

Lymon pursed his lips. "Yeah, well, if you were to ask me, I think your equipment looks pretty good—not that I'm an expert or anything."

"Oh, yeah? I've caught you studying my equipment a time or two in the past. As to being an expert, anyone who passes a high school biology class ought to have a pretty good idea of what goes where on a woman. Or, in the age of LGBTQ+, do they even care about that anymore?" She gave him a chiding look. "You been holding out on me? At this late date, are you trying to tell me that you only plug your current into male sockets?"

"I'm into the normal man-woman thing. Always have been. I was referring to your *private* equipment."

"God, I love it when you blush." She chugged more of her beer. "Lymon, when they finally put *Jagged Cat* in the can, why don't you and I go away somewhere and I'll let you run any kind of equipment checks you want."

She saw a stirring in the depths of his hazel eyes as he said, "Why on earth do you think you could stand me?"

"Because you're a man. I'm tired of all these artsy-fartsy, sensitive, soul-bleeding Hollywood types." She turned, pulling her knee up between her hands and looking him in the eyes. "Tell me, if some woman cut off a piece off your male part, would you break down and turn into a sniveling idiot?"

His grizzled smile sent a throb through her. "Lady, the woman ain't alive who could get that close to me with anything sharp. And if she did to me what she did to de Clerk, I'd be after her in a way she wouldn't want to consider in her baddest nightmares."

"You could hurt a woman?"

His expression had taken on a hard edge. "You don't want to know."

"What if I do?"

He studied his hands for a moment, then picked at a fingernail. "You might not like me as much as you think you do."

"I'll take that chance."

"Forget it."

"Lymon, I'd like to know."

He gave her a long and intense look before he said, "A bunch of ISIS commanders got the bright idea that if they used women, they could get close to us. That we wouldn't suspect them. You know, given the perspective on the sexes, and all. It worked, too. Three ladies in burkas. They walked right up the road, reached out from under their burkas, and tossed a bunch of grenades at us."

"And?"

His eyes were smoldering when he looked back at her. "Me and most of my guys walked away. They didn't. It's a simple equation."

"Does it bother you, this simple equation of yours?"

"Yes and no."

When he saw she wasn't going to relent, he added,

"It bothers anyone normal when it comes to killing people. I got out because I started to like it. As to those particular women, I waffle. Maybe they were innocent victims, told by men who had power over them to do this thing; having no other recourse, they did it. Or maybe they *wanted* to see us blown to bits. I don't know which is true. But in the final analysis, they were trying to kill me and my people. In combat you do what you've got to do."

She decided to change the subject. "So, why does Krissy think she can have my baby?"

"Krissy's nuts. Blow it off."

"Yeah, but if you'll recall, she's filthy rich as well as insane. That's a bad combination."

"Yeah, a bad combination, all right." He gave her that look that melted her insides. "Just like when security personnel mix with their clients."

CHAPTER 8

G ENESIS ATHENA. The words flashed on the screen. For background, a faint blue image of a robe-clad woman with a nice figure, a shield, and spear—Athena, perhaps?—could be seen superimposed on the forehead of a bearded man's face. Who? Zeus? What did that mean?

Christal sat in her kitchen, a half-empty cup of coffee to one side. She used her finger to move the cursor onto the words and tapped with her index finger. The letters dissolved to reveal the questionnaire.

Christal frowned, sipped her coffee, and read through the questions. They started innocuously enough. Name. Address. Sex. Occupation. Age. Level of education, and so forth.

On impulse, she pressed the *Print Screen* button and listened to her small printer whirring as it warmed up. Then, one by one, the pages slid out. She checked, just to see that it had indeed printed, and then returned to her screen.

"Do I want to do this?" She twitched her lips. "Sure, what have I got to lose?"

Under name, she typed in *Christal Anaya*.

At address, she gave her mother's post office box in Nambe. For occupation, she stated that she was self-employed. After all, what was the sense in being honest? This was just to see what happened, right?

Under marital status she typed *Single*.

Children? *None*.

Roommates? She hesitated, considering the wisdom of stating that she lived alone, and answered *Two*. Sex? popped up immediately. She added *Female*.

In the yearly income column, she arbitrarily typed in *$50,000*. Under assets, she listed that she owned her own home, valued at one hundred and fifty thousand. She said she was financing a Honda Accord. Further, she stated that she did not have outstanding loans, and owned no stocks, bonds, or investment real estate. Her sole form of income was from her employment.

Did she have a criminal record? *No*.

Had she been treated for mental disorders? *No*.

How often did she see a physician? *Once a year*.

What for? *Routine physical*.

She was asked to numerically rank her shopping venues. She listed Amazon as one, catalog as two, and brick-and-mortar as three.

How many credit cards did she have? *Two*.

Under hobbies, she facetiously typed *Stamp collecting, big game hunting, and reading romance novels*.

How many times a month, week, or day did she leave her house? She said three times a day. Did she go alone? *Yes*.

How many times a week did she date? She grinned

maliciously as she typed *Three*. Did she see one man, or several? She typed *Several* as she said, "I'm one hot chick."

The next question asked her to think carefully and answer honestly. How many people could she actually name that she would consider living with for a year in the same room? She thought for a while before typing *As of today, none.*

She was asked to imagine her bathroom. Rank in highest to lowest order which of the following were important to have. She chose: toilet-12, shower-11, sink-10, light-9, mirror-8, medicine cabinet-7, flooring-6, heater-5, tub-4, trash can-3, wall paper-2, window-1.

What on earth was that about? She sipped her coffee, perplexed at the nature of the question.

How often did she go to the movies? *Twice a month.*

How often did she stream movies? *Four nights a week.*

Who were her two favorite stars? She chose *Sheela Marks* and *Manuel de Clerk*.

If she had to choose one movie on a given night, would she choose to see Sheela or de Clerk? Without hesitation, she typed in Sheela's name.

How many times did she see Sheela on screen, streaming, or DVD in a given year, month, week, day? Christal opted for three times a year.

At that moment, a line of text appeared in bright blue, stating,

THANK YOU FOR YOUR COOPERATION IN TAKING THE GENESIS ATHENA QUESTIONNAIRE. ALL INFORMATION IS COMPLETELY CONFIDENTIAL AND USED FOR GENESIS ATHENA'S ONGOING MARKET RESEARCH. THANK YOU AGAIN FOR YOUR TIME.

Christal hit her *page up* button, but nothing happened. Then a small icon appeared at the lower left-hand corner—a box that said;

EXIT NOW.

Christal clicked it, and the screen returned her to the Sheela Marks' Web site where she had originated. The little Genesis Athena patch key was now colorless. When Christal rolled the cursor down and tapped it, nothing happened.

"Weird," she muttered.

Leaning back, she tossed off the last of her cold coffee and picked up the sheets she had copied with the *Print Screen* command. She started at the top, thinking about the answers she had given, and then stopped short.

"Wait a minute." Her frown deepened. "That's not the same question I was asked."

She stared, sure that she hadn't been asked how many close friends she had. Or to choose which of those friends she would tell an embarrassing secret.

She tapped the cursor again where it rested on the Genesis Athena patch. Still nothing.

"I don't get it. I *know* I didn't answer this question."

Scanning down the pages, she found others that she hadn't seen. If that was the case, if it wasn't just her faulty memory, what the hell did it mean?

CHAPTER 9

Sid Harness took a sip from his cup and grimaced. He knew without asking that Sam Murphy had made the coffee. Murphy came from South Dakota. He had grown up on a cattle ranch on the fringe of the Black Hills. Supposedly cowboys made coffee that would "float a horseshoe." It was bullshit. People in the West made coffee like water. If a person wanted real coffee, he had to go to Seattle or the East Coast.

With his mind knotted around that, Sid walked to his small office and flipped on the lights. He was still burping Claire's breakfast of eggs and sausage. She liked the really spicy sausage she bought at Costco.

Sid sat down at his desk and awakened his computer. His email had no more than five memos waiting. A good day. But Pete Wirthing was out for the week, so the official BS had slowed to a trickle. Some papers sat in the printer rack, but he ignored them for the moment.

Pulling up his email, Sid scanned through the

communiqués from Los Angeles and Boston. Nothing had happened on the disappearance of the missing geneticists from either city.

He read through the official junk mail sent from the office of personnel, the Justice Department, as well as the Bureau per se, and ditched it.

Then a note with Christal's address popped up on the screen. Sid grinned and opened it. Christal, now there was a lady who knew how to make a breakfast.

Hi Sid:

I'm forwarding a copy of a questionnaire that I pulled off a web page at genesisathena.com. When I filled out the questionnaire on screen the questions weren't the same. Could you do me a real big favor and send a copy down to the behavioral science guys at Quantico? Something about this isn't right. Which brings me to favor number two. Could you run Genesis Athena through ViCAP and NCIC when you get a spare moment? I'd be interested to know if it red-flags. I know I'm out on a limb here. Don't do anything that could have you standing in for an investigation from the Office of Professional Responsibilities. If you can't do this, just email me back with a simple no. I'll understand.

Forever the Best,
Christal

Genesis Athena? Sid stared at the name. He reached for the pages in the metal carrier under the printer, discarded a couple of memos he had already read on screen, and found the pages referred to in Christal's email.

He scanned the contents, then read the questions

with a greater interest. No, it wasn't quite right. He could see what had tripped Christal's trigger. Something about the questions bothered him, too.

On impulse, he reached into a drawer, pulled out an envelope, and marked the delivery box NCAVC for National Center for the Analysis of Violent Crime—the old Behavioral Science Unit at Quantico. What the hell. If anyone asked, he'd just tell them he was following up on a hunch.

Then he entered the name "Genesis Athena" into the search database to see what came up.

While the computer chewed on the name, he typed a response to Christal.

Dear Christal:

Info sent. Computer working. No problem. You owe me dinner.

Best,

Sid

Genesis Athena? What the hell was that?

CHAPTER 10

Hank Abrams kept a hand on the railing as he stood on the port side just behind the wheelhouse. That location kept him out of the wind and sea spray. The thirty-foot launch slowed on the swells as she approached the Coast Guard cutter. Hank had never been much for boats. He had managed the journey out past the twelve-mile limit and was now more than halfway back to shore. He hoped the Coast Guard wasn't going to take up too much time. His stomach was feeling just the least bit chancy with the rising and falling waves.

Sunset was burning a yellow halo across the New York skyline to the west. Several miles to the north, irregular white blocks of apartment buildings crowded the thin pale beach on the Long Island shore. The water here had a greenish-brown tinge. Hank wondered how much of the color came from raw sewage.

As the launch pulled up abreast of the cutter, Hank studied the long gray boat with its distinctive red stripe. Uniformed crewmen were watching him through binoculars. The big fifty on the bow was shrouded in weather-protected tarping. Glancing behind, Hank could see Sheik Abdulla standing in his immaculate suit, his lawyer and two bodyguards to either side and behind him.

Don't ask, don't tell. But just what, he wondered, was he not supposed to tell? For two days, he and the Sheik's personal bodyguards had been sequestered aboard the *ZoeGen* out beyond the twelve-mile limit. They had been given plushly furnished cabins on C Deck with access to the afterdeck. Food had been delivered to a nice dining room on D Deck. They had the use of a game room there with billiards, shuffleboard, and video games, as well as a small theater served by all of the streaming services. Secure doors had restricted any access to the forward part of the ship. From their area, they couldn't even see anything forward. Hank had been told to stay aft, and he had obeyed orders, taking the time to lounge, read from the collection of hardback novels, and watch the television.

The Sheik had appeared as if by magic, told them to pack, and within a half hour, they were headed back toward the wharf in Brooklyn.

At least until the Coast Guard had pulled alongside.

Should I be worried?

About what? He shot a quick look at the slim launch. If it was drugs, they could be anywhere aboard, but no one seemed the slightest bit worried as the Guardsmen made the tricky crossing from the cutter. Hank watched them clamber up and over the railing.

Hank made his way to the midships, where the Guardsmen were asking for identification. They looked so young in their gray shirts and dark pants. The Sig pistols on their web belts, however, gave them an ominous presence.

"Your identification, sir?" a young man asked, watching him with serious brown eyes. The name WILLIAMSON was stenciled on the Guardsman's breast pocket.

Hank handed over his driver's license, realizing for the first time how professional politeness could effectively tell a person he wasn't jackshit.

"What is your citizenship, Mr. Abrams?" the young man asked, his brown eyes comparing the driver's license photo with Hank's face.

"American. I'm currently living in New York." Hank could see one of the other Guardsmen carefully checking the Sheik's passport and talking into the radio clipped to his shoulder.

"What is your business aboard this boat, sir?" came the crisp question.

"I work for Verele Security. Our offices are at 175 Fifth Avenue. The Sheik"—he pointed—"is a client. I was detailed to accompany him to the *ZoeGen*." He fished out one of his business cards.

"And your business aboard the *ZoeGen*?"

Hank spread his arms. "Honestly, Officer, I cannot tell you. I'm just the hired help. I didn't even see the Sheik until a couple of hours ago."

"I see." Williamson was tapping information into a handheld computer unit. Then he glanced up and handed the driver's license back. "If you would step to the stern, sir, we will try not to detain you unreasonably."

Hank took his driver's license and walked back to where the launch's captain and mate stood. Two of the young Coast Guardsmen were still working over the Sheik's documents.

Apparently a Saudi Sheik piloting back and forth just offshore of New York City made people nervous. Especially with the off-and-on conflict consuming the Persian Gulf.

Hank watched as another crewman walked up and down the deck with a piece of electronic equipment—a sensor of some sort, no doubt sniffing for explosives, drugs, and who knew what other kinds of contraband.

"Does this happen a lot?" Hank asked the captain.

"Yeah. I told the Sheik to prepare. The way they watch the traffic anymore, I knew we'd get searched stem to stern. That ship out there"—he jerked his head —"it's just anchored off the limit. I've been ferrying people for the last week and a half. The Coast Guard's getting suspicious, but hey, we're clean and legal. What can they do?"

"Got me. I'm just protection." Hank paused. "You got any idea what happens on the *ZoeGen*?"

"You tell me. You were on that ship for two days."

"I played pool, learned snooker, watched a couple of movies, and farted around on the shuffleboard. Everything forward is off-limits. And I mean, it's shut up tight."

"Then, pal, when it comes to that boat out there, you're way ahead of me."

For the next five minutes, the Coast Guard snooped around the launch. From where he stood, Hank could tell that Sheik Abdulla's lawyer was doing most of the talking.

In the end, the Coast Guard packed up and went back to their sleek gray cutter with its whirling radars and bristling antennae. As soon as they were aboard, the diesels thrummed and white billowed out from below the fantail as she veered off.

Hank caught a glimpse of the Sheik as he watched the cutter go. A clever smile lay on his lips, his dark eyes gleaming.

The rest of the short voyage passed without interest. When the launch finally pulled in at its slip, Hank recognized Neal Gray waiting with his arms crossed. The man leaned against a large white box marked PERSONAL FLOTATION DEVICES. Hank wondered whatever had happened to "life preservers."

He liked Gray. Gray was the Sheik's man and gave orders to Hank's detail and squad leaders. He appeared to be in his early forties, a natty dresser with blond hair that he kept neatly combed. In spite of his worried blue eyes, Gray seemed efficient, organized, and smart enough to let others do their jobs without trying to micromanage. A small black nylon satchel rested at Gray's feet.

Lines were cast, and the launch made fast. Able hands attached a walkway, and the Sheik followed Hank and his retinue off the launch.

That moment of awkwardness when he set foot on cement left Hank half-reeling after the pitching boat. Neal Gray straightened, picked up the satchel, and walked over, nodding to the Sheik as he stepped up to Hank's side.

"Any trouble?"

Hank shook his head. "It was more like vacation. The Coast Guard stopped us on the way back. No big deal."

"Good." Neal reached into the pocket of his snappy

gray suit and produced an envelope. "Here you go. Instructions and a ticket. I've asked Verele if we could change your assignment, and he agreed. You're welcome to call him for verification if you'd like. Assuming you don't have any major objection, we'd like you to go home, catch a good night's sleep, and catch a plane to LA in the morning."

"What am I doing there? An advance for the Sheik?"

Gray's sober eyes took his measure. "Not an advance. Something quite different. You'll find instructions in the envelope. Actually, we need you to look someone up, make contact, and well, bring us a sample."

"A sample?"

"You'll see on the instructions." Gray smiled. "It's a little unusual, and please, we'll be happy to reward you for success." He smiled ironically and handed over the black nylon satchel. "Quite a handsome reward, if I do say so. Meanwhile, a credit card is enclosed along with five thousand dollars cash for tips and what have you."

"What kind of sample?"

Gray grinned. "Skin, actually, or a couple of strands of hair would do. Like I said, the instructions are inside. If you have any questions, call Salim. He's done this sort of thing for us before."

"That's it?"

"I'll debrief you when you get back."

"Who am I getting a sample of?"

"Your girlfriend." Neal's grin was suggestive. "Anaya. She's tripped a couple of our switches and caught the Sheik's interest. We thought you were the guy to get a line on her."

"Huh? Why me? I mean, when we parted, it wasn't exactly amicable."

"Yeah, well, I'm sure you'll think of something." In a mocking voice, he said, "Give my love to the stars."

With that, Neal turned on his heel, walking to catch up with the Sheik's party.

Hank hefted the ballistic nylon bag. Maybe five pounds. Well, what the hell, the Sheik was the guy paying the bills.

Anaya! He couldn't wait to see her face.

CHAPTER 11

Christal leaned forward after the plates were cleared and placed her elbows on the table. She gave Tony a clear-eyed appraisal as waiters bustled past their table and other diners bent to their conversations. The restaurant, called Loreto, was hidden away in what was called "Frogtown." Christal approved of that. But that was about all she could say of the evening so far.

Was Tony making some kind of politically correct statement in bringing her here? No matter. The food had been okay, and the atmosphere, if too frenetic, was still worth experiencing. If nothing else, she could tell her mother about it one day.

"So, Christal"—Tony leaned back—"you've made it. You're in LA. How does it feel to be part of the team?"

She studied him as she considered the question. He was wearing a blue Dewey and Durham blazer over a white silk shirt by Dior. The latter hung open down to the sternum. Probably to show off the golden necklace that covered his breastbone.

Tony's eyes betrayed a subtle excitement as he watched her. During the meal, he had gone to the restroom no less than three times for reasons she could only speculate on. Since he hadn't come back with white powder at the corners of his nostrils and his pupils seemed normal, she assumed it had been to double-check his appearance. That or his bladder was volumetrically challenged.

"Part of the team?"

"Sheela's team. You know, me, Rex, Dot, Lymon. All of us. I tell you, babe, we're—"

"Tony, how many times have I asked you not to call me 'babe'?"

"Yeah, well, like, it's a part of the language, you know? Part of the patois. And it isn't just that you're a knockout. I mean, you can really sail out here, Christal."

"I get seasick."

"It's like...you—huh? Seasick?"

"I was raised in New Mexico. The one time I rode a boat out on the ocean, I got sick. It wasn't pretty."

He looked confused. "What are we talking about?"

"You said I could really sail. I've seen those little sailboats down at the marinas. It looks bouncy."

"No way! You jacking me, Christal? I mean, you could have it all. Do it right and you could take off like a rocket." He flashed her the kind of smile that made an orthodontist tingle with satisfaction. "You don't know it, but you've got a quality that I think would melt the lens. It's a no-bullshit presence. A sense of self. Strong, you know? Like a 'here I am' statement. Look at me. See me. Be me. Solid chutzpah, babe."

"Right. You think I could be a movie star?" She gave him a mocking look.

He leaned forward, challenge in his sparkling blue eyes. "Christal, a lot of chicks would jump at a chance like this. You don't wanna stay in celebrity protection. I can see it in you. Not when you got a chance to reach out and pull in a chunk of the sky." He extended his arm, hand closing into a gripping fist. "Now, that's not to say it's gonna be easy. You get me? I mean, it isn't any trite figure of speech when I say it's a jungle out there."

"Let me guess, you're the great white hunter?" She arched an eyebrow. "If I just place myself in your hands, well, it might or might not work out, right?"

He gave her a grin. "I didn't do so bad with Sheela."

"Stow it, Tony. I'm not buying. If you're going to do the hard sell, try it with Patsy from Peoria. I've been around the block a time or two."

He cocked his head, the blue eyes narrowing. "You think this is all a gig to get into your pants?"

"Funny you should bring that up, but yeah, I do. And you know what? There's just room enough for me."

He threw his head back and laughed, genuinely amused. "You know, Christal, you're all right. Here you sit, in the presence of one of the most powerful men in Hollywood, and you're too cool!" He tapped long fingers on the table. "That wounds me. I'm one of the hottest movers in this biz, and you're blowing me off."

"Shit happens," she added sweetly.

"Okay, I'll bite. So...why'd you say yes to dinner?"

"Because I promised, and I broke it. I keep my promises." She glanced around at the other patrons, mostly well-dressed, manicured, and affluent. "Maybe that doesn't happen a lot in Hollywood, but I'm me. Call me a lamb among wolves."

His eyes had changed, cooling, calculating. For the first time, she realized that he was indeed a man worth taking seriously. "Somehow, I don't think you're any innocent lamb, Christal."

"Hey. New Mexico kid in from the sticks, that kind of thing."

"I heard you were a lawyer."

"I've got a law degree, and once upon a time, I passed the New Mexico bar." She shrugged. "That's not really a lawyer."

"So, what, then?"

"I was looking for challenge."

"You're kidding! Leaving a law practice for the FBI? Let me get this straight. You thought working your way up in a law firm wasn't going to be a challenge?"

She ran her napkin through her fingers, folding it into pleats. "How do I say this so that you'll understand? I had something in my gut. No, maybe it was a chip on my shoulder. Do you know what lawyers, especially young ones like me, get stuck doing? It's a world of paper, of books and research. I was tired of offices and libraries. I wanted to get out in the world, find bad guys, and bust their balls."

He gave her an evaluative stare before saying, "What did he do to you?"

"Who?"

"The guy that set you off like this."

"It wasn't any one guy. Or girl, for that matter. The men in my life, going back to my father, have been good or bad, or a combination of each. I've dealt with my share of *cabrones* as well as nice decent guys." She shook her head. "No, this was something different.

Maybe wanderlust of the blood. I wanted to be able to look back and say, hey, I did that. Can you follow?"

"Yeah, I follow. You wanted high adventure."

"What about you? Did you wake up one morning and say 'I'm going to be a talent agent'?"

"Nah. I started as the receptionist." Tony made a disparaging gesture. "Day after day, I sat there, watching the people coming through the door. Learning, you know? Producers would sit in the lobby, bitching or bragging, and I'd hear it."

He smiled. "Hey, it was cool! I was working for peanuts. You know, just for the chance to be close to the action. At first it was for bragging rights. To tell the chicks that I knew what film Emilia Clarke was going to be starring in. Or that I'd heard Harold Becker tell Miley Cyrus this dirty joke."

"You've made it a bit beyond the reception desk." She could see the gleam in his eyes. Tony liked to talk about himself.

"That's the thing, babe. I started going in and telling the boss, 'Hey, this guy's hot to sign Megan Fox.' So I sort of worked my way into the system, and pretty soon I was being invited to lunches and parties. Just to circulate, listen, and report back to the boss. Then it was planning sessions. Say, maybe the Coens wanted one of our clients; how did we know when we'd reached a contract breaker?"

A soft smile rode his lips as he stared into the past. "Then, one day, I realized I was telling the old man more than he was telling me. It was an epiphany, right? Wham! I'm actually *doing* this. Clients were feeling me out for what the boss was going to say. Did I think it was the right deal, the right role—I was dishing out the whole enchilada."

"So, you were made a partner?"

Tony shook his head. "Nah, I laid my plans. Started dealing with the clients. When the leverage was right, I walked, and I took about half of them with me." He gave her a quizzical look. "Weird. You wouldn't believe how many stayed that I thought would follow me. But the ones who did were enough. I'd learned the ropes, you know? I knew which knot to pick at and how to retie it into a killer deal." He gave her an evil grin. "And, babe, I'm *good*!"

"Was Sheela with you from the beginning?"

"Nope. She was pissed at her agent at ICM. A little bird told me. Landing Sheela was like, the best, you know? Awesome. Tricky shit. But I was at the right place, at the right time, with the right deal. Cool."

His smile was infectious. Christal sat back, relaxing for the first time. "You want my opinion?"

"Sure."

"You're a rogue."

"Damn straight."

"But a charming one once you stop dishing out that hotshot agent bullshit. Play that game with bimbos, Tony. Don't waste it on an intelligent woman."

One of his golden eyebrows rose. "So, wow! Does that mean, like, I've still got a chance with the mysterious and enigmatic Christal?"

"Don't bet on it."

His grin was impish. "I'll take that as a challenge."

"It's your funeral."

"Hey, babe, you're dealing with Tony Zell here. It's cool. I can bide my time, dazzle you with brilliance. Just wait, you'll see. I'm going to charm you like you've never been charmed before."

"Is that a fact?"

"Hey, I'm like one of those Indian fakirs with a flute. I'll get you out of your basket yet. I tell you, I can already imagine you swaying to the music."

"Uh-huh." She leaned forward, her hair spilling around her shoulders. "Just remember, Tony, I'm not one of your cobras."

"Yeah?"

"For sure. This time you've come face to face with a desert-tough New Mexican *culebra*."

"What's that?"

"More than you can handle."

He pushed back in the chair, laughing from deep in his belly. "You're a cool one, Christal. Really cool."

CHAPTER 12

Lymon hunched at his office desk going through the receipts. A cup of coffee sat within easy reach. Behind him, the computer screen glowed with his favorite screensaver, a series of motorcycles: some road racers; others touring bikes; an occasional flying motocross machine, and a trials rider balancing atop a huge boulder on a skinny Gas Gas. A Nanci Griffith CD was playing just above the audible range to keep his emotions in check.

He needed Nanci Griffith's soothing voice. If he didn't do something to calm himself through the arduous process of dealing with the bits of paper, he'd go slightly berserk and break something.

Why did paperwork have to be such a miserable hassle? He assumed it was because the people who wrote the tax laws, ran the IRS, and operated major accounting houses were both socially and sexually handicapped. Bug-eyed geeks with skinny arms and soft round bellies instead of real people.

He took a moment, imagining them: bald-headed,

wearing white shirts with thin black ties and gray rumpled slacks. They were smooth-shaven and pale-skinned. They carried shiny pens in their pockets. He could visualize their soft white fingers as they danced on the calculator keys and tape spooled out of the machines. Every now and then, they would look across at each other and grin maliciously. It was because they knew that while they might be impotent wimps, they had the last laugh.

In the end all the tough guys like Lymon Bridges were doomed to spend endless and meaningless hours of their lives pushing paper, totaling columns, balancing books, and organizing receipts instead of enjoying their tough-stud action-filled lives out in the sun.

"Maybe for fun I'll go beat up an accountant." Lymon savored the fantasy as he stapled a pile of New York receipts together for June's attention.

He leaned back, scowling at the different piles of paper on his desk. Someone had told him that the tax code was contained in bound books that stood eight feet high when stacked atop each other. If it demonstrated anything, it was a measure of the success of the American economy. Nothing else would explain a GDP that could support so many nonproductive parasites feeding off the sweat of the productive few.

Voices carried down the hallway from June's desk, and he wondered who had come in.

He was halfway through Paul's expense report when the voices grew louder. Lymon lifted an eyebrow and waited.

He heard June's emphatic "No!" and pushed his chair back before getting to his feet. Stepping into the hallway, he could see the man standing in front of June's desk. He was a handsome sort, midtwenties to maybe thirty, middle height, square shoulders, in a dark suit coat. The guy was dark-haired, shaven, but with that dark shadow to the cheeks that indicated a thick beard. He had a strong jaw, straight nose, and brown eyes that now locked with June's.

Lymon padded into June's office and asked, "Is there something here I should know about?"

June turned in her swivel chair, jerking a thumb over her shoulder. "This guy wants Christal's address."

Lymon raised his eyes. "Why?"

"Who're you?" The man had a competent way about him as if he was used to authority.

"I'm Lymon Bridges. I run this place."

The man nodded, offering his hand. "Hank Abrams. I'm with Verele Security. Uh, I suppose you've heard of us?"

Hank Abrams? Lymon kept the surprise from his face. "Yeah, I've heard of Verele Security. They do good work. Are you here for personal or professional reasons?"

That took Abrams back. Lymon could see him thinking through the possible answers.

"Professional," Abrams finally admitted.

"I see." Lymon smiled graciously. "If you will leave your phone number and address, I'll see that Christal gets them. After that, it's up to her if she decides to contact you."

Abrams gave him a hard evaluative look, then said, "I'd prefer to contact her on my own."

"I'm sure you would." Lymon kept his professional smile in place. "If I could offer some friendly advice, I'd say you might be better off to give her a little warning. Given your history, she might shoot first and wonder why you showed up after the fact."

Abrams gave him an icy smile as he put the pieces together. "I see. Thanks for the advice. That's real neighborly of you. Uh, you wouldn't have some ulterior motive yourself, would you?"

"Such as?" Lymon could feel June's curious gaze as she sat between them.

"Christal's an attractive lady."

"She's good at her job," Lymon countered.

"Are you trying to protect her?"

"She can protect herself."

"Then why won't you give me her address?"

"I already told you."

Abrams narrowed his eyes, the smile never wavering. "What's wrong? Afraid I might just hire her away?"

"It's a free market."

"If you're worried, you're welcome to contact our New York office. My boss—"

"Verele doesn't concern me. You do. Just write your name, phone, and address there on the notepad. Christal will have it by tonight. My word on that. I'll tell her you're interested in hiring her. She can decide what she wants to do."

"That's it?"

"Sum and total."

Abrams glanced back and forth between Lymon and June, smiled in ill humor, and bent, jotting on the notepad at the corner of the desk.

As he finished and twisted his Montblanc to retract the ballpoint, Lymon asked, "Who was the Arab?"

Abrams started, and for that one instant Lymon

could see him off balance. He recovered quickly, saying, "The Sheik is a client of ours."

Lymon replied, "And Sheela Marks is our client."

Abrams watched him for a moment, and then said, "From what I see in the news, you haven't been doing such a hot job protecting her recently." He flipped a mock salute. "Nice to have met you, Mr. Bridges."

He turned on his heel, stepped to the door, opened it, and left. The sound of his feet on the steps grew fainter as he descended to the street level.

Lymon ground his teeth, glaring at the door, and stepped around to rip the paper from the pad. He glanced down, recognizing the address for the Beverly Hilton.

"That was interesting," June told him evenly as she wheeled her chair around to face her desk again. "Would you mind telling me what just happened here? Turf fight? Or was that just two dominant males growling, bristling, and scratching the dirt?"

Lymon folded the paper. "It's deeper than that." He filled her in on the New York trip and then added, "Abrams and Christal were involved when they worked for the Bureau. It went bad enough to make Christal resign."

June studied him thoughtfully. "I see."

"Good. 'Cause I sure don't. What the hell was he doing here? And just why does he really want to see Christal?"

June shook her head. "I don't know, but if you think it has something to do with Sheela, maybe you'd better have a word or two with Christal, soonest."

CHAPTER 13

Christal looked up from the back issues of *Daily Variety* she had downloaded onto her MacBook. She sat at her kitchen table, staring at the screen as she scrolled through the old headlines. It was the glint of sunlight off the Plexiglas windscreen that caught her attention. She watched through the window as Lymon parked the silver BMW motorcycle, leaned it onto the kickstand, and stepped off. He was unbuckling his helmet as he walked from the parking spot next to her Tahoe.

She met him at the door before he could knock and motioned him in, saying, "Not much new on this front. I've got some feelers out, but I'm drawing a bust looking for links between Sheela and the actors targeted by the celeb hits."

Then she got a good look at Lymon's face. "What's wrong?"

He tossed his helmet onto the couch and slipped out of his jacket. His eyes were smoky, as if something smoldered deep inside. He fished a folded piece of paper from his pocket and handed it to her before he turned and closed the door behind him.

Christal unfolded the paper, seeing the company logo at the top. She stopped at the familiar script. The note stated:

Christal: Contact me immediately. Most important! Hank.

A 212 area code telephone number—a cell, she assumed—and a Wilshire Boulevard address followed.

She glanced up at Lymon. "Is this a joke?"

"I wish. He was just in the office." Lymon watched her carefully. "Christal, I don't like it. Whatever is between the two of you isn't my business. But the fact that his client was so fixed on Sheela just might be. First, we target the Sheik at the preem. Then your old boyfriend shows up as the Sheik is leaving. Then, bam! Abrams is walking in my door asking to see you. You tell me: Is this something I need to be concerned about?"

Christal took a deep breath, a cold feeling in her stomach. She perched her butt on the couch back. "Honestly, Lymon, it's nuts! Crazy! Too far out! What did he want? Did he say?"

"Only that it was professional. If it is, am I supposed to think it concerns Sheela? Is that the hidden agenda? Or is it just coincidence that he saw you in New York, got to thinking about his wife dumping him, and he talked Verele into trying to hire you so that you and he could get back together?"

Confusion came tumbling out of her brain, stopping any logical thought. "No way in hell!" She crumpled the paper in her hand. "What? Does he think I'm a complete idiot, that I'd even want to be close to him?"

"I have no idea." Lymon cocked his head, apparently seeing through her struggle for control.

"I *don't* want to see him."

"It gets worse. I think he tried to follow me from the office."

Christal stopped short, staring. "Huh? Why would he do that?"

"To find you."

"That's even nuttier than..." She couldn't finish it, seeing the concern in Lymon's eyes. "Wait a minute. What makes you think he was trying to follow you?"

"A dark-blue Ford Bronco followed me from the office parking lot." Lymon crossed his arms, pacing back and forth on the living room carpet. "It was parked back in the alley. I don't think he expected me to be on a bike. It must have been a shock when I threw a leg over the Beemer and motored off. This Bronco pulled out after me. He did a good job, but his hand was tipped. There's no parking where the Bronco had been sitting."

"Hey, Hank was trained by the Bureau. If he was following, it wouldn't have been a half-assed job."

"Yeah, trained to do a tail with a team, right? Lots of cars, passing, pulling off, keeping in touch by radio. That sort of thing. This time, he just had himself. It gets a little harder for one guy. Especially if he's having to make it up as he goes."

She glanced uncertainly at the window, half expecting to see a blue Bronco pull into the space next to the BMW.

"Relax," Lymon told her. "Splitting lanes is legal in California. He's still back on Wilshire somewhere, sitting in traffic. I went around a couple of blocks and stopped to talk to the two homeless guys that live in the alley. Stewart and John. They described your Hank Abrams. He'd just pulled in and was waiting, figuring that you'd show up, I suppose. Or maybe that if you and I were involved—"

"What?"

Lymon chuckled. "That was one of the things that crossed his mind when I wouldn't give him your address."

Christal shook her head, failing to see his humor in her current misery.

"Christal," Lymon added gently, "give him a call from a neutral phone. See what he wants. If it involves that Sheik and Sheela, we need to know."

She nodded numbly. The thought came tumbling out of her stunned mind. "What if he offers me a job?"

"I'd ask for double the salary you're getting now. Any other fringe benefits are up to Hank and Verele."

"Thanks."

"My pleasure." He hesitated. "Listen, I hate to ask you to call this guy. Anything you need, we're here for you. Me, Paul, the rest of the guys. If it gets sticky, we'll take care of you. You know that, don't you?"

She nodded. "Yeah, I'll call him Lymon. Maybe from the phone at Al's. Just give me time to get myself together."

CHAPTER 14

Hank Abrams had a sour feeling in his gut as he slowed, looked at his map, and frowned at the community gate that blocked his access to the street where Sheela Marks lived. Once again, he cursed life without FBI credentials. That badge had opened a lot of doors. It would have passed him here, too, where he didn't think a Verele Security business card would. The guy at the guard shack would have asked where he was going and double-checked to see if Verele Security was making an advance at any of the houses up the road.

"Sheela Marks is our client," Bridges had told him. That meant that he might be able to pick up Christal when she went off shift at the principal's house.

He slowed as he considered the guard shack that stood in the middle of the road and noted the cameras that had been placed unobtrusively in the ornate shrubbery to either side.

Did he want a record of his presence here? It left him feeling awkward, somehow sordid. It wasn't as if what he was doing was illegal. The fact was, there were no laws against him completing his assignment

Assault, the voice said in his head.

But it wasn't assault. Not in the classical sense. All he had to do was get close to Christal. He glanced at the small canvas kit bag on the seat behind him. He had checked out the special equipment it contained. The hand patch had been the most unusual; it stuck to the palm, and just by shaking hands, scrubbed off enough of the target's cells to be useful. The other stuff was no less esoteric, and each had its own particular uses.

Hell, if the instructions were correct, he didn't have to have physical contact with her, just find out where she lived. He'd committed the list of things he could take to memory: hairbrush, toothbrush, dirty clothes, used personal items, a sack full of her garbage, and so forth.

Theft, his legally trained mind countered.

Well, sure, by the strictest interpretation. But who would care? It wasn't like lifting a hairbrush was grand theft, for God's sake. All he needed to do was get into her house, and from there, it was easy.

Breaking and entering.

Not if Christal invited him in, he countered. Hell, all he needed was her washcloth! If she didn't invite him in, the trash would do. But it wasn't as discreet; the samples could have come from anywhere with garbage. How would they know if a sample came from Christal, or a guest? But in a pinch, it would do. He could wait until she took it out, and then he'd box it FedEx, check out of his hotel, and be on a plane that night.

He wheeled the Bronco around and reluctantly drove away from the controlled access to Sheela Marks' community. As he passed the high-dollar houses, he couldn't help but notice the tall walls that surrounded the large mansions. One by one he took the roads that surrounded the compound, figuring that the houses contained within sat on less than ten acres. He could see the roofs through the gaps between the surrounding houses. Which one was Sheela Marks'?

The cell phone warbled in its melodious tone, and he pulled over to answer it. The number was a local Los Angeles area code. It would be recorded in his "Recents" file.

"Hello?"

"Hank?" Christal's voice was controlled, toneless.

"Hey, Christal. It's good to hear you again."

"What do you want?" She sounded icy.

"Look, we need to talk. Something's come up."

"Yeah, I remember the last time you got it up. Somehow I ended up getting screwed twice."

He made a face. "Dear God, Christal. You have no idea how sorry I am. I never meant to hurt you. I never meant to hurt anyone."

"I know." She seemed to actually understand.

"If I could take my pound of flesh out of Gonzales, I would."

A pause. *"We just screwed up. That's all. He was ahead of us. I learned my lesson, Hank."*

"What lesson was that?"

"We weren't professional. That was the mistake I made that night. You can bet I'll never make it again."

He took a deep breath. "Yeah, that's two of us. That's why I need to see you." He paused. "Uh, Marsha has filed for a divorce."

"Make your offer." Her voice was emotionless.

He hesitated; obviously she wasn't into reconciliation. "What is Bridges paying you?"

"That's my business."

He winced. Then remembered Bridges' advice. "I think we can double it."

Her laughter caught him by surprise. Then she said, *"Hank, you couldn't afford me. Not that I'd work for you for any price."*

"You haven't heard my offer. Ten thousand a month." There. That ought to bring her around. At least get her to meet with him.

"You're not even close." More bitter laughter came rolling out of the earpiece. *"Have a nice life, Hank."*

"Wait! Christal, for God's sake, wait! Don't hang up!"

"You tracing this? Need to keep me on the line?"

"God, no! I swear." He shook his head, trying to figure out how it had gone so wrong. "Look, if you and Bridges are involved, that's fine. Here's the scoop: My boss is interested in seeing if you have what it takes to join our firm. That's all. No pressure, no strings. You can stay here in LA and handle our principals here."

"I'm with LBA now. I like working for Lymon. You know"—it sounded like a taunt—*"Sheela Marks is one of our clients."*

He frowned. "Would she be interested in changing security firms? Could you get me and my boss an interview?"

"Ah, so am I to believe that you want to use me to get close to Sheela? Is that it? You were always a deep player, Hank."

"Christal, just meet with me. I'll *buy* your time if I have to."

"What?"

"Pay you. Five thousand dollars. Just for the chance to..." He realized that he was listening to dead air.

With a pained look, he pressed the *end* button and stared thoughtfully through the Ford's windshield at the row of expensive houses.

He pulled up the "Recents" scrolled to the number at the top and pressed it for a call back.

"Al's Tavern. This is John." A man's voice.

Hank killed the call.

"Yeah," he grumbled, "I'm a smart guy, I'll think of something." He threw the cell phone across the car.

CHAPTER 15

Sid leaned back in his office chair at the Washington Metro Field Office and stared at the bulletin board across from him. It showed a map of the world. Here and there, pins were stuck into it, marking where geneticists had disappeared over the last five years. Of all the cases he'd ever worked on, he'd never had one like this. It just seemed to lead nowhere. His counterparts contacted through Interpol had found the same thing, and they'd been working on some cases for five years.

He needed a break, anything to get his mind off the Gordian knot that his case had become. A picture caught his eye where it rested at the edge of his desk. Sid, Tim Paris—a fellow agent—and Christal Anaya stood behind a podium receiving a meritorious service award. He smiled, reached over, and lifted the phone. He glanced at his Rolodex and pressed in the numbers.

The distant ringing was followed by Christal's voice. *"Hello?"*

"Christal? It's Sid."

"What's up?"

"I'm bummed. One of our missing geneticists, Nancy Hartlee, was found floating off Long Island. I'm just hoping that Mike Harris, the guy from UCLA who had to take a pee, and Cindy Creedmore, my girl from George Washington U, aren't doing the same." He tried to cheer up. "But I've got news for you."

"What, Sid?"

"A couple of things. You asked me to get your car out of hock at Dulles. I got the keys you mailed me and had Andersen drop me off. I found the car, paid the chit, and drove it home. It's out beside my house. Claire isn't worried about it, and it's not hurting anything sitting there. No hurry. Pick it up whenever. Uh"—he glanced at the ticket on the corner of his desk—"you owe me eighty-four eighty-five."

"Thanks, Sid! You're a lifesaver. The check's in the mail as soon as I hang up."

"How's life in LA? Still sun, smog, and too much work?"

"We're leaving tomorrow for Toronto. Sheela's on location there. We're staying at the Toronto Westin Harbor Castle if you need us."

"Good. I like Toronto. Get to Tim Horton's for me, will you? Check out those chocolate donuts they make. And drink a bottle of Upper Canada Dark. You can only get it in Ontario. Along that line, I've got something for you."

"Is it fattening or alcoholic?"

"Neither. Genesis Athena. You wanted me to stick the name into my computer?"

"Yeah?"

"Biotech."

"What?"

"It's a biotech firm. The head offices are in Yemen, of all places. Not exactly what you'd call the steaming hub of biotechnological activity, but I guess, given the political situation, they got a good deal on land or something. That, and looking at the prospectus, there's a lot of Arab ownership."

"So why would...?" There was a pause. *"Arab, did you say?"*

"Have I developed a stutter, or is this just a bad connection?"

"Sid, can you send me what you've got?"

"Yeah, Chris. Same email you told me before?"

"That's it."

"It's on the way."

"I owe you one."

"I can't wait to collect."

"Sid?"

"Yeah, Chris?"

"Has Hank been in touch?"

Sid frowned. "No. Should he have been?"

"He's here. Trying to find me. If he does call, you don't know anything. Nothing. Got that?"

"Uh, are you just being paranoid, or does this have a purpose?"

"We think he might have some interest in getting close to one of Lymon's principals. Nothing firm, mind you, and we doubt illegal, but, well, just keep it under your hat, all right?"

"Yeah, sure. Hey, you know I'd do anything for

Lymon. As to Hank, well, when he calls, I haven't heard a thing since you left DC."

"You're a pal, Sid. I love you. Take care."

And then she was gone.

"You love me?" He smiled wistfully. "If I could only be so lucky."

CHAPTER 16

S hooting costs were cheaper in Canada. In Toronto, the people more friendly, and, most ironic of all, the city lent itself to many different interpretations of the good old USA. Not to mention that the city boasted a support industry that—with the possible exception of London—was second only to Hollywood.

Sheela considered that as she sat in front of her penthouse window and looked out at the night. Her room was high in the Westin Harbor Castle. Three hundred feet below, she could see the marina hemmed by rocky jetties that enclosed a little harbor on the shores of Lake Ontario. Boats floated on black water illuminated by the city lights. She could see more dots of light out on Island Park where the last of the ferries had crossed.

To the west, just out of her view, red-and-white Air Canada planes periodically took off from a compact lakeside airport. They were small, mostly twin-engine or equipped with floats as they headed for the wild Canadian northland.

Looking out beyond Island Park and across the water, she could see several ships, their lights nothing more than yellow dots in the night. South and slightly west, across the international border, Buffalo, New York, radiated its light into the low clouds. South-southeast, she could see Rochester's telltale glow.

Toronto. *Home.* But was it? Yes, it was Canada, but it didn't feel like home. The red-and-white Canadian flags with her beloved maple leaf warmed her soul, as did the familiar sight of the big yellow Bay department store signs, the red ScotiaBank, and finding CBC on the television in the morning—although she had no idea who the hosts were these days.

The weight of the loonies and toonies in her hands weren't the same as dollars, and even though she had told the reporter from the *Globe and Mail* that it was good to be home, she now had to question the veracity of that.

Home had been Saskatchewan. Not Ontario. What was it about Canada that it seemed to be independent worlds separated by an even greater distance than she felt between Regina and LA? It was only after living in the States with its antagonistic Democrats and Republicans, that she had come to see how fragmented the notion of unity really was in the Canadian psyche. Quebec, Ontario, and the western provinces might have been three different countries, with the maritime provinces as some peripheral satellites orbiting out there in the foggy east somewhere.

She turned at a slight knock. "Come in."

The door opened, and she could see the main room

as Lymon entered with a six-pack of what looked like beer hanging from his hand. He was dressed neatly, wearing a blazer and tie, his legs in cotton trousers.

"I brought something."

"Beer?" she asked, squinting at the six-pack.

"Upper Canada Dark," he replied. "Something Christal said we had to try based upon an old friend's recommendation."

She gave him a look from under lowered brows. "I've got a screen call tomorrow at five a.m. Does that mean anything to you?"

He glanced around her room, took in the laid-back covers of the bed, smooth and folded as the turndown service had left them. Only a blind idiot could fail to notice that she was still fully dressed as she sat in her chair before the window.

In an inoffensive tone, he said, "Apparently it means more to me than it does to you. If you had been sacked out according to plan, you wouldn't have heard that faintest of knocks."

"No, I suppose not." She pointed. "The opener is over there, assuming they're not twist-offs."

He walked to the counter, pulled out two bottles, and levered the tops off, calling, "Glass?"

"No." She frowned as she took the bottle and studied it in the half-light. "You know, most Canadian beer is pretty weak. It's not like the microbrews you're used to."

"I'll take my chances." He lifted the long neck, sipped, and smiled.

Sheela lifted her bottle and washed some of the effervescent brew over her tongue. "That's really good."

Lymon stood silently, staring out at the dark lake below. "Quite a view."

"Your room doesn't have this?"

He shrugged. "I get the CN Tower, a glimpse of the white top of the ballpark, and a nice panorama of downtown." He turned. "How's the shooting going?"

"Funny you should ask." She used a toe to tap the script she'd dropped on the floor by the chair leg. "Without Manny, we've actually moved ahead of schedule. You tell me, Lymon, how does a prick like that get to be so important?"

"Women drool over him." He chuckled. "Christal said that even she had to do a double take when he walked out at the photo shoot."

"She's a pretty sharp cookie, isn't she?"

Lymon nodded. "I wish I could have hired her when I first started in this business."

"I haven't seen her for the last couple of days."

"Since we were shooting inside the Royal Ontario Museum, security was tighter than on the street. I turned her loose to do her research."

"What's she found?"

"Why do you think a biotech firm would have a link to your web site and social media platform?"

Sheela closed her eyes as she leaned back in the padded chair and sipped the mellow dark beer. "I have no idea, Lymon. Social media and the internet is Dot's domain. What did she say?"

"She said that you don't look a gift horse in the mouth. Genesis Athena throws you pennies from heaven. Their check clears each month."

"Maybe I'll ask when I do *The Hour* with Stroumboulopoulos tomorrow evening. George knows everything." She cracked an eye and glanced across at the clock next to her bed. "God, is that the time?"

"You have to be up in five hours." Lymon's voice was soft. "I was afraid that you weren't sleeping."

"Yes, Doctor. I'll just suck down my suds and collapse."

"I worry about you."

The way he said it warmed her heart. "I'll be fine, Lymon." She paused. "What's the word on your mysterious Arab?"

"Thankfully, there is nothing to report." He frowned. "Here's a curious twist. The day before we left, Christal's, uh, I guess you could call him 'ex,' showed up."

"The one from New York?"

"Yep. He wanted to see her something fierce. Offered her a job and, get this, even five grand just to meet with him." -

Sheela opened her eyes and turned her head to stare. Lymon's craggy features were softly illuminated by the light filtering through the tall window. She could see the firm set of his lips, the way he rocked up on his toes. "That worries you?"

"He was with Sheik Abdulla in New York. Then he shows up trying to get a line on Christal. Why don't I like that scenario?"

"You think he'd try to use Christal to get to me?"

"Maybe. Not that it would do him much good. If he thinks that she'd tumble into his arms and help him do evil, he's a sadly mistaken young boy."

"Did you meet him?"

"He came to the office looking for her."

"What did you think?"

"Attractive, sharp, self-possessed, but not one hundred percent on his game. He tried to follow me to Christal's. Did a shabby job of it. Not what Christal's description would have led me to believe about his talents." He paused. "Curious, don't you think? First Christal goes into protection, and then he does? Is that just coincidence?"

"Maybe." She shrugged. "What else does an ex-FBI agent do? Private investigation? Police work? There aren't that many allied fields, are there?"

"No. I suppose not. I'm just concerned, is all. It's a pattern I can't explain. If I can't explain it, it makes me nervous. The more nervous I get, the more I want to explain things."

She placed the beer to one side and stood, walking on bare feet to stand behind him. Wrapping her arms around him, she placed her cheek on his shoulder. "It will be all right, Lymon. You will keep me safe. You always have."

"Ah, yes," he eluded bitterly, "just like in that hallway in New York, and then, of course, there's my triumph in the ladies' room at the Beverly Wilshire."

"I wasn't hurt, was I?" she asked.

"You could have been."

She said nothing, tightening her hold, feeling the hard muscle lining his ribs and belly. For a long time, she stood like that, allowing his warmth to seep into her cool body.

Finally, she took a deep breath, let him go, and said, "I can sleep now, Lymon. Thank you."

He turned, brushed his lips across her hair, and walked silently to the door, where he let himself out into the main room.

CHAPTER 17

The place was called Rotterdam, a microbrewery several blocks north of the Toronto Bluejays' ballpark. It didn't look like much from the outside, just a sign, the walls made of rough-sided ruddy brick. Inside, it was raucous, popular, and filled with the young and vigorous. Through gaps in the back wall, Christal could see shiny stainless steel vats where various kinds of beer and ale were brewed. The white wooden walls had been scarred by years of occupancy. Posters hung here and there, and a series of large blackboard menus listed various brews and foods, all chalked in with different-colored block letters.

A hockey game ensorcelled a clutch of husky young men at the far end of the main room. They wore numbered jerseys and were accompanied by two rather nubile young women wearing cutoff shorts and stretch shirts a size too small for the breasts they'd stuffed into them.

The wreckage of a fish-and-chips dinner basket was

pushed off to Christal's left, and a half-full glass of the establishment's famed stout sat to her right. The bar napkin before her was stuck to the table, but still served to fulfill its God-given purpose as a notepad.

On the napkin top, she had printed GENESIS ATHENA. Then she had defined the terms. Genesis: to produce, to give birth to, to create. Athena: ancient Greek goddess of knowledge, first in war, symbol of the city of Athens, goddess of wisdom and knowledge, born fully formed from the forehead of Zeus.

She considered the relationship of the two words together. Athena, sprung full-blown from the forehead of Zeus; how had she been born?

"Use a fire axe?" she muttered, thinking about extracting Athena from Zeus's forehead bone. Did that mean heads had anything to do with the assaults? Mel Gibson's razor scuzz came from the head. But that flew in the face of Sheela's tampon and urine. Nor did it fit the harpoon shot at Brad Pitt's butt.

"A sample?" she asked under her breath. At that moment the room exploded with cries as someone scored a goal on the hockey game playing at the other end of the room.

What was it that Lymon had said about Hollywood celebrities? That they paid for their success with pieces of themselves? Pieces, like had been taken from Manny de Clerk's penis? She frowned, thinking of witches and the desires that led them to possess.

Lymon's words returned to haunt her: *"Under all the flashbulbs, fancy dresses, and long shiny cars, the world is feeding off of her blood and sucking at her soul."*

Christal reached into her purse and pulled out the

Genesis Athena flier that the kid had handed her at the benefit:

GENESIS ATHENA MAKES DREAMS COME TRUE.

YOU CAN BRING HER INTO YOUR LIFE.

Below was the image of Sheela Marks smiling out at the world.

"All right, I'll bite." Christal reached into her bag for her cell phone and dialed the 1-800 number on the flyer. She pressed *send* and waited through three rings before an automated voice said, *"Greetings! Welcome to Genesis Athena, the home of the stars! Please use the keyboard on your telephone to enter the first name and then push the pound sign before entering the last name of the celebrity or star that you admire the most."*

Christal turned the phone so she could punch SHEELA#MARKS.

The automated voice said, *"According to your selection, you have chosen—"* Another voice supplied, *"Sheela Marks."*

Christal smiled. Then the first voice resumed, *"If this is correct, please press one."*

Christal pushed the *one* on her keypad and heard the tone.

"For our free celebrity bio, press one now."

Christal repeated the operation.

"If you consider yourself to be Sheela's greatest fan, press one now."

Christal did.

"Sheela Marks has something special. When she smiles, the world is bathed in light. If you dream of her night and day, press one."

Christal made a face as she complied.

"We think you might have what it takes to join Sheela Marks' most exclusive circle of admirers. If you agree, press one now."

Christal pressed.

"Please enter your name and address starting with street, box, city, state, postal code, or zip now. Speak slowly and clearly for our voice recognition software."

Christal, caught off balance, sputtered, "Uh, I'm Lisa Bridges, 12256 Wilshire Boulevard, Suite Two, West Hollywood, California, 91210." She had only a moment to wonder if giving the LBA office address had been the right snap decision.

"Lisa Bridges, 12256 Wilshire Boulevard, Suite Two, West Hollywood, California, 91210." The voice repeated it perfectly. *"If this is correct, press one now."*

Christal punched the button.

"Enter your phone number now and press pound."

Christal entered her phone.

"Thank you for calling Genesis Athena and sharing your love of Sheela Marks. We will be mailing our Sheela Marks packet to you today. Please look for it in your box. If you do not receive it within the next week, please call this number again." A pause. *"We'll be sharing your dreams of Sheela."* Then a click indicated the end of the conversation.

The group at the far end whooped again as two hockey players slammed headlong into each other and tumbled onto the ice.

CHAPTER 18

Sid Harness glanced at his watch. Twenty-eight minutes after noon. He still had two minutes before Lymon was supposed to call. Sid used the time to peel back the paper that wrapped his turkey-and-provolone sandwich. He was sitting at a white vinyl-clad table in a Subway off Thomas Circle. Looking out the window, he could just see the statue of the corroded general sitting on his dark bronze horse. Traffic wheeled around below the general's feet. He was scowling out, theoretically, with the same grim determination that had held the line at Chickamauga, Franklin, and Nashville.

The lunch crowd clogged the small restaurant, and behind the glass counter, two dark-skinned people, perhaps Pakistani or Iranian, hustled back and forth, slapping meat, lettuce, peppers, cheeses, and tomatoes onto buns.

It was a good place. Loud, crowded, and hectic. If anyone overheard, they'd only get bits and pieces. Sid had wedged himself into a small corner table, his back to the room. He sipped at the Coke he'd bought and could barely hear the Commerce Department secretaries bitching about their boss at the crowded table behind him. The good-looking blonde kept banging his chair back with hers.

Sid's phone rang a half second after he'd taken his first bite. Swallowing, he washed it down with the Coke and opened his cell. "Harness."

"Sid? Lymon."

"I was just sitting here, thinking I ought to be billing you by the hour."

"Okay." Lymon paused. *"Is that legal?"*

"Hell no! But then, neither is what I'm doing on your account. You'd think I was working for LBA instead of you-know-who." He glanced around uneasily, satisfied that people were more interested in slamming lunch and getting back to the grind than eavesdropping on wayward FBI agents.

"Did you get what I need?"

"If I got your message correctly, you wanted to know where the toll-free number you gave me was physically located. Your tax dollars have allowed me to ascertain that that phone number is answered at 98376 Virginia Avenue in Broomfield, Colorado."

"Colorado?"

"That's what the divine oracle that lives inside the computer said. If you need to know more, you're going to have to cast tea leaves, or do a little old-fashioned detective-type footwork."

"Right. Thanks, Sid. What about the Sheik?"

"He's a curious guy. Turns out he's not actually from Saudi Arabia. Hails from warm, sunny, sandy

Qatar. That cozy little country about midway down the east side of the Persian Gulf."

"I know where Qatar is. We spent a week floating out in the harbor there, remember? R and R compliments of the good old USN."

"Yeah, I do seem to recall that, but then I have the keen brain of a highly trained federal agent. You're just a marshmallow celebrity guard guy these days."

"Do you want to get to the point?"

"The Sheik's rich—owns a fleet of tankers and freighters that handle about ten percent of the shipping going in and out of the Persian Gulf. He also has major investments in real estate around the world. You might be interested to know that he's big in your business."

"Yeah, pictures, I know."

"He likes being seen with pretty women, especially movie stars and high-profile models. He likes to squire them around the world in his private 757." He lowered his voice. "Just between you and me, I heard that he does sensitive things for both the Bureau and the Company down at the big L."

The big L was Sid's personal slang for the Central Intelligence Agency in Langley.

"I see. Anything that you can tell me that might relate to my client?"

"No. He seems to be a legit businessman who has decided that the future lies with the West rather than the dogmatic rag-heads who want to go back to the Middle Ages. No conspicuous ties to terrorism, Al Qaeda, ISIS, bad guys in Iran, or anything that would blacklist him."

"How about biotech? Is he invested in that?"

"Odd that you should mention it. Yeah. He owns

several companies that are into genetic engineering. They're agricultural. You know, drought-resistant corn and tomatoes, that sort of thing." Sid paused, wondering why it hadn't registered when he skimmed the memo he'd requested on Sheik Amud Abdulla. *Genetics?*

"Sid? Christal is here. She wants to know if you got any answer from the guys at Quantico about the questionnaire."

"Put her on."

He waited and heard Christal's voice. *"Hey, Sid. What's happening?"*

"My cold turkey sandwich remains undigested in front of me. It's a hot day in DC. My investigation is spinning its wheels in loose sand. I think Peter is going to make me shelve my kidnapped scientists if I don't have anything by the end of the week."

"Kidnapping cases don't suit you. What did the shrinks say?"

Sid pulled out his notepad and a pen. "When we're done, I'll attach the report in an email. You'll have to read the fine print, but head shrink Tom Tanner thought it was a test. You know, the sort psychologists give people to profile their personalities. He said that the changing questions were routine. If you answer something that gets a hit, the program changes to ask you more specific questions. Uh, say you've got a neurosis about being compulsively neat. It tailors itself to determine just how fucked up you really are."

"All this is in the report?"

"Yeah, I'll email the attachment from my personal phone as soon as I get back to the office. Do me a favor, huh? Delete it after you read it. I don't want anything coming back to haunt my sleep."

"For you, Sid, anything. Lymon and I will burn it in the trash can. Then we'll flush the ashes down the john."

He grinned as he took a bite of his sandwich. Through a mouthful, he said, "You know, Chris, spy work really suits you."

CHAPTER 19

The green room for *The Hour* at the studio in downtown Toronto was well stocked. Christal glanced past Lymon as Rob Sawyer, a Canadian science fiction author, opened the refrigerator and removed a can of pop. Sawyer was up next, having just won a Canadian literary award.

She reclined on a gray fabric-upholstered couch and glanced up at the television monitor as a round of applause broke out. The television in the corner of the small room showed Sheela as she walked out on stage clad in a pastel blue Ungaro wraparound.

People in the green room went silent as Sheela walked up to Stroumboulopoulos and kissed him lightly on the cheek.

"That's my Sheela," Dot whispered. She sat in the chair opposite them, a sheaf of papers in her hands, reading glasses down on her nose as she watched Sheela take her seat and smile out at the live audience. The orchestra was playing the theme to *Blood Rage*. When the music died away, Stroumboulopolous began teasing Sheela about her Oscar and why she had come to Toronto to shoot *Jagged Cat.*

Christal glanced at Lymon, seeing the longing in his expression as he watched Sheela on the monitor. "You okay?" she asked in a soft voice.

"Yeah," he muttered, tearing his attention from the screen. "It's been busy. What's Sid's report look like?"

She'd deleted the file after reading it. "I failed the test, Lymon. That's why the web site cut me off. It makes perfect sense."

"Explain."

She glanced around the crowded room. Everyone in the green room was fixed on the TV and Sheela. "You've got to see the questionnaire for what it really is: a tool for evaluating the people taking it. Whatever Genesis Athena is looking for, I gave it the wrong information."

"Okay. Such as?"

"Well, for instance, I listed the wrong interests under hobbies. I think I said something flippant about stamp collecting and big game hunting. That's not what they were looking for."

"Right." Lymon frowned. "What do you think they're after?"

"I think they wanted obsession. That's why the bathroom questions were so important. I answered practically; their psychologists were looking for some different order in the importance of bathroom fixtures."

"Huh? You lost me." He crossed his arms.

"All right, let's say that someone compulsively filled out that questionnaire. After a toilet and sink, they might say a mirror was the next most important thing."

"Why?"

She was fishing, knowing that she was out of her

league. "Because an obsessive person might need to see themselves, to constantly be reassured that their hair is in place, that nothing is stuck in their teeth."

Lymon grinned. "Okay, so we should have had Tony take the test."

"Yeah, maybe." She frowned. "But my guess is that your old friend Krissy might have been a better choice."

Lymon started, his gaze prying at her. "Krissy's a nut. She's obsessed with..." He whistled softly. "Jesus, is that what you're getting at?"

"Look, it's just the way my mind works, okay? Grandma said I had the gift. It's the closest I can come to an explanation for a hunch like this."

"How often are your hunches proven right?"

"Often enough that I don't question them."

"So, you're thinking Genesis Athena is designed to recognize obsessive-compulsive disorders?"

She nodded. "I'm not sure why, Lymon. That part eludes me. I'm booked on a United flight to Denver in the morning. Maybe it will make sense when I find their offices. Broomfield? That's a curious place for their headquarters, but maybe by going there, I'll figure it out. If I find out it's a mental institution, some of the pieces will have fallen in place. If not, we'll see what comes in the mail when we get back to LA, but I'm betting that their Sheela packet will have something in it that will act as a lure for the lunatic fringe."

Lymon was staring off into the distance. "Did Krissy ever answer your email asking about her having Sheela's baby?"

"No."

"We could have nailed her on that. Even sending an email is in violation of her restraining order."

"Do you think Genesis Athena is run by one of Sheela's wacko fans?"

"After seeing the 'share-la-Sheela' site, I guess I can believe anything. My inclination is that it's probably harmless." Worry lined his brow. "I'm more concerned about the Arab angle and what Abdulla wants. He's rich, powerful, and sniffing around Sheela. He's a threat; I can just feel it."

"Yeah, me, too." Christal rubbed her arms uncomfortably. "You weren't the one who got eye-raped right there in front of God and everyone."

Lymon nodded in concern. "On that line, maybe your buddy Hank is Abdulla's new bird dog. Sid said that the good Sheik likes pretty girls, right? If you'd taken that job, you might be jetting around the world in posh luxury rather than sitting here waiting on the George and Sheela show."

The crowd burst out laughing as Sheela made a joke about the tampon theft. It seemed that the story still hadn't died.

"Get a life, boss. I'd rather be a maid at a Motel Six in Albuquerque than spend a single second in that guy's presence. Grandma would have said he had *el mal ojo,* the evil eye. The man's bad news. End of story."

"Here, here."

Yes, evil, a voice whispered in Christal's head. *And he wants you!*

A cold shiver ran through her. Out of nowhere, she asked, "Do you think he's behind the celeb hits?"

"What? Where did that come from?"

"I was just thinking how creepy Abdulla was, and it popped out."

Lymon glanced up as Stroumboulopoulos and

Sheela laughed together. They had moved on to telling some joke about ice fishing in Saskatchewan. Christal decided it was something peculiarly Canadian in humor.

Lymon said, "I could see some obsessed male Arab having an interest in a pretty woman's tampon. Kinky, but possible. As to Mel Gibson's razor scuzz and shooting a dart into Brad Pitt's butt? Well, there you've got me."

"You know," Christal mused, "Hank works for Abdulla. Maybe we should have met with him. We could have stripped him naked, hung him up by his thumbs, and squeezed him for information. I think he'd have spilled his guts with the right persuasion."

Lymon gave her a careful scrutiny. "Are you always this edgy?"

She fixed a plastic smile. "Only when I imagine the expression on Hank's face when I flick my Bic under his scrotum."

"You must really like the guy."

"I hate people who lead me astray. Mostly because they remind me how stupid I can be. If I'm ever stupid, Lymon, don't remind me of it, okay?"

"Yeah. Images of butane lighters are filling my fertile imagination." He lifted an eyebrow, hazel eyes attentive. "I've been meaning to ask: Do you think it's a coincidence that Hank goes into personal security just after you do?"

"I don't know," she answered honestly. "I had no contact with him after I left the Bureau. The only link between the two of us would have been Sid."

"And he wouldn't have said anything to Abrams." Lymon wiggled his shoulders as he scrunched lower into the seat. "The coincidence bothers me. I don't know, Christal; it's like we're dancing around the peripheries but not seeing what ties the whole puzzle together."

"If it's a puzzle," she countered. "I mean, you're just assuming that Genesis Athena, Sheik Abdulla, the celeb hits, and Hank are related."

He mulled it over. "All right, you're the one with the weird spooky gift and the brouhaha grandma. What's your take? Are they?"

"Related," she muttered, unhappy with herself for saying it. "For the life of me, I don't know why, but I think when it comes to me, it will all fit like a glove."

A wild burst of applause broke out as Sheela stood, waved to the crowd, and took the host's hand.

"What about her?" Lymon's voice was barely a whisper. "Will she be safe, Christal?"

Christal paused, lowering her voice to match his. "You should marry her, Lymon."

"Sure," he breathed.

"Julia Roberts married Danny Moder, her camera-man. And Anne Heche married her cameraman, too. Sharon Stone married Phil Bronstein, a newspaper editor."

"Christal?"

"Huh?"

"Shut up." He rose too quickly to his feet, lifting his sleeve to say, "Paul, she's on the way. We'll meet you at the door within five."

In her earpiece, Christal heard, *"Roger, boss. Paparazzi are here in a drove. Tell Sheela to be on deck and ready for them."*

Christal rose, straightened her tweed skirt, and

followed after Lymon. She would be slightly behind Sheela and to one side as they left the building. Dot had gathered her things and stepped into line as Lymon explained about the paparazzi.

Sheik Abdulla's face hung in the back of Christal's mind.

"El mal ojo!" her grandmother's voice spoke from beyond the grave. *"He is evil, child, and he wants you!"*

CHAPTER 20

Hank Abrams sipped coffee from a disposable Tim Horton's cup and glanced around the spacious lobby of the Westin Harbor Castle. At this time of morning, the place was like a tomb. Only the desk clerk stood behind the polished counter. Passing the registration desk, he lifted one of the house phones and punched O.

After three rings, a voice informed him, *"Hotel operator."*

"Yes, could you connect me with Christal Anaya's room, please?"

"One moment."

Hank pursed his lips and scowled uncertainly as he monitored the lobby. It had taken him two days to discover that Sheela Marks had packed up and flown to Toronto to film scenes on location. He'd scrambled to get here, then scrambled for another day and a half to find Christal's hotel.

Damn it, I'm headed for a fuckup again.

He hated the feeling of inadequacy that had

plagued him since the Gonzales fiasco. When he rubbed his cheeks, he could feel stubble. Hell of a thing. He used to be perfectly groomed. The way he lived now, rustling from one hotel to another, he barely had time to wash his clothes.

Now he had her located. All it would take was a touch, just a moment in her presence, and he could call it quits and return to New York. He ran the gimmick through his head: He'd say he was with building maintenance, eh? The phones had gone down—been hacked by pranksters, eh? Was she Melinda Arbuckle in room 4312? When she said no, he'd ask to which room he'd been connected.

The phone rang five times before the operator broke in to state, *"I'm sorry, sir. It appears that Ms. Anaya isn't in her room. Would you care to leave a message on her voice mail?"*

"No, thanks." He grimaced as he hung up and glanced at his watch. It was a quarter to five. Where the hell was she? Christ, at this time of morning, the old Christal would have been lost in REM sleep.

He started to turn when the elevator dinged and Christal stepped out, a black nylon suitcase hanging from a strap at her shoulder. She was dressed in a professional pantsuit with a light gray cotton jacket.

Hank turned, facing the wall with the phone to his ear. From the corner of his eye, he watched as Christal crossed the lobby, her heels clicking on the polished floor. She stepped through the glass doors at the main entrance and out to the curb.

Hank hung up the phone and hurried after her, stopping just short of the door, where he could glance past the aluminum jam. The doorman had hailed a cab and was holding the door as Christal slipped into the back seat.

Hank waited until the cab began to roll before stepping out and running up to the doorman.

"Shit!" he cried in despair as he watched the cab take a right onto the street beyond. He turned to the surprised doorman. "Did Chris say where she was headed?" He reached into his pocket and pulled out a set of keys. "She left these, and she's going to be really upset when she realizes they're gone."

The doorman hesitated an instant, seeing the worry on Hank's face, then sputtered, "You'd better hurry, sir. She's on her way to the airport. I heard her say the international terminal."

"Great! Thanks!" Hank turned on his heel, sprinting for the line of cabs that waited in a line at the curve of the drive-in.

Hell! If she was flying somewhere, he had to at least figure out where. If it was back to LA, well and good. He could catch up with her there. If it was somewhere else, did he dare let her out of his sight? What if he lost her again? Verele would think he was a complete bumbling incompetent.

The cab driver—a Sikh, given his turban—was half out of his door when Hank yanked the passenger door open and cried, "International terminal at the airport!"

He slammed the door and shook his head, wiping at the coffee he'd spilled on his pants. The Tim Hortons' cup was half crushed in his hand.

CHAPTER 21

Number 98376 Virginia Avenue was a white, prestressed concrete building in a small industrial complex just off 128th Avenue on the far northern fringes of Denver, Colorado. The buildings were new, with long expanses of darkly tinted glass. Thin strips of lawn were encompassed by white cement walks that bordered the parking lot. The grass had the manicured look of a professional lawn service, and several young trees were growing around a small pond with a delightful little fountain.

Christal pulled into the lot and took one of the visitor's spaces two down from the handicapped slot with its blue sign.

She killed the phone's map function that had guided her to the address and checked herself in the mirror. The afternoon sun was already starting to cook the inside of the car. Christal ran a brush through her gleaming black hair, decided that nothing offensive was in her teeth, and dropped the phone into her purse before stepping out into the hot air.

God, have I really been up for twelve hours already? It didn't seem right that she could feel used up, and it was just after midday here. The flight in from Toronto had been turbulent, just uncomfortable enough that the pilot had kept people strapped in for most of it.

The DIA airport had been plugged with people. As she'd waited in the bowels of the B concourse for one of the shuttles, someone had said that only two of the automated trains were running. The entire time, she'd felt as if eyes were locked on her. But when she had glanced around, it was only to see a sea of faces, all looking harried and irritated.

At least Avis had been up to their usual proficiency. Her car, a Toyota Crown Limited, had been waiting after the shuttle bus dropped her at the right space. From there, the drive through Denver had been stop-and-go as the highway patrol cleaned up a wreck on I-76. The jam had given her time to really consider her plan of attack.

"All right, Genesis Athena, here I come." She walked up to the black glass door, gripped the aluminum handle, and pulled it open. Cool air washed over her as she stepped into a small lobby. Three chairs and a compact couch seemed to have surrounded and captured a small wooden table off to the right. In the corner, a potted plant lived in tropical splendor under the fluorescent lights. To her left, a stairway led up to the second floor, while a hallway was blocked off with a wooden double door.

Christal noticed a building directory on the wall beside the stairs and walked over. White plastic letters were inserted into a black background and denoted the occupants in different suites. Five businesses called the building home, but none of them was named Genesis Athena.

"The plot thickens," she whispered as she studied the choices. She immediately discarded the two engineering firms, decided that the fishing lure company was out, and hesitated as she studied the last two.

She discarded AlpenGlo Publishing and went with Cy-Bert as the most likely candidate. It was located in Suite 201. Christal climbed the textured cement stairs and passed through the fire door. Cy-Bert occupied the first suite of offices to the right. The door was wooden with a brass knob. A slit of window beside it gave her a view of a reception area and several doors leading into the rear.

Christal stepped in and walked to the desk, where a young woman in her early twenties looked up from a Kat Martin romance she was reading.

"Hello. Can I help you?" Excited blue eyes met Christal's.

"I hope so. I'm Christal Anaya," she replied as she laid a business card on the counter. "I'm with LBA. We're a security firm in Los Angeles. It is our understanding that Genesis Athena has a telephone number that is registered to this address."

The blue eyes grew serious, and the girl pursed thin pink lips. Christal could see the dusting of freckles on her nose. "Genesis Athena...let's see." She wheeled to one side and tapped at a computer console. After several seconds, she said, "Oh, yeah. Here it is." She turned the monitor so that Christal could see the name gleaming on the blue screen. The familiar phone number was listed, as well as an address.

Christal bent around so that she could read it. "Is that address right?"

"Uh, yeah," the young woman admitted. "Uh, I guess so. You'd have to talk to Bill and Simon. They run Cy-Bert. Uh, they're not here now. They're running a marathon in Boulder today."

"Do you mind if I write that down?" Christal was already jotting: Genesis Athena—643 Sa'Dah Street, Aden, Yemen.

"Uh, I guess."

Christal could feel a big chunk of the mystery slide into place. Yemen? That fit what Sid had told them. She asked, "So, how does a Yemeni company have a Colorado telephone address?"

"Oh"—the young woman waved it away—"we have over six hundred clients here, you know? It's like we do all the phones for them. You know, like if you want to have a number and give out information? We do all the ordering and things for telemarketing companies."

"Such as?"

"Well, like, you know, if you sell stuff, right? Like old vinyl records, or clothes, or stuff? You can call one of our numbers and our computers take your order. You know, they ask for, like, which product you saw in their catalog? Then you type in your account number, the item number, and your credit card number, and confirm your address, and the company warehouse sends you the thing you ordered."

"I see."

"Pretty cool, huh?"

"Do you have a number for Genesis Athena in Yemen?"

The ditzy blonde hesitated. "Wow. I don't know if I can give you that. It's like a company secret. Like, what if you're from another company that does the same thing that ours does?"

"I'm not. As the card says, LBA is a security firm. Our only interest is in keeping our clients safe. I swear, I'm not here to steal your clients. If you have any questions, you can call our California office and get confirmation."

The blonde considered it for a moment. "Well, okay. You seem nice. It's like, we send the monthly bill out FedEx, and a check shows up the same way. I remember that now that I think about it. I have to sign for it."

"Do you do the setup here? You know, write the questions and add the voices?"

"We can." She glanced at the blue screen, her finger running down a line of numbers. "But not for Genesis Athena. They do all that themselves." She grinned. "But I got to be the voice for ColoHigh Fashions once."

"Wow!" Christal forced a smile. "So, I'm to understand that you're just a phone service? That's it?"

"Yeah, that's us. If, like, you guys at"—she squinted at the card—"at LBA need a system, we'd be, you know, really glad to be it. But you'll have to talk to Bill and Simon."

"When they get back from the marathon."

"Yeah, like, isn't that cool? You know? They're old—in their late thirties—and they can still run!"

"Yeah, cool."

Christal thanked the girl and turned. When she walked down the stairs, she shook her head. *Genesis Athena really is in Yemen, for God's sake?*

Yemen. Just catty-corner across the Arabian Peninsula from Qatar. Sheik Amud Abdulla called Qatar home. She was chewing on that thought as she climbed into her rental, closed the door, and started the engine to stimulate the air-conditioning.

She lifted her cell and punched in Lymon's number. He answered on the third ring.

"Bridges."

"Lymon? Anaya. Listen, I'm sitting in front of our address in Colorado. You're going to love it. The place is just a phone service. Genesis Athena isn't here."

"So, where are they?"

"You ready for this?"

"Shoot."

"Aden, as in Yemen. Sid was right; it wasn't a ruse." She related her visit to Cy-Bert and gave him the mailing address she'd taken from the computer.

A pause. *"Did you determine if our friend Abdulla has any connection?"*

"All they've got is a telephone contract with Genesis Athena. You should know, however, that if you ever need a phone service, the airhead at the desk will be happy to write LBA a contract. Lymon, my best guess is that this place is a cutout."

"So...what do you think this means for us?"

"Well, for one thing, I think it's a cinch that whoever Genesis Athena is, they don't want to be easily found. And that, boss, really has my whiskers quivering, as Grandma used to say."

"I'll bring this up with Dot when I see her this afternoon."

"Right. Uh, what now? Do you want me back in Toronto or to head for the barn?"

"*Sheela's wrapping her shooting here tomorrow morning. It's up to you, Christal.*"

She was considering that when a dark-blue Chevy Lumina pulled into the parking lot and rolled to a stop two spaces down from hers. The guy was jerking his door open as he killed the engine.

Christal blinked twice and gaped. "Lymon," she said in a sober voice, "Hank Abrams just drove in and jumped out of his car. He's headed right into the Cy-Bert building."

"*What? Are you sure?*"

She put her Toyota rental into reverse and backed out, making sure she cleared the lot before she floored the accelerator.

"*Christal?*" Lymon was barking from halfway across the continent. "*Christal? Are you all right?*"

For the moment, she couldn't answer. Hank hadn't looked right. He'd been unshaven, his clothes rumpled and his hair mussed. That grainy expression reminded her of a man who wasn't sleeping well, someone haunted by depression and frustration.

"*Christal? Are you there?*"

"Lymon, I'm spooked," she added as she took a right onto 128th. "How the hell did he know I was going to be here?"

CHAPTER 22

The lounge at the Beverly Hilton had only a few patrons. Hank Abrams sat at a small table next to the far wall and hunched in the cloth-backed chair. He stared uneasily down at the glass of Glenfiddich, neat. Strains of sixties and seventies music drifted down from the speakers. Behind the bar, the bartender—dressed in a puffy white shirt and black slacks—was tapping the screen on his register.

Staring into the amber fluid, Hank fought the desperate desire to upend his single malt and chug the contents. As of that moment, he could still expense the high-dollar scotch, but whether he'd be able to in a matter of minutes was anyone's guess.

God, what a relief it would be to down one after another and dull the growing ache in his soul. For those blissful hours, he could be smashed out of his head. The worry, the frustration, and disappointment would be gone.

Shit, six months ago, I was the fair-haired boy in the Bureau.

Now it was all gone. He'd had a gorgeous and talented wife, a nice house, a solid job. People had looked up to him as he rode the rocket to stardom.

How had he lost it all?

Christal!

He closed his eyes, his hands grasping at the air, knotting until his forearms hurt.

Every failure, every fuckup, had Christal at the bottom of it. Jesus, what was she, the anti-Christ?

"Oh, yeah, like she was just here!" the cheery blonde had said. "*I mean, like, you should have seen her on the stairs, you know?"*

Hank rubbed his eyes. A sour churning in his stomach left him half-sick, a tickle of nausea at the bottom of his throat.

He looked up when he caught movement in his peripheral vision. Neal Gray, immaculate in a charcoal Brooks Brothers suit, white shirt, and matching tie, approached the table and pulled out the opposite chair.

"You look like hell," Neal told him as he took the drink list and scanned the offerings.

"I haven't gotten much sleep the last couple of days." The question had been burning inside him. "When I called you from Toronto and told you she was headed for Colorado, how the hell did you know she'd be going to that place?"

Neal looked up as the bartender approached and laid a napkin on the vinyl table. "Can you make a margarita? Nothing fancy, just on ice."

"Yeah, sure," the bartender replied and turned back to the bar.

Neal leaned back, his fingers twisting the edge of the napkin into a spike. He gave Hank an appraising look as he coolly studied him. The man seemed to see right through the front, penetrating Hank's skin to read the growing desperation and fear. "Hank, your call from Toronto surprised us. How did you learn she was headed to Denver?"

"I managed to get close enough when she was checking in at the United counter. People don't look around when they're talking to the desk agents. It's as if they don't want to look suspicious or something. I overheard."

He couldn't stand it any longer and blurted, "Look! I'm not a fuckup! I know it looks like I can't carry out a simple assignment, but the bitch won't even see me! Shit, I offered her five grand just to meet with me, and she turned it down flat! And then, this Toronto thing, how was I supposed to know she'd be flying off with Sheela Marks? God, I swear, she's a fucking devil!"

"Hank"—Neal's voice was even—"take a break here. You're being too hard on yourself."

Hank gasped. It was too soon to believe he was off the hook. "I was ahead of her! Then, bang! I'm stuck in traffic behind a wreck on a Denver freeway. By the time I figure out just how to get to this place, she's already been there!"

Neal smiled. "Christal Anaya really gets to you, huh?"

Hank swallowed hard. "There are times, I swear, if I could reach out and wrap my hands around her throat..." He stared at the tendons standing out on the backs of his hands, his fingers tightening on the air above his scotch.

Neal leaned back. "It's okay. You did all right, Hank. Sure, we'd have liked to have had our sample by now, but warning us that she was headed to Colorado made up for that."

"It did?"

"She was already on one of our lists. She flagged one of our computer websites a couple of weeks ago. The lady is digging around at the edges of one of the Sheik's companies." Neal paused. "Tell me, do you think she's capable of industrial espionage?"

Hank leaned back, considering. "Christal? I don't know. I mean, she's not one to break the rules. She's kind of by the book, if you know what I mean."

Neal studied him. "You really thought I was coming to can you, didn't you?"

Hank swallowed hard. "Yeah."

Neal leaned forward. "What have you got left, Hank? Besides this job, I mean."

"Not much."

"Your mother's in a nursing home in upstate New York. Your support is the only thing between her and Medicare, which won't cover the costs. Uh, just between the two of us, how do you think this thing with Marsha is going to work out? Will you get anything from the settlement?"

"Her firm's handling the divorce," Hank murmured. "She's offered a settlement if I don't fight it. Fifty grand, cut and dried, and I don't contest it."

"You going to take it?"

"Neal, if I fight it, she's going to clean me out. I'll be in hock to the lawyers alone for the next twenty years." Then, unable to help himself, he spilled the whole story about Gonzales, Christal, the night they'd screwed in the van.

After he'd run dry, Neal sat back, a pensive look on

his face. "And they never figured out how Gonzales got a camera into the van?"

"No."

After a long silence, Neal's blue eyes narrowed. "Tell me something, Hank. How much of a stickler are you for the rule book?"

Hank straightened, a tickle of anxiety in his breast. "Where's this going?"

"Nowhere illegal, if that's what you're thinking." Neal grinned. "You might say that where we're going, there are no laws...but the pay is *real* good. I can assure you it's not drugs, or weapons, or any of the usual 'high risk' ventures. We do nothing that violates the law within the territorial borders of the United States." A pause. "How would you feel about making a hundred and twenty grand a year—not counting bonuses—as a starting salary?"

He perked up. "What's the catch?"

"From our perspective, it might just be you." Neal smiled up at the bartender as the man placed the margarita on the table. Neal handed him a credit card. "If you'd run a tab, I'd appreciate it."

"Yes, sir." The bartender retreated.

Neal sipped his drink and looked up. "Do you believe in quid pro quo? If I do something for you, you'll do something for me?"

"Like in the Mafia?"

Neal laughed. "We're trying to make up our minds if we want to invest in you for the long term. How would you feel if we looked into this Gonzales thing? Figured it out, if you will. Would that be worth anything to you?"

"Damn straight, it would."

Neal caught him off guard when he asked, "So, how does a top agent have such a hard time catching up to an unsuspecting woman? We thought you'd have obtained the sample within the first forty-eight hours."

Hank took a deep breath, feeling the axe hanging over his head. "You'd think she was being protected by LBA rather than just working for them. Look, I can handle this. All I need is—"

"Christal Anaya has become a problem," Neal interrupted easily. "My people really need to talk to her. If you're with us, we'll let you in on the ground floor of something really big. It will mean leaving Verele...going to work for the Sheik."

Hank frowned, feeling the earth turning soft under his feet. "I don't understand. I'm just supposed to use one of your little gizmos to get a skin sample, right?"

"The plan has changed since then. It changed when Anaya walked into that telephone service in Colorado. There are bigger things afoot here. Things worth billions that I can't tell you about. Yet." Neal leaned forward, an earnest look on his face. "She's been jerking your chain, hasn't she? Come on, admit it: She's the reason you're in this mess."

He felt the resistance run out of him. "Yeah."

"My people need to talk to her, Hank. That's all. Just find her, help me and my crew get to her, and well, we'll talk about it later, all right?"

"You just want to talk?" Something had to be missing.

"Yep." Neal shrugged. "Hank, what the hell have you got left to lose?"

CHAPTER 23

They occupied a spacious photographic studio in West Los Angeles. The photographers had just finished and were in the process of packing their reflectors, dismantling their lights, and casing their cameras.

Christal watched as Sheela smiled and shook hands all the way around. The small group of Spanish businessmen, one by one, took their turns holding her hands and lavishing their thanks. Rex cleared his voice from the side—a signal for Dot, who smiled like a queen as she disengaged Sheela from her admirers and led her back toward the dressing room.

Rex stepped in smoothly, saying, "Gentlemen, that was fantastic! We have rarely had such a professional and flawless shooting session."

A babble of accented voices chimed in agreement. Christal smiled to herself. She'd listened to the three Spaniards as they had talked during the shoot. Their Castilian accent hadn't masked the sexual innuendo as they ogled Sheela during the photo session.

While the photographers continued to disassemble their equipment, a crew began collapsing the series of backdrops. The stage had alternately consisted of scenes from downtown Madrid, Toledo, Seville, and other Spanish cities. One in particular was of the Escorial illuminated by a wash of yellow light. Sheela had modeled various fashions before each, and the photographers had shot roll after roll of photos for the new catalog, billboards, and other media.

Electric fans on either side had created breezes to ruffle Sheela's hair and toss her coattails. That had been the last scene. Christal watched as the techs rolled the big backdrop into a long tube.

Rex caught Christal's eye and gave the slightest nod of his head before shooting a meaningful glance toward the dressing room.

Christal picked up her purse, walking wide around the tripods and stepping past the fan to take the narrow hallway to the rear. The dressing room was a haphazard affair: panels set up to screen Sheela from the main room.

Dot stood with her arms crossed, watching as Sheela slipped out of a long-knit MaxMara dress and handed it to a young woman who replaced it on a hanger and hung it on a wardrobe rack in the rear.

"How'd we do?" Sheela asked as she pulled on her slim denim Blujeanious pants and straightened.

Dot glanced back at Christal, nodded, then turned her attention to Sheela as she reached for a red-patterned top by Guess. "Under all the hype, they're happy. Rex is going to stay behind and stroke their collective manhoods."

"Figuratively, I hope."

"Yeah, me, too," Dot said dryly.

"Whatever it takes." Sheela wearily pulled the top on and fluffed her red-blond hair over her shoulders. She glanced at Christal; with stunning quickness exhaustion had replaced the sparkle she'd shown during the session. "What do you think?"

"I don't see how you keep from falling over." Christal stopped short. "You about ready?"

"Get me home, James." Sheela stifled a yawn, grabbed up her Marc Jacobs purse, and pointed at the door. "Dot, I'll see you tomorrow at my trailer on the lot. You can brief me on my schedule then. I'm going home to fall into bed."

"See you then," Dot agreed.

Christal lifted her cuff mike and said, "Paul? We're on the way."

"Roger. Uh, Christal? There's a guy out here, looks like a lost electrician. He's across the alley...maybe ten yards away. He's got a toolbox and seems to be killing time. Just thought you should know."

"Right. I'll keep an eye out when we step out the back door." She gestured to Sheela. "We're ready."

Christal led the way down the narrow hallway to the sign that read EXIT. She pushed on the crash bar and stepped out. The alley was just off Santa Monica Boulevard, bounded by dented Dumpsters, bits of paper, and a couple of empty bottles. The alleged electrician stood across the alley and stared at her from across the hood of the polished Escalade limo. He had on a yellow hard hat, a leather tool belt filled with pliers, hammers, and such, and wore a gray sweatshirt and blue jeans over brown work boots.

"Come on, Sheela," Christal stepped over and opened the rear limo door.

"Ah, I love this job," Sheela was saying as she stepped outside. "The glamour of the alleys, hotel kitchens, back doors, and—"

The flash took Christal by complete surprise. She blinked, wheeling to see the "electrician." His toolbox was open at his feet, and a large Nikon filled his hands. Instinctively Christal placed herself between Sheela and the paparazzo. The flash continued to pulse as the automatic camera captured Sheela's rapid duck into the limo.

"Hey!" Christal cried, her anger rising. "Just who the hell do you think you are?"

"It's a free country," the paparazzo called back, grinning from behind his lens. "God bless the First Amendment!"

"Maggot!" Christal slipped in behind Sheela and pulled the door shut as she clicked the locks down. "Shit!" She felt humiliated.

"Tricky," Paul called over his shoulder as he slipped the car into gear. "I've never seen that workman ruse before."

Sheela leaned back and closed her eyes. "It's all right. It was only one guy this time."

"God, they're like a bunch of mangy coyotes," Christal muttered as she studied Sheela with worried eyes. During the photo shoot, Sheela had been electric. Then, in the dressing room, she had gone from glittering, smiling energy to sacked lint in an instant. Now she looked hollow and half-digested.

"You need some time off," Christal said softly. "It's none of my business, but given your schedule, I

wouldn't have traded a day off for that photo session—
no matter what it paid."

Sheela barely smiled, cracking one eye to study
Christal. "So, you think I looked that bad?"

"No, you were stunning. I would have thought you
lived for that moment alone. Now you're even more
hammered than before."

"Christal, I had to do it. What, you don't think
today was worth a million and a half? Not to mention
they're boxing up everything I wore today and shipping
it to the house. Freebies, you see. All the better if I
happen to be wearing one of the pieces when the
cameras go off."

Christal blinked. "You're kidding! A million-five and
a whole fall wardrobe for six hours of photos?"

"That's right." Sheela closed her eyes.

"Man, am I in the wrong business? I guess a check
like that makes up for all the hassle. On the way over
here, I thought you were going to fall over from exhaustion. Then, all of a sudden, you were just burning at a
hundred and ten watts."

"It's a trick. A thing you learn." Sheela shrugged it
off. "As to the shoot, doing it is partly prestige. My face
is going to be all over Spain. Gwyneth Paltrow, George
Clooney, Sharon Stone—a lot of American actors have
done the El Corte Ingles shoot. It's the most prestigious
department store chain in charming Espana. Doing
their shoot is one of those notches you cut into your
pistol on the way up."

"But you just flew in with the mourning doves."
Christal glanced at her watch. "Uh, you didn't even get
to go home before coming here."

Sheela gave her a wan smile. "What's the matter,

Christal? Fame and fortune not all that you thought it would be?"

"It never is, is it?"

"No." Sheela lowered her voice. "We had to schedule that shoot for this morning. I'm due on the set tomorrow at five. We only had today as a travel day. Bernard wants to finish up my scenes this week. It will put him—four million and two weeks ahead on time and budget—and he's going to need every cent in post production to fix all the Manny scenes."

"That encounter with Copperhead really did him in, huh?"

"There wasn't that much there to start with." She seemed to be talking in her sleep. "He's a pretty face. No guts. They don't make many men with guts these days."

"Lymon included?" Christal ventured.

"Lymon is definitely excluded. He's the only man I—"

"Yeah, I know." Christal glanced out the tinted window as they turned onto Santa Monica Boulevard. Sunset was burning yellow through the smog and glistening off of the surrounding traffic. People were walking along the sidewalks, passing the businesses that alternately sold donuts, video disks, tattoos, lotions, cameras, and furniture from behind glass windows and beneath colorful signs. When she looked back, Sheela was watching her through heavy lids.

"You know?"

Christal nodded, feeling a pull on her long hair where the seat trapped it. "Is it really so impossible?"

Sheela closed her eyes again. "You remember that guy with the camera back there? *People* or *Us* or

National Enquirer will hand him a couple of hundred for that string of photos." A pause. "Do you have any idea how much they'd pay for a shot of Lymon and me in an intimate situation?"

"A bundle, I suppose." She softly snapped her fingers to get Sheela to look at her before she made a slight nod toward Paul and lifted an inquiring eyebrow.

"He knows," Sheela answered softly. "But thank you for your discretion." She straightened, stretching her arms out in front of her. "Why am I telling you this? God, I *am* tired. It's a warning of what I might blurt when I'm half-asleep."

"It's okay." A beat. "Look, Sheela, if you ever need a confidante, I can keep my mouth shut."

Sheela cranked an eye half-open again. "You know, you could make a fortune with what you could learn. Any of the big rags would pay a bundle for an inside story on Sheela Marks."

Christal laughed out loud. "I could make a fortune smuggling coke in from Colombia or doing hits for organized crime." She paused, giving Sheela a wry smile. "Sorry. Not a chance. Look, I'm a native New Mexican. We're genetically predisposed to both poverty and loyalty. I guess I'll just have to keep your secrets. Anything else would be a denial of my ethnic and cultural heritage."

Sheela smiled at that. "You're just all right, Christal Anaya. A good friend. I don't have many friends."

Christal considered her words. "If I'm going to be your friend, I've got to tell you, I think you're killing yourself with this schedule. You keep it up, and something's going to snap."

"I get a break as soon as we wrap *Jagged Cat*. If I get

too woozy, there are always ways of keeping sharp."

"Chemicals?"

Sheela's eyes remained closed. "I hear censure in your voice."

"Yeah. How many stars OD or wind up so brain-fried on that stuff that they kill their careers?"

"Most," she whispered softly. "It's so easy. Just a little pill...and you're back. Sparkling like a Bulgari diamond and feeling as smooth as an Olay body rub. Suddenly, you're riding a jetting wave that carries you up and up, rising out of a dull grayness."

"And then it smacks you like a bug on a bumper unless you take another one."

"People just don't understand. I can't quit, can't call in sick. Too many people depend on me. Tomaso, Dot, Rex, Tony, Bernard, the studio." Her voice weakened. "I carry them all, Christal. Without me, they're nothing."

"You can't carry them all forever."

"I'm running out of me," Sheela murmured softly. "Running out...empty inside..."

"Hey, just get what sleep you can. I'll wake you when we're home."

Sheela said, "Thank you, Christal," before she nodded off.

Christal studied her face, wondering at the classic lines that had smiled down on millions from the screen. The woman made magic for the multitudes, was worshipped around the globe. So much so that a Spanish department store would chase her down and pay her a million and a half for wearing their clothes in front of a camera. All that, but Sheela couldn't be with the man she loved?

Is it worth it?

CHAPTER 24

"You all right?" Lymon asked as Sheela wobbled on her feet. He caught her arm, steadying her.

She blinked and looked owlishly around the paved lot behind the studio. A row of trailers lurked along one of the high walls, each with a thick black electrical cable, water hose, and flexible sewer line running from beneath to fixtures in the pavement. The early-morning sky had an orange tone, deepened by pollution and the fires burning up in the Angeles forest. The weather guys said the wind would be changing sometime after noon to blow it all inland.

Sheela tightened her grip on Lymon and shook her head as if to rid herself of a bothersome insect. "Just tired, Lymon. Look, get me to my trailer. That's all. I've got time to sleep while the grips and greensmen do their thing."

He tightened his hold on her arm as he walked her toward her trailer. His BMW was perched on its center stand just under the trailer's awning. "You worry me."

She gave the motorcycle a hollow-eyed stare. "That was one of the most memorable days of my life, Lymon. No matter what, never forget that."

"It was just a ride, Sheela."

"Yes...pure paradise."

As they walked by the silver machine, the trailer door opened and Rex leaned out. "Good! Back before I'd thought you'd be."

"What are you doing here?" Sheela's voice reflected weary acceptance.

"Tomaso wouldn't let me see you last night," Rex muttered. "You're going to have to do something with that guy, Sheela." He jammed a thumb into his chest. "I'm *not* the hired help. I'm your manager, not some pastry chef he can...hey, you okay?"

"Tired," she said, leaning harder against Lymon. "I just need a nap."

"Too many twenty-hour days," Lymon added, knowing it wasn't his turf but unable to keep his trap shut.

Rex cued on the protective tone in Lymon's voice, his eyes sharpening as he noticed the way Sheela had clamped onto Lymon's arm. "Yeah, well, I've got business. Tony's had two offers. One from Jerry Bruckheimer, another from Donald Petrie. They're both casting for projects that you attached yourself to. Preproduction starts for both within the week. We've got decisions to make."

Lymon almost lifted Sheela up the steps and walked her back to the small bedroom, elbowing Rex to the side in the process.

"Sheela? You hear me?"

"Later," Lymon said gently but shot Rex a look that would have chilled milk.

"God, give me a break, Rex," Sheela added. "I almost didn't get through that last scene. Bernard's pushing like a maniac. I owe him in return for scrapping that bullshit he'd written into the script."

Rex made a sweeping gesture to include the two brad-clipped scripts and a clutter of paper that he'd placed on the table in the small booth. "Yeah, well, what about—"

"Later!" Lymon snapped and maneuvered Sheela into the small bedroom.

She smiled up at him. "Thanks, Lymon. Wake me a half hour before my call, all right? Hot coffee? And maybe time to run through my lines before I have to walk over for makeup?"

"Yeah, you've got it." He smiled at her, running his thumb over her eyebrow. "For now, you sleep."

"You'll be here?" Her fatigued eyes pleaded with his.

"I'll be here. And the coffee will be ready. Strong and black."

"See you soon," she murmured and turned before flopping on the bed. He wasn't sure, but he thought she was already asleep as he pulled her pumps off her feet.

He closed the door, passed the mirror-lined dressing room, and found Rex in the small kitchen. The manager was seated half out of the booth, his tie loose over a powder-pink Robert Graham shirt, suit coat hanging open. Rex was watching him as if seeing him for the first time.

"Cut her some slack, Rex. She's walking wounded."

Rex's eyes had turned a cold blue; the set of worry

and distaste lay on his lips. "Lymon, what the *hell* are you doing here?"

"Doing?"

Rex waved a hand at the bedroom. "You acting as her assistant now, as well as her bodyguard? Maybe thinking a little Whitney Houston and Costner gig is going to fall into your lap?"

Lymon managed a narrow smile as he bent, opened the fridge, and pulled out a can of the nasty light beer that Sheela kept there. He popped the top, took a. swig, and made a face. He tapped the can with a finger. "You know, if it wasn't for marketing, they'd never sell this swill."

"Is that a fact?" Rex was looking even more hostile.

"Yeah, but you hire a firecracker ad agency, pay some big-name football players enough, write a cute script for them, and you can even convince all those hard working blue-collar stiffs that watered-down pilsner tastes good."

Rex might have been looking at a bug. "So, just what are you trying to sell me?"

"Nothing, Rex. Not a single thing."

"Right. What is this shit you're pulling with Sheela?" His expression hardened. "You're the hired help, Lymon. The muscle. Period. You getting me?"

"You're not telling me anything I don't already know." Lymon took another swig of the beer and sat down across the table from Rex, meeting his eyes across the scripts and paperwork.

Rex broke contact first, leaning back and slapping his hands on his legs. "I don't want her hurt."

"Then give her a break." Lymon indicated the paper cluttering the table surface. "Come on, tell me the truth: Can't that wait until next week? The lady is killing herself. She wasn't kidding. She was like shredded paper in that last scene. She could barely manage her lines. She was on the verge of collapse. Bernard didn't notice. He thought she was spot-on—given that she was supposed to be whacked-out after running from the police for days—but everyone else in the room was holding their breath with their fingers crossed."

"Wait just a fucking minute! Who appointed you as her keeper?" He blinked as if struck by something. "God, you're not in love with her, are you?"

"Fuck you, Rex."

"You poor deluded idiot! You listen to me, and you listen well. If you're in over your head, it's time for LBA to move on, and I'll find someone else to see to Sheela's security."

Lymon felt himself starting to bristle. "I don't work for you, Rex."

"Oh, yes you do, buddy. I'm the guy who brought you in, remember? It's my signature on your check. I run Sheela's affairs."

Lymon rolled the fragile aluminum can between his fingers. "Okay, go ahead and fire me." He glanced back at the closed bedroom door. "But do it after she finishes shooting, will you? Like, maybe after the cast party? The studio has rented Dan Tana's for all of Friday."

"Then, you're history, pal."

Lymon arched an eyebrow. "We'll cross that bridge when we get there. But I don't think so. You're forgetting, you may sign my checks, but the lady back there brings in the bucks. In the end, we both work for her."

Rex smiled thinly. "You don't want to push this,

Bridges. When it comes right down to where the shit hits road, she'll back me. She *needs* me a hell of a lot more than she needs you. She might be the talent, but I'm the brains behind her business empire."

"What? Make her choose? Me or you? Bullshit! I stopped playing that game in the fifth grade. She needs both of us. Just as we are, not fighting over her like twelve-year-olds." He leaned forward, pointing a finger. "So, here it is. You do what you do, and I'll do what I do, and we'll both do what's best for the lady, all right?"

Rex watched him in distasteful silence for a moment, then said, "Yeah, right." He used his left hand to scoop up the stack of papers, pointedly leaving the screenplays behind. "When you think it's all right, could I make an appointment with Sheela to go over her investment portfolio? And maybe you could schedule those two scripts into her free time? Bruckheimer and Petrie really need an answer...if you think you could get around to it."

Lymon shook his head. "You're being an asshole, Rex."

"And you're not?" He stopped at the trailer door. "Who's the asshole here? Me? You're the one who thinks you can romance Sheela. Let me remind you of something. If you remember Houston and Costner in *The Bodyguard,* you'll recall that it didn't end well for either of them."

CHAPTER 25

Hank was walking down yet another hallway to another meeting. This time it was a hallway at the Hilton, but the eerie feeling of trouble had started chewing on his gut. He stopped at the door and knocked softly as he glanced up and down. A maid stepped out to the cart he had passed and gave him but a cursory notice as she lifted a stack of towels.

Hank hesitated for an instant when the door opened. Instead of Neal Gray, a striking woman stepped back, saying, "Come in."

Hank walked past her, fully aware of her fascinating gray eyes and hair like freshly spun copper. She had pulled it back into a French braid that hung partway down her back. She wore an elastic tank top that flattered her breasts and tight brown cotton slacks were molded to her legs in a way that left little to the imagination. Expensive sandals hugged her feet.

The lady-killer smile he gave her was instinctual. She smiled back, eyes measuring but interested. Ah, she was one of those—one of those few women who were completely satisfied with themselves. She knew just who and what she was, and God help the man who tried to play silly games with her. She'd shut him down like a Disney ride in the rain.

"Hank Abrams," he said as she closed the door behind him.

"April Hayes," she returned. Her accent was cultured, educated, perhaps with a hint of Midwestern twang, but he couldn't be sure.

He entered the room to find the couch occupied by a short-statured, dark-haired woman with an intense face. She wore a white blouse and gray jeans. Her shoes were loafers. "Gretchen Smith," the shorter woman told him as she stood to shake his hand. Her dark-brown eyes were probing, antagonistic. He pegged her as just the opposite—a woman who had never found herself. The intense expression was meant as cover for a deep-seated insecurity.

"My pleasure." He looked around, trying to keep from glancing at April again. "Is Neal here?"

"In a moment," April told him easily as she walked to the small bar. "Drink?"

"Scotch, if you've got it."

"We do." She shot him a knowing smile that sent a tingle along his backbone. "Single malt, neat, with a water back, right?"

"Right," he agreed, playing along with the game. He tried to ignore the head-to-toe scrutiny Gretchen was giving him. "How long have you been with Verele Security?"

Gretchen's face went sour. April's smile remained warm and welcoming as she said, "We're not. We work for Genesis Athena." She poured from a bottle of Glenlivet. "I was in law enforcement. LAPD." She handed him the scotch, their fingers touching for the briefest of instants. It felt like electricity.

He saw her pupils react. Interesting. For a moment, their eyes held. "So, you didn't like LAPD?"

Her smile teased. "I was on the fast track to detective. A chance meeting with the Sheik changed my direction, my paycheck, and the amount of bullshit in my life."

"Cool!" Gretchen quipped as she seated herself on the couch again. "It's life-story time."

Hank turned, a pleasant smile on his face as he took in the woman. "And you? Been with the Sheik for long?"

Gretchen frowned as she looked up at him, trying, no doubt, to figure what he was angling for. "Three years. Genesis Athena hired me because of my brain." She said it as if that was her only asset.

At that moment the door to the rear opened, and Neal Gray stepped out. Hank caught a glimpse of an ornate bedroom, the sheets rumpled and askew. So, did that mean that Neal and April were an item?

"Hey, Hank," Neal greeted. He was wearing a white shirt, narrow gray tie, and wool slacks. His taffy-blond hair was mussed uncharacteristically as if he hadn't run a comb through it that morning. "Did you meet everyone?"

"I did." Hank sipped his scotch. "I've got to confess, I thought it was you and me."

"This is the LA team." Neal was grinning, a secret in his eyes. "They handle some of our special operations. Counterparts to Salim and his group back East. April and Gretchen have collected some of our most promising specimens."

"Specimens?" Hank asked.

"Like you were doing out here. At the time, it seemed like you were a more logical choice to go after Anaya."

"You might say we're proactive," Gretchen declared. "Do you have a problem with that?"

"Uh, no." Hank tried to keep his face neutral. God, what was she? The Wicked Witch of the West's evil doppelgänger?

"Our mutual problem," Neal said as he took a seat, "in this instance, is Christal Anaya." He glanced at Hank. "She was a pretty good investigator, wasn't she?"

Hank took a chair across from the coffee table, choosing the spot so that he would be in April's immediate line of sight. He smiled, affecting a knowing attitude. "Christal Anaya is one of the best field agents I've ever worked with. She has an uncanny ability to fill in missing data. It's...I don't know, almost like magic. The first time you hear her begin to fit things together, you'd swear she was nuts, but as the data begin to come in, you discover she's been right all along."

"Intuitive?" Neal asked.

"Spooky intuitive," Hank agreed. Then he smiled, using the boyish one that women found so attractive. "You know, her grandmother was a witch."

"What?" Gretchen asked in a grating voice. "That's absurd."

Hank glanced first at Neal, then at April. The woman was watching him with level gray eyes, her fine face betraying nothing. He shrugged. "Say what you will, but there are times when you work around

Christal that you can't help but wonder. She does have an ability that almost goes beyond science when it comes to solving cases."

"So," Neal mused, "if she's digging at our corporate secrets, do you think it's a good bet that she'll figure them out?"

Hank shifted, affecting complete assurance. "If Christal were sniffing around doors that I wanted kept closed, yeah, I'd be worried."

April shot a communicative glance at Neal and arched her eyebrow as if to say, "I told you so."

Neal, for his part, frowned and laced his fingers together. "Maybe it's lucky for us that Hank's here."

"I just hope I can help."

"Do we know where she is?" Gretchen asked pointedly. "I'm tired of putting up with the bitch."

"I'm on it," Hank added. "It's just a matter of—"

"We've got her," Neal replied softly. "She's staying at a Marriott Residence Inn near here. Word is that she's checking out next week. My sources say that she's probably going to be looking for an apartment on her off time."

Hank started, jerking up straight. "How the hell do you know that? I've been chasing my ass off trying to get a line on her."

Neal's smile was the Cheshire Cat kind. "It's all right, Hank. We've got our sources. When you tailed Anaya to Colorado, you brought the seriousness of the situation to our attention."

"Thanks for telling me," he said dryly.

"I just tapped my source this morning," Neal added. "It's not one I use except in extreme circumstances."

"Maybe you should read your memos," Gretchen

muttered. "We've bumped into Anaya twice now. It was all in the reports."

"But nothing that would have indicated a direct threat to Genesis Athena," April amended, obviously to Gretchen's displeasure. "Our contacts with her have been in what we assumed to be the parameters of her job with LBA."

"What about de Clerk's?" Gretchen shot back. "Why the hell was she there? Huh? His security was supposed to be off that night."

"It was," April snapped. "I think he made a date with her and forgot."

Hank watched the interplay with interest, but Neal stopped it when he raised his hands. "Forget it, ladies. I've checked. It's a matter of the right hand not knowing what the left was doing. So, forget it. Let's move on to Friday night."

Gretchen leaned down and picked up a cardboard folder. This she opened, removing a diagram and spreading it on the table. It looked like a floor plan to Hank. He could see a unit, parking lot, stairs, windows, and doors marked. A big green mass was labeled TREE.

"This is Anaya's room at the Residence Inn," Gretchen began. "It's a piece of cake. We can leave the vehicle in the lot here." She pointed to the parking lot. "I've already called the manager. Two of the units on either side of Anaya's will be empty on Friday night. I took the liberty of renting them. The third room in the building"—she indicated the room diagonally—"is already rented, so we'll have to keep the noise down."

Gretchen seemed to be enjoying this.

She continued, "We can enter at any time. The lock takes a standard magnetic card. The tree beside the walk will provide us with some cover from the main office. Even if we're seen, no one is going to pay much attention."

Hank leaned forward. "Let me get this straight. We're going to break into Christal's room?"

Neal looked up. "Do you have a problem with that?"

Hank pursed his lips, aware that April was watching him with hawklike intensity. Did he dare let her think he was bothered by a little thing like breaking and entering? Besides, it was a hotel. And better yet, it was his chance to show Christal that she shouldn't be prying away at one of their clients.

He smiled as he imagined Christal's face when he stepped out into the room. "I think it would be wise to do this when she's gone. If you walk up and ring the bell, Christal's not going to let you in."

Neal's expression was neutral. "According to my source, Sheela Marks and her cast are going to be at Dan Tana's for most of the evening. Anaya shouldn't be off shift until sometime in the very early morning, but we should be ready early—just in case."

"Good." Hank leaned forward, looking at the diagram. "Then I suggest that we have coffee ready when she walks in the door. Not only that, but we need someone outside to follow her up the stairs in case something tips her off and she bolts." He pointed. "This unit next to hers shares the same stairway, right?"

"Yes," Gretchen told him distrustfully.

"Good. And we've rented it?"

"Yes."

"Then when Christal opens her door, it wouldn't be out of line for someone to step out right across from her as a blocker in the event she runs."

"I like that," April said as she leaned forward. "Good call, Hank."

Gretchen looked even more sour.

"That's it, then," Neal said and glanced up at Hank. "Anything else about Anaya that I should know?"

Hank shrugged. "She's going to be really pissed about this. You'd better not count on her just taking a warning and backing off. She's not that kind of agent."

Neal's lips puckered, and he nodded. "I'll keep that in mind. Any other questions? No? Then I'll see you at eight tomorrow. We'll do a drive-by and check in to our next-door rental as soon as we know Anaya's gone. See you then."

They all stood, Hank feeling good about himself. He was headed to the door, his mind knotted on Christal and how she was going to take a rebuke from strangers.

"Abrams?" April asked, matching his step. "You got time for a drink?"

Something about her appealed to him. Maybe it was the danger that lurked in the corners of her dry smile. Or perhaps she was just a damn good-looking woman, and she was coming on to him. Or was it the hint of challenge that lay so deep in her smoldering gray eyes?

"Sure. They make a mean margarita here. Or, if you prefer, we could go somewhere else."

"I know someplace private."

Hank bowed. "It'll be my pleasure."

As they walked out into the hall, she gave her head a slight tilt. It reminded him of Lauren Bacall. "You never know," she said, "we might both enjoy it."

CHAPTER 26

Weary to the bones, Sheela rubbed the back of her neck as she walked from the studio to her trailer. The lot was hot, baking under the sun. She had heard that a peculiar high-pressure system had built over the Mojave, that it was kicking the scorching desert air back over LA.

The weather guy didn't know what high pressure was.

A headache ground away at the back of her brain, and her eyes burned, perhaps from the smog, or perhaps from the fatigue that lay so heavily in her blood, muscle, and soul.

She had finished her last scene, God willing, if some editor didn't find a flaw that would cause Bernard to recall her.

But that would be sometime in the amorphous future. On beyond zebra, in another lifetime that started after she woke up from a zombie's somnolence that would start after the festivities on Friday.

The cast party was a thespian's tradition that

reached back into the dim and distant past. A celebration of the hard work, the good times and bad, that had occasioned a group of strangers to become a short-term family.

I'm done!

She smiled wearily and looked down at her purse. The amphetamines lay unused, but for a couple of tablets. She was still in control. Her body might have felt like scorched toast, but her self-discipline had held.

The pills in her purse mocked her. She could feel them, whispering, calling, chiding her. Relief lay just a swallow away. She'd be fresh again, ready to take on the world instead of being this brain-dead hulk of ambulatory tissue.

Sleep is almost yours.

She waved as she passed a flock of extras dressed as Civil War Confederates and rounded the corner that led to her lot trailer. The awning cast a solitary square of shade over the lawn chairs and small table. The muted puttering of the air conditioners rose from the long line of trailers.

Sheela plodded up to the steps and opened her door —then sighed wearily as she stepped inside and waved halfheartedly at Rex, who sat at the table in the small booth.

She told him. "I wrapped my last scene. Bernard's doing some short intercuts with the extras, and then he'll get what he can out of Manny, but it's not my problem anymore." She grinned. "So, it's Thursday afternoon, and I'm headed home to fall face-first into bed."

Rex smiled. "Glad to hear that. You and I have some things to talk about."

"Not now, Rex. I can't think...let alone pay attention."

He tapped the two screenplays on the table. "Did you get a chance to go through either of these?"

"Get real!"

"We need an answer. Tony thinks you ought to bail on the Petrie property and go with Bruckheimer. I tend to agree. The role suits you better."

"I want some time off," she said as she slumped into the booth across from him. "Rex, I'm roadkill. It took everything I had to get through *Jagged Cat*. I can't keep up with this schedule."

He tilted his head. "I thought I got you something for that."

She reached into her purse and pulled out the little pill bottle. "I took three. I don't like them."

His flat stare bored into her. "Sheela, do you know what it means to be on the A-list?" He tapped the screenplays again. "I've talked to the producers. You've got your choice. Twenty million up front, or fifteen percent of the box office. Your decision."

"Rex, I—" She shook her head. "They start preproduction next week, right?"

"Bruckheimer wants you on Thursday for a preliminary meeting. Petrie has his scheduled for Friday."

She closed her eyes, whispering, "I just can't do it."

She could feel his gaze, hard, unbending. "Sheela," he said softly, "I've gotta know which one."

"Neither," she told him as she nerved herself to look him in the eye. "Tell Jerry if he'll wait for a month, I'll do it."

"What?" Rex snapped. "You want me to tell Bruckheimer to put a two-hundred-million-dollar project on hold while you take a nap?"

"You heard me!" The shrill note in her voice surprised her. She hesitated, rubbing her masklike face. Her skin felt wooden from the caking of makeup. "God, I'm sorry, Rex. I don't mean to be a shrew."

He smiled, half-forgiving. "It's okay, Sheela. Yeah, get some rest. I'll drop by tomorrow and we'll make a final decision. About nine, then?"

"Why are you pushing this?"

He stood, collecting his papers. "Because you're hot. Come on. You're in your thirties now. This is Hollywood, babe. Get it? You've got ten years. That's it. When you hit forty, you're history. By the time you turn forty-one, they're gonna need an archaeologist to dig you up."

She blinked, feeling the twinge of fear.

"Hey," Rex relented as he snapped his briefcase closed on the papers. "It's okay. We just gotta make hay while the cutting's good." He pointed to the pill bottle. "They're there if you need them." A smile. "You can rest next decade, right?"

"Yeah, right." Shit, the way she felt now, she wasn't going to wake up until she was forty-three.

"Sheela," Rex cooed in a gentler voice, "it's not just you that we're talking about. Crying 'Me! Me! Me!' won't cut it."

She could feel the sense of guilt come toppling down, like stones on a swimming woman.

Rex got halfway to the door and stopped, his briefcase under his arm. He turned, a pensive look on his face. "Tell me, this 'time off' thing...did Lymon suggest it?"

"He's worried about me."

A flicker crossed his eyes. "Yeah, I'm sure he is."

Then Rex was gone.

Sheela rolled the bottle of pills between her fingers. If she only took one, she could finish the scripts this afternoon. She fought for a deep breath, feeling sick. Pieces of her were shrinking.

Going away.

Getting ever smaller.

Everyone depends on me. The whole fucking world.

CHAPTER 27

Friday afternoon had started hot under a searing sun. Christal pulled her Tahoe into the circle drive and tried to park as inconspicuously as possible. She glanced at her watch, seeing that it was five till one. The eucalyptus and oaks cast cool pools of shade that barely masked the heat rolling down from the San Gabriels.

Christal took a moment to check herself in the mirror. Good, nothing in her teeth, and she looked presentable. Not bad for as rapidly as she'd gotten ready for this assignment.

"Christal?" Lymon had asked, curiosity in his voice. *"I just got a call from Sheela. She wondered if I could send you over at one this afternoon. Said there were some things she wanted to discuss with you."*

When she'd prodded, Lymon had given no more details, but had sounded puzzled himself.

"Christal?" he had finished. *"Be quick, huh? She's got a heavy schedule tonight. Try not to take too much of her time. Let her get all the rest she can."*

So, here she had come, shuffling through the half-coagulated LA traffic to Sheela's opulent mansion. She had checked in with neighborhood security and then buzzed in at Sheela's gate.

Crystal stepped out of her Tahoe and walked up to the huge wooden doors. She hadn't even rung when Tomaso opened the right-hand portal and welcomed her.

"This way, Ms. Anaya," Tomaso said, leading Christal not to the meeting room that she was familiar with but up the stairs. She lagged, trying to see the artwork. The familiar colors of the Southwest were warm and reassuring. A single glowing Reid Christie painting showed sunlight glowing off bison where they grazed in an emerald pasture. In another, by Santiago Perez, a colorful New Mexican rider dashed his horse below a saint-filled sky.

"I didn't know Sheela had such an interest in this kind of art," she offered as Tomaso led her past the closed doors to the end of the hallway.

"Yes, she tries to go to Santa Fe at least once a year." Tomaso smiled, lifted a hand, and knocked before opening the door and announcing, "Ms. Anaya to see you, ma'am."

"Thank you, Tomaso," Sheela called as Christal stepped into the...what? Ante-bedroom? Christal took in the huge TV, the books, and videos. Looking straight back through the opened doors, she could see Sheela's huge bedroom; to the right, she caught a glimpse of the well-equipped dressing room.

"Christal!" Sheela rose from a chaise and crossed the floor to take her hands. "Thank you for coming."

Christal started to smile and hesitated, fixing on the

puffiness in Sheela's red-rimmed eyes. "Hey, you all right?"

"Tired as hell," Sheela muttered. "Can I get you something? A drink? Have you eaten?"

"Yeah, I fixed a bite at my place. The Residence Inn is neat that way. Each of the suites has a kitchen. They're little apartments, actually."

Sheela motioned to the chair across from hers and resettled herself. "Did you see the news this morning? About what happened in Paris?"

Christal leaned forward in the overstuffed chair. "You mean that business about Princess Diana? Yeah."

During the night, someone had broken into the forensic lab that curated specimens taken from the body of Diana, the Princess of Wales, during the investigation after her fatal car crash in 1997. The Sûreté was investigating, and was particularly curious as to how a French radio station had been tipped off within hours of the break-in. News clips had shown outrage throughout England as the story broke. The Spencer family had already voiced their dismay. No statement had been forthcoming from the royal family on the matter.

"What do you think?" Sheela asked softly.

"I don't know yet." Christal made a gesture. "Maybe it's related, maybe not. She wasn't Hollywood. Not a film star like you and the others."

Sheela nodded. "I want to know what you've found out. Everything. Lymon has been giving me reports, but I want it from the horse's mouth."

Christal laid it all out, then added, "I think it's all coming together. And I don't like where it's going."

"How's that?"

"I think Sheik Abdulla, Genesis Athena, and the bizarre thefts are part of the same thing." She winced slightly. "It's as if I can feel it all moving in unison. Kind of like something breathing just out of sight. You can't help but know it's a monster of some kind. Lymon's right. There are too many coincidences. Why Hank? Why did Sheik Abdulla cancel everything at the last minute to fly to New York just to see you? Why is Genesis Athena in Yemen, while he has his offices in Qatar? You, Talia Roberts, Manny de Clerk—all the big stars. All high profile. It's like a fan wish list from *Us* or *People* magazines."

"So, you think the Sheik is...what? Gaining leverage for pictures by stealing my tampon? Or just angling for magazine ink?"

"No," Christal clarified, "but I think he's figuring to make a great deal of money. That, and it's an ego thing. Something to do with control and power."

"Ah, we're back to witches again?"

Christal cocked an eyebrow and nodded. "Yes...and no. I've got a gut feeling that it's similar, but with a different twenty-first-century twist. Power and greed —just like in ancient Southwestern witchcraft—lie at the bottom of this. It's about feeding a craving hunger, and the hunger is called desire."

"It frightens me that I've been in this business long enough to think you're right." She rubbed her face, a dull pain behind her eyes.

"The way you look...you taking uppers?" Christal asked and immediately regretted it. Damn it, her mouth had been getting her in trouble all of her life.

Sheela pointed to the scripts on the floor at her feet.

"Rex is after me to make a decision. Hell, I can't even remember what I read."

She picked up a pill bottle from the table, rolling it between her fingertips. The little pills inside rattled like Death's whisper. "If he wasn't pushing so damned hard I...God, there's just not enough of me to go around." Her eyes sharpened. "It goes against my principles—taking these things."

Christal studied the fragility in her eyes, in the set of her shoulders. The woman was close to falling into a thousand pieces. What the hell was the matter with these people? "I may be out of place asking, but why are you doing this? I mean, treating yourself this way?"

"People depend on me." She said it with all the sorrow of the saints. Then she asked, "What do you think about honor, Christal?"

"That's not a question I get asked every day."

"I guess today is your day."

Christal straightened, rubbing her hands together. "Very well, honor is the root of integrity. It comes with certain core principles that govern every waking moment of our lives. I'm a Catholic at heart—from the old church, the one that says you're going to have to pay for every sin you commit."

"Do you have principles, Christal?"

She smiled wryly. "Unfortunately. Damn things keep getting in my way. The last time I violated them, I got slapped down pretty hard. That's why I'm working overtime. Penance."

Sheela fixed in a dull stare. "Do you depend on me?"

"God, no! What kind of silly question is that? No. Sorry. I have my own life, thank you."

Sheela stared into the distance, and Christal saw

the brittleness, the cracks that were running through her psyche.

This was a glimpse of what Sheela Marks would look like when she was old and worn through by life.

"Doesn't Rex see what's happening to you? Doesn't anyone care if they push you into the abyss?"

A chilling smile lay on Sheela's lips. "I'm property. A trademark. Like Rex says, I may only have ten years left."

"You'll be charred carrion if you don't do something for yourself."

"I let everyone down once. Never again."

Christal leaped to her feet. "Maybe I ought to go down, lift Rex up by his tie, and have a little talk with him. Shit, he's treating you like you're his dog. So what if runs you to death, he's Rex fucking Gerber, he can always get another dog, huh?"

Sheela laughed, the sound of insanity barely hidden in the peals. And then, to Christal's amazement, Sheela's swollen eyes began to leak tears.

"Hey, it's okay." Christal dropped to her knees and took Sheela's hands. Mother trucker, what did she do now? Sheela's tears left her uncomfortable, embarrassed. She'd never been a good one for hand patting and consolation. "Sheela?"

The woman sniffed, pulled her hands away, and wiped at the tears. Sheela pulled herself together with Herculean effort. "Sorry. I don't know where that came from."

"It's okay."

Sheela shook her head. "Isn't it funny? Surrounded by all these people, and I have to call you to fall apart in front of." A grin. "I could have a therapist, like all the rest. You can't throw an apple core into the bushes here without hitting one." A pause. "Somehow that just doesn't suit my practical Saskatchewan upbringing."

"My New Mexican one either."

A pause. "Would you do something for me, Christal? Something personal?"

"It would depend. Don't forget that I come from a law enforcement background."

Sheela looked up, desperation in her eyes. "I need to get away for a couple of days. I need to go someplace where no one can find me. I just need time to myself. Can you help me with that?"

"Sure. I mean, maybe. I'd have to know where you were going. My first concern would be for your safety."

"I'll be very safe. I'll have protection close at hand."

"I'd have to tell Lymon."

"Yes, but only him."

"Okay, so, just where is this safe place?"

She sounded like a little girl when she asked, "Could I come and stay with you for a couple of days?"

"*What?*"

Sheela took a deep breath. "I just want to be a real person for a while. If I don't get out, find something to grab a hold of, I'm going to lose myself."

Christal shook her head as if to throw the idea off. "You want to come stay with me...in a hotel?"

Sheela nodded, her eyes down. "What if I told you that there was no one else I could depend on?"

"What about Lymon?"

"I'm asking this as one woman to another. I *need* to get away for a couple of days. Away from Rex, away from Tony, someplace where I can just sleep, watch TV, read a book, and be anybody but Sheela Marks." She looked up, eyes glittering with desperation.

"Yeah, I'm in. Let's do it," Christal declared hotly. "And if Rex or Tony show up blustering, I'll eighty-six their asses right out of the place."

Sheela seemed to melt in relief. "Thank you."

Christal nodded, feeling the pieces of something falling into place deep in her mind. "One condition."

"What's that?"

Christal pointed. "You toss those pills into that toilet back there—and my place is yours."

Sheela stood, walked back to the dressing room toilet, and upended the bottle. Pills cascaded into the bowl before she ceremonially pressed the lever to flush them. When she reentered she looked more alive, a faint sparkle in her eyes. Artfully, she tossed the empty plastic bottle to Christal. "Done."

"Just one little problem: How are we going to do this? Sneaking you out of here is going to be like breaking you out of the federal pen."

Sheela hesitated before she said, "I've got a plan."

CHAPTER 28

"**B**oss, we've got a problem," Christal announced as she burst into Lymon's LBA office and closed the door meaningfully behind her.

He had been at wit's end, double-checking the figures his accountant had forwarded. The federal government wanted a bigger chunk than he had expected for the quarterly taxes. Bigger to the tune of fifteen thousand dollars. He'd been wondering how he was going to broach the question of a bigger bill to Rex.

Thus it was that the last thing he needed was Anaya stomping in with "a problem." He gave her what he hoped was an appropriate glare of reprimand as he tapped the fingers of one hand on the adding machine and shuffled the piles of paper stacked here and there with the other.

"Have you ever considered knocking politely and asking permission before barging in like one of Hannibal's elephants?"

Anaya didn't register it as she plopped herself into the chair next to his desk. "It's about Sheela." She looked around. "Is this place safe? Can we talk?"

"Yeah, provided your vocal cords work, which they seem to. You mind telling me what's so important that you can interrupt my private self-flagellation at the IRS's behest?"

"Sheela's on the verge of a breakdown." She raised her hand. "Hear me out, huh? You remember when she asked me over this afternoon? She needed someone to talk to. I was it."

"Why you?" He sat back, slightly irritated.

"Because I'm...I'm safe. A neutral party. She doesn't have to worry about offending me, about biasing a preconception. I'm peripheral enough that if I betray her, the blow won't kill her soul. You get it, boss? I'm an expendable nobody."

"Rex has been at her again?"

"Yeah, he's pushing really hard over some movie deal that Sheela has to make her mind up about yesterday."

"That son of a bitch."

"We're on the same wavelength there, boss. No doubt about it."

Lymon closed his eyes and sighed before reaching for the phone. "Thanks, I'll deal with it."

"No." Christal surprised him by placing her hand on his atop the phone. "It's taken care of."

"Would you mind explaining that?" Damn it, not only was Sheela his client, but *he* was in charge of LBA, not some two-week-old employee.

"Here's the deal: Sheela's going to spend the weekend at my place."

"What?"

Christal raised her hands. "Don't get on your high horse." Her dark gaze bored into his. "Lymon, you weren't there. You didn't see the expression on her face. One wrong knock, and she's going to shatter. Just the same as if you dropped a Swarovski crystal onto a slab of concrete."

"I wish you'd talked to me before—"

"Rex has her on uppers," Christal continued. "He's trying to squeeze everything he can out of her."

Lymon ground his teeth.

"So, we have to make this happen. Sheela's got a plan. I want to put a couple of wrinkles into it."

Lymon gave her a dead stare. "Christal, this isn't just an exercise; you're playing with dynamite."

"I know," she answered honestly. "She's everyone's golden goose, but they're so busy gnawing on her drumsticks that she's going to be bones on the plate before anyone gives a damn. So, Boss, this weekend she's coming to my place to just be a regular person."

Lymon leaned back in his chair. "I don't know whether to strangle you or give you a raise."

Christal rose, bracing her hands on his desk as if she were about to leap over it. "Answer me something, Boss. You care for the lady, don't you?"

"I have professional responsibilities."

"What about your responsibilities as a man?"

Lymon glared at her, fighting the desire to stand up and bust her across the mouth. "You're treading on dangerous ground here."

"Yep." Her hard gaze bored into his. "Can you really tell me that you're willing to sit there and let the woman you love self-destruct? Huh? Seriously?"

He had butterflies in his stomach as he said, "All right, smart-ass, what have you got in mind?"

CHAPTER 29

For the *Jagged Cat* party, Bernard had rented Dan Tana's, a small two-room Italian steak house in the nine thousand block of Santa Monica Boulevard. The Friday night gathering was intimate, the cast's chance to share the final familial bonds they had forged during the short but intense shooting schedule.

Red-and-white checked tablecloths, red leather booths, and hanging Chianti bottles decorated the rooms. Celebrity artwork, movie posters, and photos lined the crimson walls. The fare was New York steak marinated in a special Italian tomato sauce; rolls—many of which were used as projectiles—and all the wine the cast could drink.

Sheela had hooted and clapped as Bernard conducted the impromptu awards ceremony. For her gag gift, she had received a bent carving knife to commemorate the scene where she chased her father around the kitchen. Then she had turned to the familiar faces, told them what a pleasure it had been to work with them, and blown them all kisses before retaking her seat and listening appreciatively to the others as they took the floor and received their gag gifts.

Manny de Clerk sat in a booth in the back, surrounded by his agent and manager, a somber look on his face. He had just smiled and waved when Bernard gave him a framed photo.

Poor Manny. Sheela had covered her sympathy with a smile. When the real world had broken through his fake self-image, he had cratered.

What about yourself? she asked. *If someone penetrated the walls you've built, could you do any better?*

She swallowed hard and rolled the cloth napkin between her fingers. Her heart was beating, anticipation sending tingles through her muscles. God, she felt like she was a girl again, stealing her father's motorcycle.

Silly! You're a grown woman.

One who was sneaking away for a weekend of sin. Or so she hoped.

She glanced across the room to the door, knowing that she was coming up on time. She could still back out, call Christal and tell her that she'd changed her mind.

"Anyone else got anything to say?" Bernard demanded. "No? Then I guess that does it for me. Again, thank you all. You're the best, most professional cast I've ever had the pleasure of working with. God bless you all."

They all applauded, whistled, and stomped.

"If anyone's interested," Bernard answered, "I'll be serving drinks up at my place. You're all welcome."

More whistles and cheers.

As they stood, Sheela made the rounds, kissing cheeks, hugging, making the pleasant chatter expected of her. She reached into her purse, thumbing the button on her cell. Plugging her other ear with a finger, she said, "Paul? I'm ready."

"I'll be there soonest," he said. *"The door security will call for you when the limo is out front."*

Sheela mingled in the knot at the door, smiling, feeling alive for the first time since she and Lymon had gone tootling around on the Indian. Sapping fatigue lay there, deep in her brain and body, but the adrenaline rush held it at bay.

What's happened to you? she wondered. *When did your courage dissolve into water?*

Thank God for Christal. *"You can depend on me."* The woman's words repeated as if engraved on Sheela's soul.

What was Lymon's reaction going to be? He'd be pissed at first. She smiled at that, both pleased and irritated that he was ever the professional. Just once, couldn't he let himself see beyond his duty? Dimming the noise and bodies around her, she imagined the two of them, alone, intimate, just holding each other.

"Manuel de Clerk?" the door security called.

Manny's agent acted like a battering ram, clearing the way to the door. Sheela could see flashes as the paparazzi captured Manny, one hand raised, fleeing down the cordoned rope lines to the open door of his limo.

Shit, they were like locusts. She frowned, looking down at her black leather pants and tall black boots. Would they guess? No. It was too far out.

"Sheela Marks!" came the call.

She excused herself, smiling, as she stepped to the door—and out into the strobes and clatter of the cameras. Two of the security guys made sure that no one crossed the velvet ropes leading to curbside.

"Sheela!" "Ms. Marks!" "Look this way!" "Sheela, over here!" She smiled, waving, trying to oblige them all, knowing full well that the wrong expression was captured forever.

The limo door was open, and she slipped inside with one last wave. The door shut, and she held her posture as Paul pulled away from the curb. Only then did she collapse.

"Thank you, Paul," she called.

"No trouble, ma'am." He kept his head forward. "The bag is on the floor as you requested."

She experienced a flood of relief. She was only moments from freedom.

CHAPTER 30

Marc Delangelo slipped from the crowd blocking the sidewalk in front of Dan Tana's. He raised his hand, waving; a bright red Porsche Boxster, the top down, swerved toward him.

He vaulted into the seat, pointing. "There, that limo. That's her."

Jennifer, his girlfriend, glanced at him in the illumination cast by Santa Monica Boulevard. "You're sure it's her?"

"Yeah." He grinned. "She's up to something. I've watched her a lot of times. She doesn't dress like this unless something's up. I mean, leather pants? That's not her style. And that denim long-sleeved shirt? This is Sheela Marks, not Gwyneth Paltrow."

"So?"

"So," Marc replied, "if we keep them in sight, I think we're going to catch America's sweetheart doing something really cool. And, like, that's a couple of months' rent if I can get it on camera."

Jennifer glanced at the infrared camera that he pulled from a bag. "You'd better. I'm still pissed at what you paid for that thing."

"Hey, babe, it's the coming thing!" He gestured ahead. "You just stay a couple of lengths back from that limo."

CHAPTER 31

enesis Athena. Christal rolled the name around in her head as she pushed the plastic grocery cart. According to her watch, it was just after ten, and the store was almost empty. A few other patrons cruised up and down the brightly lit aisles of the Raley's. They were casually dressed, no doubt picking up the last few things before the weekend. That, or like Christal, they worked unusual hours.

She glanced at her watch, figuring that Sheela would duck out of the *Jagged Cat* party as early as she could. She had promised to be at Christal's by eleven. The woman who had pleaded so passionately and with such a look of desperation in her eyes wouldn't be partying until all hours of the night.

Christal had checked to be sure that Sheela made her party at Dan Tana's, then had taken her Tahoe to do some last-minute shopping. It had occurred to her in a stupendous flash that she was about to have a most auspicious houseguest—and her refrigerator was stocked with what she considered the barest necessities of survival: refried beans, tomatillos, cheese, poblano and jalapeño peppers, corn tortillas, eggs, and burger. Whatever Sheela liked, Christal could just about be assured that the famous actress' spice cabinet didn't just consist of cayenne pepper, cumin, cilantro, and garlic like Christal's did.

Genesis Athena.

The thought intruded as if trying to lever itself into her mind. An image flashed: that bit of Manny de Clerk's foreskin. Christal was trying to force it away and concentrate on Canadian-friendly recipes when her eyes fell on the sausages in the meat cooler. Reddish and mottled—like a bloody tampon. Where in the hell had *that* come from?

She could hear her grandmother's voice whispering encouragement from just beyond her perception.

"What is it, Grandmother? What are you trying to tell me?"

Christal stopped short, a coldness washing through her as her brain made the curious connection. Foreskin? The mottling on a tampon? *Tissue!*

Menstrual blood contained bits of tissue from the sloughing uterine lining. And what was razor scuzz but bits of skin and beard hair? *Tissue!*

Sandra Bullock's hankies and toothbrush? They'd be loaded with cells. Some from the nose, others the delicate cheek cells inside the mouth. Just like Talia Roberts' sheets—full of skin cells and hair scuffed off by friction as she slept.

They'd taken a more direct and blunt approach with Pitt. They'd chopped a piece out of Brad's butt— and collected their tissue samples!

She could sense the answer, just beyond her grasp,

like the perfumed hint of flowers born on a summer night's breeze. She thought of Sheik Amud Abdulla. What did a man who was obsessed with control and power do with bits and pieces of other people's bodies? Power was the key, wasn't it?

What does a witch do with the pieces he collects?

"He uses them to gain more power and control," she mused aloud as she passed the processed meats and picked a small frozen turkey out of the freezer. She'd bet that Sheela hadn't had a stuffed turkey dinner any time recently.

What kind of power would a man like Abdulla seek?

"Wealth," she answered. "But how does he get more wealth from pieces of other people's bodies? How does he sell that to others? And better yet, what kind of control does he achieve?"

And therein lay the rub.

Nevertheless, Christal smiled as she walked the aisles. She almost had it! She could feel the lightness of it. Abdulla accrued the wealth and control, and Genesis Athena was the vehicle through which he did it.

But how? Why did the questionnaire screen out people like Christal? Who was it meant to pass? And why?

When she picked that final lock, the whole thing would fall into place. She tossed a small sack of pine nuts into the basket for stuffing, then added black rye bread. She'd make Sheela a stuffed turkey like she'd never had before.

It wasn't ransom. None of the celebrities would pay to get their bits of tissue back. Nor had any demands been made. So, what did Abdulla get? What was the prize contained within those often microscopic bits of flesh?

DNA.

But they'd thought of DNA. Considered it and abandoned it. Abdulla could have obtained his samples at minimal risk. With ludicrous ease, actually. Evidence recovery teams recovered DNA every day from crime scenes all across the country. People left DNA everywhere they went. Instead of swiping Sheela's tampon in that ridiculously involved sham in the ladies' room, Copperhead could have waited and simply stolen Sheela's champagne flute when she set it down. A moderately competent technician could have recovered more than enough cells from the smear on the glass to develop a complete DNA profile.

"So, why grandstand?" Christal mused. What could be gained by taking such terrible risks? The smallest of mistakes could have landed Copperhead and Mouse in the can. Then the whole thing would have been compromised.

"Or would it?" She frowned as she rolled her cart to the checkout and began placing items on the conveyor for the checker. It wasn't like the police could have held either Copperhead or Mouse for more than a night until they made bail for trespass. They could have claimed it was a prank gone wrong, apologized, paid the fines and restitution, and walked.

Christal tapped her credit card on the screen and wheeled her load of plastic sacks out into the warm night. The sky was glowing a yellowish brown. The Los Angeles Basin, it seemed, never experienced true darkness.

And I am just starting to see the light!

Christal slipped behind the wheel, a giddy thrill running through her. It was all coming clear. Sheik Abdulla was a witch, all right. Just a different kind than the ones she had grown up hearing about. He, too, wanted souls to control. It was only the way of it that eluded her.

She turned on the map light and pulled the small blue notebook from her purse. Steadying it on the steering wheel, she began jotting down the basics. God, it was all coming together. And in a moment of epiphany, she had it!

Why hadn't anyone anticipated this? It was the logical next step given the leaps and bounds at which genetics and biotech had been evolving.

She scanned the notes, thinking back to the expression on Sheela's face that night they'd stolen her tampon. At the end of her list, she printed one last haunting question before jamming her notebook partially into her purse.

"I'm going to get you," she promised as she slipped the big Chevrolet into drive and headed for her apartment. "By the time Sheela leaves on Sunday, Mr. Sheik, I'm going to have you by the *cojones.*"

Christal was thinking of just how much she'd enjoy it as she walked up to her unit, shifted the bags, and reached for her key. She didn't know anything was amiss until she stepped through the door.

CHAPTER 32

Lymon caught up with Sheela's limo as it turned onto Coldwater Canyon. He pulled up beside the driver's side and gave Paul a thumbs-up. Through the reflection on the car's side window, he could barely make out Paul's nod and grin.

Glancing behind, Lymon couldn't see anything out of the ordinary in the traffic. Switching lanes, he maneuvered to the car's right side and stayed even with Paul as they slowed for a red light. He rolled to a stop across from the right rear passenger door and looked over expectantly. Even before the Escalade came to a complete stop, Sheela opened the door, the floorboard extending. She stepped out, helmet on her head, and slammed the door shut behind her. In a flash, she was behind Lymon, her arms tight about his middle.

"Let's go!" she cried, glee filling her voice.

When the light turned, Lymon waved at Paul and rolled the throttle, letting the big Indian bellow as he pulled away. He signaled, pulled into the right lane, and turned off on a side road. "Want to go straight to Christal's, or ride for a while?"

She was laughing, the little-girl sound of it filling his soul with joy.

"God, Lymon! I'm really doing this! I feel free! Free, free, free!" She whooped, raising her arms to the night and jiggling the bike.

"Hey! Let's not wreck us in the process, all right?"

"God, no! This is too good to be true!" She snugged her arms around him and squeezed the breath out of him. "I want to ride for a while. But we do have to go by Christal's first. I told her I'd be there at around eleven. She'll worry if we don't check in."

"Right." Lymon flicked the turn signal and bent them into a turn, heading around the block and back toward Christal's.

"Hey," Sheela said as she leaned her chin on his shoulder.

"Hey," he answered gently.

"It was really good to see you pull up alongside. When Christal told me to stow my helmet and leathers in the limo, I was just hoping against hope."

He sighed. "Yeah, well, I'm an accomplice now. Rex will skin me alive if ever figures this out."

"Rex can go screw himself," Sheela muttered. "Lymon...should I fire him?"

"He's the best in the business."

"At what price?" she wondered. "When I talked to him this afternoon, he hinted that I might want to think about changing security firms. He said you stiffed him for another ten thousand in your bill."

"Yeah, and I'll bet he didn't tell you I ate five thousand of the twenty the IRS hit me for. I divided it with you since part of the fault was Rex's for prepaying me last month. He didn't think of what that would make the quarterly earnings look like. If I'm down at the end of this quarter, you'll get the benefit then, too."

"Do we have to talk business?"

"No." He signaled for a left and slowed to wait out traffic at the entrance to Christal's Residence Inn. At the first break in the oncoming cars, he slipped the clutch and pulled into the lot, aware of a Porsche hot on his heels. He noticed that the sleek car pulled into the registration space and a young man leaped out, watching the Indian as Lymon rounded the end of the speed bump and idled toward Christal's.

People noticed the Indian. It was unique, with the styled fenders and the huge engine. People didn't walk up to it thinking it was just another Harley.

He started to pull into the space beside Christal's Tahoe, then noticed the van, its side door open. A knot of people were hurrying down the walk toward them, a limp-looking body propped in their midst.

"What the hell?"

"It looks like someone had one too many to drink," Sheela said as Lymon slowed and put a foot down.

The bike dropped into its loping idle, shaking beneath him as he watched. They were loading the person into the door. Lymon saw a swaying of long dark hair. Something about the woman's slim form...

"Hey!" He let the clutch out, rolling forward. "What the hell's going on here?"

A man turned. Tall, blond-headed, he looked handsome in the glow of the sodium lights. "Nothing that's your business. My wife just drank a little too much, that's all."

Lymon eased to a stop several feet from the van, craning his head to see inside. He could feel Sheela tense behind him.

"Christal?" he wondered under his breath.

His only warning was a blur as the man leaped, caught him on the shoulder with both hands and shoved with all his might. The blow tumbled Lymon, Sheela, and the Indian onto the pavement.

Lymon's body slammed hard, his helmet cracking loudly against the asphalt. He got his hand under him, pushing up, only to feel the weight of the Indian trapping his calf and foot.

"Son of a bitch!" He heard an engine roar, looked up past the bike, and saw the van careen back, lurch to a stop as the side door was slammed shut. Then came the squeal of tires as it rocketed ahead and hammered over the speed bump. The last he saw, it vanished into the night.

"Sheela? Are you all right?"

"Fine." She was wiggling behind him. "Shit! What happened?"

He flopped like a trapped fish, got a hand up to press the chicken switch on the handlebar, and heard the big twin chug to a stop. "Someone just took Christal." He threw himself desperately against the weight of the big motorcycle. "I don't fucking believe it!"

"Hang on," Sheela muttered. "I've about got my foot loose."

Lymon turned his head at the sound of footsteps. He could see the young man running across from the registration building. He held a big blocky camera before him, stopping to shoot a couple of pictures before saying, "Hey, shit! Sheela Marks! What a hit!" Then he lifted the camera to shoot another couple of frames.

CHAPTER 33

F riday night in the summer was always a busy time at the police station in Beverly Hills. This one proved no exception. Lymon barely managed to keep a shackled drunk from puking on Sheela as they made their way down the hallway.

The interview room they were escorted to was soundproofed but filled with recording gear. The room, painted off-white, wasn't more than ten by eight with the proverbial one-way mirror framed into one wall. A thick and heavy metal table dominated the center; each leg had been bolted securely to the cement floor. The cubicle felt decidedly cramped with six people in it.

"I don't get it," Lymon growled as he shifted from foot to foot. To Sheela, he looked like a caged lion. Something in the set of his face—in the rage behind his eyes—both fascinated and repelled her. Her own adrenaline was still rushing through her like a tonic.

Two uniformed cops sat on the other side of the battered gunmetal gray table and stared uneasily at

Sheela where she leaned against the far wall. In reply, she met stare for stare.

The paparazzo, a freelance photographer named Marc Delangelo, glowed, while his girlfriend, Jennifer Schmidt, looked sheepish as they sat in two of the plastic chairs.

"I got it all." Marc was beaming. "I mean, I ran half a roll of those people carrying that woman to the van."

"It's dark," Hurley, one of the cops, protested.

"It's an IR camera, man," Marc cried as he tapped a finger on the heavy camera resting on the table. "I don't need flash, get it? I can shoot in any light."

The second cop—Randisi, according to his tag—said, "Look, you've got no proof that this Christal Anaya was abducted. These might have been friends of hers who were taking care of her."

"She was new to town," Lymon replied. "She didn't have friends here."

"Yes, she did," Sheela interjected. "She had me!" A fire was burning within her. "And she had you, Lymon. Then there's that FBI agent."

"Sid Harness. But he's in Washington."

"FBI?" Randisi asked.

"A mutual friend." Lymon was grinding his teeth.

Sheela pushed off the wall and stepped over. "Look, Officer, maybe she wasn't abducted. We'll have a better idea when we process Mr. Delangelo's film."

"Hey, it's *my* film! My personal property. Protected under the First Amendment."

"It may be evidence," Hurley corrected.

Sheela felt her blood begin to boil as she turned on the photographer. "What's it worth to you? Huh? I'll give you fifty thousand right now. Sight unseen. Hell, you might have left the lens cap on. Forgot to put film in the camera. Who knows?"

Delangelo swallowed hard. "Seventy-five thousand."

"Bullshit!" Lymon exploded, wheeling around.

The look behind his eyes sent a cold shiver down Sheela's spine. She raised a hand, blocking him. "Easy, Lymon. Take a breath."

He did, fighting to keep the maniacal rage from boiling over. She looked past him at the two cops. She could read their expressions: wary, as if sensing the stakes and unsure who to finger for the coming explosion.

"Gentlemen," Sheela said professionally, "I would appreciate it if your crime scene people could go over Ms. Anaya's apartment. I realize that you might have budget concerns, but if you will call your chief, I believe I can find some sort of reasonable compensation for the department."

The two cops glanced at each other, and Randisi made a slight tilt of the head. Hurley stood, nodded, and let himself out into the hall.

Lymon was thinking now; she could see it. He said, "You've got a file on Christal. She pressed charges a couple of weeks ago during the Manuel de Clerk thing. She identified the same woman at de Clerk's who took Ms. Marks' tampon at the Regent Beverly Wilshire. If I were you, I think I'd start there."

Randisi watched them through half-lidded eyes, his fingers tapping on the statements they had just signed.

"Hey, I'm outta here," Delangelo muttered, "Come on, Jennifer."

"You'll leave when I tell you to," Sheela barked,

using her stage voice. "I'm not done with you."

"Bullshit!" Delangelo cried. "I'm sitting on the biggest shot of my life here."

Sheela walked up to stare into his eyes. "What if I told you there was more here than the simple abduction of a security agent? What if I told you that you're sitting on the biggest story of the decade?"

"Are you shitting me?"

"Oh, it's not COVID, the Trump indictment, or Putin's assassination, but it's something that could make your career. If you're interested, you'll play ball. If not, I'll write you a check for seventy-five thousand for that camera right now."

He hesitated, frowned, and she read him like a comic book. He didn't even have complicated illustrations.

"This is bullshit."

Sheela narrowed a hard eye. "You in or out?"

Delangelo glanced at Jennifer, who was shaking her head no. He licked his lips, the frown line deepening in his forehead. "Seventy-five thou? No shit?"

"Done." Sheela stuck out her hand. "Rex will have a check for you in the morning. Security will let you through." She reached for the camera.

"Hey." Randisi gestured at the camera. "That's not leaving this room until I say it is."

Sheela tossed him the heavy camera. "How long will it take your people to develop infrared film?"

He caught it by instinct and grunted as the weight rocked him back in his chair. "We can have it in a couple of hours if it's a rush."

"It's a rush," Lymon said, leaning over the table to stare into Randisi's eyes.

CHAPTER 34

Hank stared down at Christal's bound body and wondered how it had all gone so wrong. The van slowly worked its way through the desultory late-night traffic. He rode in the back, seated on one of the benches while April held his hand. Her fingers were drawing designs on his palm. Something about her excited him in a way that no other woman ever had. She was a mixture of dare, challenge, and sensuality. Hell, she was Sharon Stone in *Basic Instinct*. Hank had never understood that character until he looked into April's saucy gaze and saw her soul sway with his.

He needed only to close his eyes, and his dick began to tingle. Images of their afternoon lovemaking replayed in his head. He could see her golden body, so perfect, rising and falling sinuously as she held his wrists down. When she'd come, her breasts had tightened, straining at the air. In that instant, his body had exploded with a pulsing orgasm that left him bucking under her weight and every nerve on fire.

So, does it matter? We've got Christal. She'll talk. That's all we want. Just a little talk.

He turned to smile at April, his guilt assuaged, and then he looked down at Christal, remembering another night, another van. That time, he'd lain atop her. He remembered moaning when he came. Remembered her tightening around him to make it better. How were they supposed to know they were being recorded? That a few days later, surrounded by his colleagues, he would watch his bare buttocks rising and falling in a black-and-white nightmare. The camera angle had recorded Christal's face, had caught her open mouth, her eyes closed in delight and her throat working as pleasure pulsed through her.

As he stared down in the dimly lit van, her slack expression reminded him of that night.

We just want to talk. He swallowed. *Yeah, sure.*

Shit, what had he done? He glanced at April, words of protest rising, only to be blunted and fall away in confusion as she leaned over to kiss him on the lips.

The plan had worked like proverbial clockwork at the Residence Inn. He had watched Christal climb the steps a little before eleven that night. Three bags of groceries hung from her hands. Slipping them onto her left arm, she fished her key card out of her purse, slid it into the lock, and walked into her apartment.

Hank had stepped out the door of the opposing unit and had been right behind her, his presence as a blocker unnecessary. Christal had flipped on the lights and walked into her room. It was only when she turned to close the door that he had seen the surprise in her eyes.

"Hank?"

"We've got to talk," he told her, stepping inside after her and spreading his arms as if to prove he was no threat. He watched the sudden anger on her face and raised his hands higher, distracting her as Neal stepped out of the darkened kitchen and walked up from behind on crepe-soled shoes.

"We've got nothing to talk about." Christal's hands knotted on her grocery bags. Some thought flashed in her eyes, an understanding that something was dreadfully wrong. She started to turn when Neal reached out and pulled her back. As she started to scream, Neal had neatly inserted a syringe into her neck and depressed the plunger.

"What the hell?" Hank asked, worried for the first time. "What did you just do?"

"Just a little oil for the system." Neal back-heeled Christal to the couch, keeping one hand pressed over her mouth as she bucked in his strong arms. The grocery bags tumbled to the floor. The turkey made a hollow thump. Cans and bottles rolled across the white vinyl. Her purse bounced off the corner of the couch and spilled open.

April and Gretchen entered through the still-open door, each smiling down at Christal. "Got you at last, bitch," Gretchen snarled. She drew back a foot for a kick.

April stopped her, saying, "Not now." She glanced at Hank, praise in her gray eyes. "Nice work, Hank. She never suspected a thing. You're good."

"Glad to be of service." But the syringe? That hadn't been part of the plan. The first stirring of unease built inside.

Christal's struggles had gone weak, rage draining

from her dark eyes to be replaced by a dreamy look. Neal took his hand from her mouth and looked down at the blood welling on his palm. "She bit me."

"Hope you've had your shots," April chided.

Christal's face had gone slack, blood on her lips.

Hank, uneasy, muttered, "Must have hurt like hell."

"Not the worst I've ever gotten." Neal walked over to the sink, found the paper towels, and began dabbing at his hand.

April leaned down, staring into Christal's eyes. "We're from Genesis Athena."

Hank saw something change in Christal's face.

"Ah, you know," April said in a friendly voice. "That's why you went to Colorado, isn't it?"

Christal blinked and frowned as if having trouble following the conversation.

"Do you know what Genesis Athena is?"

Christal mumbled, "You're...witches."

April laughed at that. "Do you know what we're doing?"

Christal blinked hard, made a face, and said, "S... Stealing...souls."

April patted Christal's shoulder. "Oh, we're stealing more than that." Then she straightened. "All right, let's get her to the van."

"The van?" Hank asked, surprised. "You said you wanted to talk to her."

April walked up to him, her slender fingers arranging his collar. "We do, but not here. Someplace more private."

"Jesus, do you know what you're playing with? One wrong move, and you're involved in felony abduction."

She turned, asking, "Christal, if we give you some answers, will you come with us?"

Christal blinked, seemed to be struggling with the question, and slowly nodded.

April's eyes illuminated. "There, see? You can't abduct a willing participant. It's that easy."

And it had been, right up to the moment the lone motorcycle had pulled up. Hank had looked, half expecting the silver bullet-looking thing that Bridges rode, but had seen instead some sort of sleek cruiser with two riders. Hank had never been big on motorcycles, and this one had picked a lousy time to rumble up. And he wasn't sure that Neal knocking the bike over had been the smartest move, either. Technically, that qualified as assault.

Doesn't matter. I'm in the shit now.

It should have bothered him more than it did. He glanced across, seeing April's eyes on his.

"Do you think the guy on the bike is going to be trouble?" Hank asked as he glanced back over his shoulder at the traffic.

"Nah," Neal called from the front seat. "It'll be days before anyone comes looking for Anaya. It's not like he got a good look at me. For the moment, he's stomping around, making macho threats to save face with his woman. Thinks he just pissed some guy off by sticking his nose where it didn't belong."

"You know," Hank reminded, "I made my living in the Bureau interviewing people like the guy on that bike. Between him and the woman, they could put together a pretty good picture of what happened."

"Hank," April whispered, "trust us. We're good at

this. If a problem crops up, we'll solve it. We're not doing anything illegal."

He started to say something, aware of the weight of Christal's body at his feet, but April had reached over, her hand slipping along his thigh to send tingles through him. "For later." Her whisper deepened. "Trust me, you'll never regret it."

Hank closed his eyes and nodded, trying to keep from moaning as her fingers found him through the soft fabric of his pants. In that state, he wasn't looking out the window as they drove into the private airport.

CHAPTER 35

In his dreams, Sid was sledding across sparkling blue Bahamian water. He rode some sort of engine-powered surfboard. Dreams were magical that way. His super surfboard didn't even need surf as it jetted across the crystal waves, a foamy wake washing behind. He kept looking over to the white beach backed by lush green trees. A woman stood there, her gaze fastened on him. She was a beauty with long black hair and sparkling obsidian eyes—her perfectly tanned body covered only by a skimpy yellow bikini. Sid grinned and waved, angling the surfboard toward her, knowing that paradise lay there, just across that short stretch of water. As he neared, she reached up, slipping the straps of her bikini from her brown shoulders and—

The phone rang. The dream shredded and left Sid clawing for the nightstand. He jerked around in his bed. Bits of beach, sun, water, and girl drained away as he fumbled for the receiver and rasped, "Yeah?"

"Sid? It's Lymon."

"Fuck! It's...uh," He got one eye half focused on the digital alarm clock beside the bed. "Five in the morning!"

"Christal's been kidnapped."

"What?" Sid sat up, aware of Claire groaning as she rearranged her pillow and curled away from him. "Who'd kidnap Christal?"

"There was a paparazzo there. He got pictures. A whole roll of them. It's a bunch of people loading Christal into a van. She looks drugged, drunk, or otherwise not herself. Oh, and Sid?"

Sid ran a hand over his face. "Yeah?" His mind was staggering, trying to comprehend through the cobwebs of sleep. He kept stumbling over how nonsensical it sounded.

"One of the guys manhandling her into the van is Hank Abrams."

CHAPTER 36

Lymon rode his big Indian into the circular drive fronting Sheela's house and pulled to a stop behind Tony's Z8 BMW. Rex's red Ferrari squatted like a menacing wedge at the edge of the steps.

"Well," Lymon quipped as he kicked the sidestand out and turned off the ignition, "the Bobbsey Twins are here."

"Right! Just what I need after the last twenty hours." Sheela straightened a leg and stepped off before she began fiddling with the D rings on her helmet. "Maybe they're busy at the pool and we can sneak in without them knowing. We'll tiptoe up to my room and crash."

"After what we've been through, do you think you could sleep?"

"Sleep? In the classical sense? No. But I'm going to fall face-first onto the floor if I don't lie down." She lifted her helmet off and shook her head to free her braid. Her face looked lined and gray, making her appear ten years older. "I'm worried sick...and I don't think I've ever felt this exhausted and wrung out."

At that moment, Rex Gerber opened the front door.

"Trick or treat," Lymon said softly as he stepped off the bike and undid his own helmet. He could feel the heat in Rex's gaze as he followed Sheela up the steps. Something in the man's look reminded Lymon of the time he'd got an under-aged date back to her father's house two hours after midnight. On irate impulse, Lymon said, "Hi, Dad," as he passed Rex.

"Yuck it up, asshole," Rex muttered. Then he turned to Sheela, who stepped into the coatroom and hung up her helmet and leather jacket. "Sheela, can I have a word with you?"

It surprised Lymon when she whirled, a finger spearing toward Rex's face. "I'm not up for your bull-shit right now, Rex. Someone kidnapped Christal last night."

Rex backed away from the finger, frowned, and then blinked. "What?"

"You heard me. Lymon and I saw it." She reached back and began pulling her hair out of the French braid. "We've got pictures."

"Kidnapped?" Rex repeated.

"Someone got into her apartment last night and carried her away. We've spent the whole night alter-nately talking to the police and the FBI. Like I said, we've got it on film. And Rex, you're going to love this. The woman that Christal calls Copperhead, the one that sliced a chunk out of Manny's dick and copped my tampon? She's there. So is the mousy one, the one Christal said was called Gretchen. The paparazzo that snapped the pictures was using a really good infrared film."

"You're not kidding?"

"Sorry, Rex." Lymon set his helmet on the foyer's marble table. "It's as real as it gets."

Rex seemed to mull over the words, then nodded to himself. "Well, I'm sorry to hear that. I liked her. Lymon, I hope you get her back."

"That's it?" Lymon propped hands on his hips.

"Well...she's your employee. I don't see where this should involve Sheela."

"But it does," Sheela shot back. "I hired her. I made the decision that day in the meeting room. We sent her after the people who tried to mug me in the hotel in New York. Then she stumbled over them at the Wilshire, and again at Manny's. Now, it appears, she made them a little too nervous. She's in this mess because of me."

Rex put out placating hands. "Yes, yes, all right. We'll put the best people we can on it. But Sheela, let's talk to Dot first, see what kind of spin we can put on this. There ought to be a way to make a win-win situation out of it."

Sheela blinked, wavered on her feet, and would have flown at Rex but for Lymon's restraining hand. "Easy, Sheela."

Rex backpedaled, smiling. "Hey, I'm sorry. I didn't know it was so rough. All night with the police? The FBI? Damn, Sheela, I wish you would have called. I could have come down, lent my weight to—"

"Shut up, Rex. I'm tired. It's been a long two weeks, okay? When a guy named Delangelo shows up, please have a check for seventy-five thousand for him. I bought his camera."

"Seventy-five thousand? *For a camera?*"

She waved him off, starting for the stairs, only to have Tony walk out of the main room, a script in his hand.

"Hey, cool! Sheela, babe, we gotta talk! I've been on the phone with Jerry. He *really* wants to spot you for *Giant*. You read the script, right? I mean, it cooks! I think you ought to jump on this. It's got your fingerprints all over it."

"Tony...fuck off." She started up the stairs, then hesitated, looked back, and said, "Lymon? You coming?"

"Right behind you," he added, shooting Rex a neutral glance.

"What the hell's that all about?" Tony asked.

"Someone put the bag on Christal last night," Rex said. He sounded confused.

"Huh? What do you mean put the bag on?"

"As in kidnapped. You got that? Someone abducted Christal."

"No way!" Then a short pause. "Abducted? Seriously? Weird shit, man."

Lymon shook his head, following on Sheela's heels. At the top of the stairs, he glanced back. Tony had a deeply pensive expression, his brow furrowed as if processing unsettling information. The look in Rex's eyes barely veiled the anger and frustration seething within.

Anger? Sure. Lymon seemed to have the inside track. But where had the frustration come from?

When he closed the bedroom door behind him, he

stopped short, suddenly terribly unsure. Where the hell was this leading? Sheela seemed completely oblivious to how this was going to look to the folks downstairs. And it got worse when she called, "Lock the door."

Lymon found the latch and watched her as she collapsed onto the chaise and bent to pull her heavy boots off. After the last one thumped onto the floor, she stared at him, face haggard, eyes listless, hands dangling limply from her knees. "I'm worn through, Lymon. I have nothing left. If I have to deal with one more crisis, no matter how small, I'm going to break down and weep."

He walked over and offered his hand. "Come on, let's get you to bed."

Instead she lifted one leg suggestively. "These leather pants are a bitch. Pull."

He did, helping her to slide them off. Then she stood and began unbuttoning her blouse as she walked toward the rear. "Come on, Lymon. It's not the way I always dreamed. It was always supposed to be a romantic seduction with expensive cognac, candlelight, and soft music."

He followed her into her refuge, staring at the beautiful furnishings. The room was soft, white, and large. Against one wall a fluffy canopy bed sported huge frilly pillows. The dressers held knickknacks and photos of her family and old friends. The only celebrity to be seen was Morgan Freeman. When Sheela saw him looking at it, she added, "He saved my life once. Talked me through a bad situation."

Sheela dropped her shirt on the floor and walked over to the bed. Her nimble fingers unplugged the cord from the back of the phone. She tossed one of the big pillows to the side and threw back the covers. Unabashed, she undid her bra and let it slip away before pulling an oversized T-shirt from a top drawer. She glanced at him as she pulled it on. "Are you as tired as I am?"

"I couldn't sleep."

She crawled under the covers, patting the bed. "Come lie here beside me. Clothes on or off, I don't care. I just need you close, Lymon. I have to know you're here."

"Sheela, if I crawl in there—"

"It'll be like necrophilia," she replied, closing her eyes. "I'll be asleep before you can pry my legs apart."

He frowned, kicked off his boots, and slid under the covers, feeling awkward in his clothes. It seemed sacrilege to be wearing street clothes while encased in her spotless white linens—but a whole lot safer than the alternative. A curious giddy feeling tightened at the base of his throat. The sheets were smooth, scented, and his hard body sank in the bedding.

She made a purring sound. "Promise me you'll stay close?"

"I promise."

She snuggled against him, her hand slipping across his chest. He was remembering her body as she changed into her sleep shirt. She'd looked like a goddess. But an image of Christal wedged into his weary brain. Here he was, safe and comfortable beside the woman he loved. And Christal? Where was she? Scared? Frightened? To torment him, his imagination pictured her bound, gagged, as one man after another crawled on top of her naked body.

"She's my friend, Lymon," Sheela whispered as if

she shared his thoughts. "She never asked anything of me. Didn't want anything from me. Just you and her...in the whole world."

"We'll find her," he said softly.

"Just hold me." Sheela pressed her body against him.

"I might embarrass myself," he said, kissing the side of her head.

"Lymon, I'm so tired, but it's nice to know." A pause, then a sleep-softened, "I love you."

"I love you, too."

She was asleep that quickly.

Lymon lay there, painfully aroused, his heart thudding against his ribs. How could he feel like that while Christal was undergoing...what?

He blinked up at the ceiling, forcing himself to imagine Christal's face, wondering where she was.

Be safe, Christal. He swallowed hard. What if they found her body in a ditch somewhere out beyond San Bernardino? No one should die like that. Alone, frightened, degraded, and abandoned.

Sheela's breath purled on his cheek.

The shit's in the fire now.

CHAPTER 37

In for a penny, in for a pound, Hank Abrams thought. Where had that saying come from? How many years had passed since anything worthwhile sold for a penny a pound? He looked down from the Gulfstream g650's window. The Rocky Mountains were glowing in the morning light.

April slipped into the seat beside him. She flipped her burnished red hair over her shoulder and gave him that challenging smile that made his blood race. "Neal and Gretchen are asleep in the front seats. Anaya's going to be out for at least another couple of hours." She pulled her muscular leg up, propping it on the seat back in front of her. "So, how's it feel to be in the mid-six-figure salary bracket?"

He shot a look past April to where Christal lay propped uncomfortably across the aisle, her mouth hanging open. Drool had dried on her shirt. Her arms were bound to her body with silver duct tape. Her eyes, half-open and slightly dried, reminded him of a dead woman's, the stare empty.

"That's what she's worth?"

April seemed to find that amusing. "Probably a lot more. The Sheik found her enchanting. He's got a thing for women. He's fascinated by blondes and redheads, but—I think it's something cultural—he just craters for a brunette."

"Wait a minute. You mean we stole Christal for... what? A harem?"

April twirled a long lock of hair, amusement in her eyes. "I like you, Hank. You really have a sense of indignation. A harem? No. At least, I doubt it. Maybe, if Anaya's into it, she might make a play for him. The Sheik's a little different. He's a watcher."

Hank swallowed hard. "You're telling me Genesis Athena is a cover for sex trafficking?"

She turned, leaning so her face was close to his. Her steely gray eyes were alive with excitement. "Nothing so crude. We just need to find out what Anaya knows. If she's not a threat, we'll take a sample, reimburse her for her time, fear, and inconvenience, and let her be on her way." She ran a finger along his temple. "God, what do you think we are?"

"You tell me." He took her hand in his, pulling it down and folding it in his so she wouldn't remind him of his sexuality—or hers. "I think it's time you tell me just what Genesis Athena is. Why you take so many risks getting your samples."

"That's how we drum up business. It's the hook that brings in the clients."

"Clients?"

April freed her hand and settled back in her seat. "What you became part of last night is one of the world's newest and potentially most profitable businesses. I told you, we don't do anything illegal."

"Just kidnapping and transportation across state lines. That's major jail time that we're into right now."

April shrugged. "Not if she's released with compensation. Like I say, the Sheik's interested in her."

"Yeah, so what? He watches her? Then gives her a couple of bucks and lets her go?" He snapped his fingers. "Just like that, Christal Anaya forgets she was lifted from her apartment and hauled across the country against her will?"

"Most likely." April watched him speculatively. "You see, we don't want her body. We just want her DNA."

"Excuse me?" Then it hit him. "That's what the little devices you gave me were for?"

"Uh-huh, and had she not barged into our phone service in Colorado, we'd have taken our sample, added her to our catalog, and she'd never have been the wiser."

"So, what do you do with the DNA? Patent her genetics?"

"Sometimes, yes, depending on different genes people have."

"I thought that was the province of biotech labs. That drug companies and universities were filing those kinds of patents. And wasn't there some kind of lawsuit? The one with Myriad Genetics back in 2010? That you can't patent someone's genes?"

April leaned back and took a deep breath. Hank couldn't help but watch her breasts swell beneath her thin silk shirt. "You're thinking about US patents. Hank, there's a whole world out there. Genesis Athena is an international company. We have labs in the Persian Gulf, in Africa, Europe, and Australia. We even have a ship, a large—"

"ZoeGen," he whispered.

"That's right. You've been aboard. With the Sheik, right?"

"Uh-huh."

"So," she asked, "now that you're getting the idea, are you in, or out?"

"Why me?"

"You're Bureau trained. You did a good job with Anaya. We watched you. That was smart action on your part when she dropped everything and went to Toronto. Even smarter when you followed her to Colorado. Sometimes in multinational companies like ours, simple things are forgotten. We didn't think of putting a warning system in place in Colorado. Now, we're notified immediately if anyone walks in the door and starts asking questions about Genesis Athena. Finally, you were right about the planning at Anaya's. You handled her perfectly. She never knew what hit her. In short, if you decide to throw in with us, we think you'll be a formidable asset."

"And how does Verele fit in?"

"He's legit. His company provides security when we have people in New York. That's all. He doesn't ask questions; we don't speak out of turn."

"So, what happens if I say yes?"

Her nose wrinkled with her smile. "I've been looking for a partner. Gretchen's good, but, you know, she's got issues. I like you, Hank. I think you've got potential. I mean, you were great in the sack. It's been a long time since I've made love with a man who wasn't intimidated by me."

"Besides great sex, what's it pay?"

"We receive a hundred thousand a job plus royalties."

"Royalties?"

"Two percent of what the company makes per specimen. For Talia Roberts alone, Gretchen and I stand to make a couple million."

"Huh?"

"Remember when her sheets and trash were stolen? That was us. I did the parasail jump from the helicopter. We got plenty of good solid DNA out of her sheets and the tissues she used to wipe her makeup off."

"Jesus Christ!"

"We'd love to do him, too. Imagine what he'd be worth! The problem is finding a sample. And you've got to prove who he is. You know, people won't fork out the kind of money we're talking about unless they know they're getting the real thing."

"Wow."

"The clincher is there's no law against taking another person's DNA for profit."

"Yeah, but there's a whole slew of laws against cloning. Not just in the US, but around the world."

"Not in Yemen," she reminded, "and certainly not on the high seas. That's what I meant when I said that we're not breaking any laws, strictly speaking." She jerked her head toward Christal. "And we'll make sure that she doesn't bear a grudge by the time we're through. Trust me on that."

Hank glanced unsurely at Christal. "And if I say no?"

"We ask you to sign a nondisclosure agreement, pay you a hundred grand for your silence, time, and consideration, and hope you'll think it over and change your mind. I'll give you a number where you can reach us."

He chewed his lip for a moment, aware of the challenge in her eyes. "So, how's Gretchen going to take you finding a new partner?"

April leaned close and kissed him. "She'll get over it."

"Uh-huh."

She traced her tongue around his ear. "When we get to the *ZoeGen* I've got a private cabin and a couple of weeks of vacation. It'll be like being on our very own cruise ship."

"I hate waiting that long."

She rose up in the seat, glancing forward. "You ever had sex at forty thousand feet?"

"Nope. The Bureau made us fly economy. It's tough when you're folded into a center seat next to a little old lady."

She reached over and unbuckled his seat belt, pulling him after her. "Come on. There's a fold-down bed back here. We'll have to be quiet, but they'll be out for hours."

"Are you crazy?" he asked, glancing back at where Neal and Gretchen's heads were lolled two rows away.

"It's the only way to be." She led him back to the rear and folded down the little couch across from the tiny galley. Before he could protest, she had his belt unbuckled, his pants unsnapped, and his fly down.

Her eyes were agleam, and her lips had parted in anticipation. His hands—of their own volition—began fumbling at the snap on her jeans, then shoved them down over her round hips. Heart hammering, breath hot and racing in his lungs, he peeled her shirt off. She clamped her mouth on his, her tongue flicking and teasing. He bit off a moan as her grip tightened painfully on his erection.

Then they were on the cushions.

He was staring into her eyes, saw her pupils expand, dark and eternal, at his entry. She shuddered, her muscular body arching as she tightened.

"Join us, Hank," she whispered.

"Yes. *God, yes!*"

CHAPTER 38

Lymon checked his watch. 2:16 flashed at him. He turned his head. Sheela lay curled on her side. Her red hair spooled over her pillow in a soft wave. She was sleeping hard enough that she didn't move as he slowly lowered his feet to the floor and padded out to the anteroom to put on his shoes. He closed the doors behind him before using the toilet in the dressing room.

He stepped into the hallway, glancing down toward the stairs, and saw no one. On silent feet, he passed the paintings and sculptures and started down the curving stairs.

"Lymon?" Rex's sharp voice barked as he walked over to the little marble-topped table and reached for his helmet.

"Yeah, Rex?" Lymon turned. Rex stood by the doorway that led through the parlor and out to the pool.

"You and I had better talk." Rex made a jerking movement with his head. "Outside. Just the two of us."

Lymon bit off a rueful smile and followed Rex out to the poolside. There, Sheela's manager had set up camp. Melting ice cubes floated in a half-empty glass of scotch. Two scripts were piled atop each other and file folders held copies of stapled contracts. Rex dropped onto one of the white lounge chairs. He waved to the chair across from him.

"She's still asleep?" Rex asked gruffly.

"Yeah. And, please, leave her alone. She needs the rest."

Rex's hard stare bored into his. "What are you doing, Lymon?"

"Taking care of my client."

"Really? Sneaking around so you can slip your dick into your client? Is that how you take care of her, Lymon?"

Lymon leaned forward, anger welling. "Rex, I'm going to tell you this once. I don't have sex with my clients. I never have, and I never will."

"Yeah, right." He threw a gesture toward the house. "What the hell just happened up there? You read Grimm's fairy tales to each other, made tea, and—"

"Do you have trouble with the English language, Rex? I told you, I do *not* have sex with my clients. Period."

Rex just stared at him like he was some kind of bug. "You're fucking fired. Get lost. I don't want you here anymore."

"That's not your decision."

"Lymon, I've told you before, you don't want to cross me. You don't want to put Sheela in the position of choosing between you and me. You'll lose, pal."

"Don't be an asshole, Rex." Lymon sat back in the

chair. "I'm not playing this game. I've got a bigger problem. One of my people was taken last night. Now, if you're finished swinging your dick, I'm going to check on what they've found out about Christal, and what I can do."

Rex's flat stare didn't waver. "Stop the bullshit, Lymon. Oh, yeah, you're concerned, all right. Have any trouble getting it up while you were worrying about Christal? Or did that just make it all the more exciting?"

"You're a real shithead, Rex." Lymon pointed a hard finger. "And since you can't seem to understand that I could have just caught forty winks up there, here's how it lays out. If I ever..."

Lymon shook his head. "Forget it. It's none of your business." He got to his feet. "I've got things to do."

"Lymon!" Rex called from behind him. "Lymon! Don't you walk out on me!"

Lymon shut the door behind him, nodding to Tomaso, who was coming toward him, another scotch on a tray. He said, "Sheela's sound asleep for the first time in weeks. If Rex demands to see her, tell him to go to hell. You got that?"

Tomaso, generally so very in charge of himself, started. "Sir?"

Lymon gave him a pat on the shoulder. "Just do it, all right? If you don't, he's going to kill her."

Tomaso's dark eyes held his for a moment, and he finally nodded. "Yes, sir."

Lymon made his way through the house, out past the foyer table where he collected his helmet, and into the yard. Afternoon light cast a yellow glow through the trees as he pulled his cell phone from his pocket, turned it on, and punched the number for the West LA station handling Christal's case.

Come on, Christal, let them tell me you've been found safe and are at the station giving a statement.

But she wasn't. The police had nothing to report.

CHAPTER 39

Sid was starting to think he'd been taken for a ride. The Uber driver he'd hired at LAX didn't speak English. Sid didn't speak Spanish. He had to hope the address he'd typed into the phone, and the little triangle on the dash screen would end up being the same place. He hadn't remembered that it took so long to get from the airport to Wilshire Boulevard. But then, he'd been riding with Christal last time, sharing conversation, laughing, enjoying the odd moments of just looking at her and thinking how much she meant to him.

So he fumed, his suitcase propped under one arm, while traffic moved, stopped, and moved again. The slightly pungent tang that periodically rose from the floorboards suggested that the greasy-looking stain between his shoes must have had its origins inside a human digestive tract. When he rolled the window down, all he could smell was traffic. And the driver called back that he was doing something to the *frio,* whatever that was.

He wished he'd chosen the upgrade to a black car. Instead, he was cramped in the back of a Honda CR-V.

Sid tried to think about other things.

So, it was with relief that the Uber finally took a left onto Wilshire, proceeded another three blocks, and pulled up at the curb beside a fire hydrant.

"Estas aqui," the driver told him. *"Es el numero, no? Mas o menos?"* He pointed at the address on a jewelry shop window and then the dash screen where the little triangle that represented the Honda now blinked.

"Yeah, we ought to be three doors down." He hoped he was right. Lymon had taken him in the back way. The obnoxious odor rising from the floor made his decision for him.

He opened the back door, and hung his travel bag over his shoulder. His phone dinged as the receipt was emailed. The ratty-looking red Honda pulled away from the curb, and Sid took stock of the sidewalk. He started down the block. Not every business had a number over the door, but Sid had the general idea.

LYMON BRIDGES ASSOCIATES was printed in block letters on a sign screwed into a brick wall. Sid sighed with relief, opened the aluminum-clad glass door, and thumped his way up the wooden steps. At the top, he opened a security door and stepped into Lymon's office. He could smell coffee, the odor of wood and dust, and the slight mustiness of carpeting.

June's fortress of a desk stood empty, its surface cluttered with a computer screen and keyboard, a blotter, a stand of pens and pencils, telephone, and all the other *impedimenta* of a good cleric.

Soft voices were coming from the rear. Sid dropped

his bag on the leather-upholstered couch beside the door and walked past June's desk.

He found Lymon's office with Lymon himself behind the desk. June was half-perched on one corner, staring down at the computer monitor. Another guy, a darkly complected, fit-looking young man, lounged in Lymon's office chair. They all looked worried as they glanced up.

"Sid?" Lymon cried in surprise, rising to his feet.

"What's the matter with you? Don't you check your answering machine?" Sid asked. "I called just before my flight left DC."

"Text his cell phone next time," June said tartly. "Landlines are for dinosaurs and telemarketers."

He got a good look at Lymon's face, seeing the stress. "What's the news?"

"Nothing," Lymon answered, then gestured around. "I think you know everyone here but Salvatore."

"Sid Harness," he said, taking the man's hand and feeling the bundled strength implied by the grip.

"My pleasure. I've heard a lot about you." Salvatore fixed a dark gaze on his.

Sid jabbed a thumb in Lymon's direction. "He lies."

Salvatore grinned. "Then, so does Christal. She told the same stories."

"What are you doing here?" Lymon asked, coming around the desk. "How did you get here?" He looked puzzled. "Why?"

Sid shrugged. "It's Saturday. I've got a slew of annual leave coming. I thought you might need a little help on this end. Having a tame FBI guy in the closet can be helpful." He scuffed his toe for effect. "And on top of all that, Christal's my friend."

A knowing smile molded Lymon's lips. "Yeah, I thought so. You eaten?"

"Not on airplanes these days. I grabbed a pastry at the Starbucks down the block from my house. That was a little before seven this morning."

Lymon turned to June. "Call Al's. Have him make up a to-go order of burgers." He looked at Salvatore.

"I'm on it, boss." The muscular man rose to his feet, nodded to Sid, and stepped out.

June picked Lymon's phone off the cradle and tapped numbers by memory.

"What happened?" Sid asked as June spoke carefully into the phone.

"Here're the photos. Take a look for yourself." Lymon led him to a worktable in the office's back corner.

As Lymon narrated the events, Sid fingered the photos. Each had that slightly off-color of an infrared shot. The image quality was remarkably good. The guy taking the photos had started with a party walking down the sidewalk. Sid could see a figure being carried. From the postures, Christal was completely limp. Alive or dead? He couldn't tell.

The series of photos led to an open van door, then pulled back, showing a motorcycle pulling up.

"You and Ms. Marks?" Sid asked.

Lymon nodded. "Sheela was going to spend the weekend with Christal."

"Huh?"

"It's complicated."

Sid read the look in Lymon's eyes, let it go, and flipped through the rest of the photos. The most telling was of a tall man shoving Lymon and Sheela over, while in the background, a familiar face was caught full-on. Hank Abrams had been in the process of dragging Christal's limp body into the van, but had looked up in time to see the blond guy push Lymon's bike over. Hank's expression reflected worry and distress.

"What do you think?"

Sid thumbed through the rest as the van motored off. "Is that a license number?"

"Yeah, a Ryder rental. The local FBI is working on it."

Sid tapped the stack of photos against his palm. "How'd you get all this?"

"Sheela managed to buy off the paparazzo who shot this. Look, it was just fortuitous. The guy caught on that Sheela was doing something, tailed us, and took these photos."

"What?"

Lymon's shadowed eyes held no humor. "It's how people live out here, Sid. Sheela wanted time to relax. She talked Christal into letting her spend the weekend in her hotel room. We just happened to ride in at the right moment to see it all happening."

"You're sure it's Christal these guys were after? Maybe they got wind of it, thought they were getting Sheela?"

Lymon bent and picked up a gaudy green flyer. Sid took it and unfolded the paper. The big letters jumped out at him. "Genesis Athena." Looking up, he asked, "You think that's what this is all about?"

Lymon crossed his arms, glanced at June, and shrugged. "It's the best we've got."

"Why?"

"Answer that, my friend, and we'll know what Christal was on the verge of discovering."

"What about Hank?" Sid asked.

"I called his boss this morning. Verele says he knows nothing about any kidnapping. According to him, Hank is no longer in his employ. He says he took a position with a client."

"Sheik Amud Abdulla?" Sid said, remembering.

"Look, I know Verele. Verele Security isn't into breaking the law. My take is that Genesis Athena offered Abrams a better deal. I think the good Sheik just lifted Christal. Did she tell you about the first time he saw her?"

"About that night in New York? A little. I did some research for her."

"We know." He tapped a file folder that lay closed on the desk. "Genesis Athena. What is it, Sid? What's the Sheik doing? Why'd he grab Christal? What did she discover that scared them so?"

Sid could feel June's probing gaze as she studied him. He shrugged, glancing at the woman. Lymon had a thing about surrounding himself with attractive women. "You got me, cowboy. I just ran some stuff through the computer."

He heard the rear door open and close down the hall. Salvatore had been really fast. "She faxed me some papers, a questionnaire. I had the psych guys down at Quantico look at it. They thought it was a test of some sort. A sort of psychological evaluation."

"To evaluate what?" a fine contralto asked from behind him.

Sid wheeled—and stared into the most bewitching blue eyes he'd ever seen. They pinned him like a study moth, and it took his floundering mind a moment to realize that he knew that perfect face. Had seen it staring down at him with rapt wonder from the screen.

"Jesus Christ," he mumbled.

"Not even close." The goddess was offering her hand. "I'm Sheela Marks. And you are?"

"Sid Harness," Lymon called from behind when Sid's words failed him. "He's a very dear and very old friend."

Sid swallowed hard, managed to shake Sheela Marks' hand, and watched as Lymon pushed past, a frown on his face.

"What's happened?" Sheela asked.

"What are you doing here?" He looked past her to the tall handsome man who waited in the hallway. "Hello, Paul."

"Mr. Bridges," the man replied respectfully.

And then Sheela Marks put her hands on Lymon's shoulders, looking into his eyes. "Lymon, I have to know what's happened. Have the police called? The FBI? They won't talk to me, but I know that you have connections."

"Nothing, Sheela. Not a word. No one has called here or even to her mother in New Mexico, for that matter." He seemed to harden. "She might have just dropped off the face of the earth."

Sid could feel the electricity flowing between them, could read the body language. For a long moment they looked into each other's eyes, and then Sheela Marks said, "I have to find her, Lymon. No matter what it takes."

CHAPTER 40

Gray dreams began to shred, giving way to a terrible sweetly metallic taste that clung to Christal's dry tongue. She shifted, vaguely aware that her body had the gritty feel of numbed cotton. A faint ache lurked behind her eyes.

For the moment, it was fine to lie in the safe grayness, hanging halfway between wakefulness and the fragments of fleeing dreams. Some voice deep within urged her to surrender to the dream again. Fall back into the mist of unconsciousness. It would be so much easier that way.

Easier?

Than what?

A slippery premonition goaded her to blink. A white haze glared when she flicked open her gritty eyelids. The fluffy muzziness in her brain refused to give way to thought.

She pulled her hand up, hearing it rasp across linen. Rubbing her eyes, she blinked again. Shit, was she hungover?

Her tongue moved dryly, and swallowing was almost impossible. The first saliva tasted foul—really foul.

She made a face.

Pushing with rubbery muscles, Christal sat up, aware that she wore only panties and a brassiere. Her glazed vision had trouble coming into focus, so she massaged her rheumy eyes with her palms until she could make out the small white room. Her new cosmos consisted of a solid metal door, a table with a plastic drinking glass and water pitcher, a round window, and her bunk. A smaller wooden door led where? To a closet?

"What the...?" She struggled with her brain. Thought seemed to be such a flexible problem.

Where the hell am I?

Christal pinched the bridge of her nose, trying to pin her mind in place. Home was the Residence Inn in West LA. She had been doing what? Getting ready for Sheela to come and stay the weekend with her.

She had been where? Headed home after doing some last-minute shopping. She could remember walking the supermarket aisles, selecting things to cook, things she thought Sheela might like to try.

Then a faint memory stirred. First it was the emotional recollection of fear followed by the hazy images of Hank Abrams, his hands up, a pleading expression on his face as he glanced at something behind her shoulder. A hand had clapped over her mouth, dragging her back. The sting in her neck...

"God, where am I?" She swung her feet over the edge of the bunk and stared down. Her shoes were resting side by side on the gray-carpeted floor. Her clothes were neatly folded on a small nightstand at the head of the bed.

She swayed as she stood, bracing one hand against the cold wall, and felt unforgiving steel beneath. A hard rap with her knuckles confirmed the fact. Her slim brown fingers contrasted against the white paint.

Steadying herself, she turned to the round window and stared out in disbelief. The sun was either rising or setting, capping endless waves with yellow, hollow troughs dark and rippling as the muscular swells rose and fell.

Shit! She was in the middle of the Pacific! On what? A ship? She pressed her nose to the glass, bending her face this way and that as she tried to see to either side. An infinity of water rolled off to the golden horizon.

She made a face as she poked and prodded her stomach and abdomen. Why the hell were her insides so tender? Taking inventory, she could see a bruise on the back of her hand. From what? An IV? Her arms and shoulders were sore. What the hell had they done? Dragged her like a corpse?

The effort of pulling on her pants almost tumbled her face-first onto the floor. Finding the sleeves in her blue blouse almost defeated her. Her coordination wasn't what it should be. Christal took a deep breath, stretching, feeling the dull ache in her muscles. Then she grabbed the handle on the metal door and twisted. Locked.

She glanced around, cocking her head. What the hell had Hank done to her? She tried the smaller door, opening it to find a compact toilet and sink.

She turned back and hammered on the big steel door with the flat of her hand, yelling, "Hey! Open this up!" The heavy portal seemed to suck up the worst of her violence.

She stopped, listening, as panic rose in her breast. She could only hear a faint humming, the noise that of distant engines.

"Hank! You asshole!" She hauled off and kicked the door, feeling a spear of pain in her foot.

How long did she stand there? Her room had grown dark. So, the sun had been setting? Then she'd lost an entire day? Or had it been more? A terrible fear, like nothing she had ever known, prickled like needles along her spine.

She noticed the switch on the wall, pressed it, and was relieved when the recessed safety light in the ceiling came on. She tried the pitcher. It contained water. Gratefully she drank, aware of her dehydration. Then, opening the toilet door, she stepped in and relieved herself. Urinating proved uncomfortable enough that she checked for blood and was relieved to find none. The bathroom wasn't much bigger than a phone booth. Outside of the sink, a toilet paper dispenser was the only furnishing.

She stood, pulled up her pants, tried the sink, and was rewarded with hot and cold water.

"So, I won't die of thirst," she muttered before walking back to stare out the porthole at the darkness. She turned off the light to see better. Out there, on the ocean, she could see no lights, nothing but an endless darkness.

Swallowing hard, she whispered, "Dear God, I'm scared."

CHAPTER 41

Given his name, FBI agent Sean O'Grady, from the LA field office, should have had red hair, freckles, and mischievous green eyes. Instead the Bahamian native looked anything but Irish with his smooth black skin, angular jaw, bony face, and African features. He had agreed to meet with Lymon and Sheela through Sid's intercession. The "tame FBI guy" was already proving his worth.

O'Grady and Harness sat across the booth from Lymon and Sheela. O'Grady had picked a Studio City Burger King for the meeting. The wreckage of the agent's dinner consisted of a crumpled Double Whopper wrapper, empty box of fries, and a soft drink cup, half-full, on the plastic tray.

Sid sipped at a cup of coffee and kept a notebook in his hand. Lymon and Sheela shared an order of fries, having eaten earlier. Sheela had dressed in stealth mode, wearing a loose Lakers T-shirt, faded jeans, sunglasses, and a scarf over her head. She looked more like a housewife than an internationally known film star.

"We got this," O'Grady said, reaching into the pocket of his coat to pull out a little blue spiral-bound notebook. "Recognize it?"

"Yeah...well, maybe," Lymon granted. "Christal used one that looked something like that."

O'Grady passed it across. "Flip through to the last page."

Lymon thumbed through the pages, seeing Anaya's neat script. He noted that true to her Bureau training, each notation recorded the place and time of her writings. The last page—dated as 22:15 hours on the date of her abduction—consisted of a series of quickly jotted notes under the heading "Genesis Athena."

He read:

Genesis Athena. Athena sprang full-blown from the head of Zeus. Sheik didn't pick that at random. DNA is the key. He's the twenty-first-century version of the traditional Southwestern witch. But he is stealing more than just a person's soul—he wants it all. DNA from the rich and famous? What the old-time witches would have given for this technology!

?: If DNA is so easy to get, why make such a production of stealing it?

?: How much would an obsessed fan pay for a celebrity baby?

?: How do I break this to Sheela?

Lymon frowned, glanced at Sheela, and tried to decipher her pensive expression.

"That mean anything to you?" O'Grady asked. Sid had stood, stepping around the table to peer over Lymon's shoulder.

Under his breath, Lymon whispered, "Son of a bitch."

"What?" Sid asked, bending closer to stare at the page on the notebook.

"Where'd you find this?" Lymon tapped the notebook as he looked up.

"The floor. When the ERT went through Anaya's room at Residence Inn, it was under the couch along with a tube of lipstick. The only prints we've lifted off it are Anaya's. We went through her place from top to bottom. In the process, we got a blood sample on a paper towel, a couple of smudged prints, several hairs, and some evidence from the registration desk that we're running down. Rubber from the scratch they laid in the parking lot matches the compound in the rental van's tires."

O'Grady smiled. "Someone hosed the inside of that van down with bleach and a high-pressure system before they returned it. The credit card it was rented under led us to a PO box in Long Beach. Somebody named Lily Ann Gish had rented it."

"Lillian Gish," Sheela said softly.

"You know her?" Sid asked, slipping back into the booth beside O'Grady.

Sheela gave him a faint smile. "It's an alias. They're playing with us. Lillian Gish was one of Hollywood's first superstar actresses back in the black-and-white silent film days."

"Same name Copperhead gave Manny, wasn't it?" Lymon asked, trying to remember everything Christal had told him. He glanced at O'Grady. "You might check the police report. See if that matches."

O'Grady nodded, writing in his notebook. "That business in the notebook press any of your buttons? About the DNA, I mean?"

Sheela took a deep breath. "I can tell you how much an obsessed fan would pay for a celebrity baby."

"How much?" Sid asked.

"As much as they could leverage," she answered flatly. "People would mortgage their houses, sell their cars, take out all the loans they could." She turned her sunglasses on Sid. "Some would sell their souls, not to mention their bodies, and the very blood in their veins."

Sid frowned. "And the business about DNA?"

"Christal thinks the celeb hits were about stealing DNA," Lymon supplied. "But if you'll recall, we've had that conversation...and discarded it."

"Stealing DNA?" Sid asked absently, his face tightening in that old expression Lymon knew so well. Damn it, he was onto something.

"The problem is," Lymon continued, "like Christal says in her notes, why go to the trouble and risks? You can steal someone's DNA without sticking your neck out. You want Sheela's DNA? Swipe the napkin off her table at Morton's when she's done with lunch."

"Do you think that's really it?" Sheela asked softly, her head lowered.

Lymon glanced around the table and shrugged. "Hell, I don't know."

"It's wild but possible," Sid muttered, reading

Sheela's deflated posture. "You'd be surprised what people can do with DNA these days."

"You mean beyond just identifying a perp or solving a case?" O'Grady asked.

Sid made an open gesture with his hands. "I've been working a series of kidnappings. Geneticists. In the process, I've had to learn something about the science. Some of the things they can do? You wouldn't believe it. Remember Dolly, the sheep? That was just the tip of the iceberg."

Sid had their attention, so he leaned back, one arm on the seat back. "Look, you've heard the bits and pieces on the news, right? Neanderthal DNA? Those extinct marsupial wolves in Australia? The frozen mammoth in Japan? The news is always telling us about something. Remember the calf they cloned from a piece of steak? The jellyfish genes in the monkey?"

"Man, those are just animals," O'Grady muttered derisively.

Sid gave him a flat look. "You think there's a difference between cloning a sheep and a human?"

"Well, it ain't the same thing. I mean, man, people are a whole lot more complicated than any sheep!"

Sid slowly shook his head. "That's your emotional reaction, Sean, not reality."

"Well, bro, you fill me in, then." O'Grady had set his bulldog chin.

"When you're dealing with DNA, a sheep is every bit as complicated as a human being. Sometimes, even more so. One of the guys we've been looking for cloned extinct marsupials in Australia. Used DNA extracted from museum specimens. Now, that, let me tell you, was complicated shit compared to taking a sample from living tissue, isolating the DNA, and inserting it into another woman's egg."

Sheela seemed to be wilting as Sid talked. Lymon placed a hand on her shoulder. "What is it?"

In a small voice, Sheela said, "It's all starting to make sense, Lymon. All of it. Christal just handed it to us."

"How's that?" O'Grady asked. "You know why she was abducted?"

Sheela barely nodded as she stared down at her lap, head bowed as if in prayer. "Marketing."

"Huh?" Sid asked. "How does stealing Christal equate with marketing? Marketing what? Felonious behavior?"

Sheela took a deep breath, lifting her head and removing her dark glasses. She looked from one to another, the deadness in her eyes affecting Lymon as no words could. "DNA is easy to obtain—I understand that. But if someone like Krissy wanted a Sheela Marks baby, how do you prove you can actually provide it?"

Lymon felt a cold wash of understanding. "Oh, my god!"

"That's right," Sheela said woodenly. "You've got to be able to *prove* the DNA comes from the person you say it does. The customer has to know beyond a doubt that you've got the real thing; that he or she's not being bilked."

"I'm dense," O'Grady growled. "What the hell are we talking about?"

"The reason for the celebrity hits." Lymon swallowed hard. "It's advertising. Don't you get it? If you're going to offer your client a chance to have a baby with Manny de Clerk's DNA, you have to prove it's the right stuff. I mean, you can't show someone a pile of DNA and say, 'That's it. Meet Manny's DNA.'"

"Son of a bitch," Sid whispered, a half-vacant expression on his face as his mind worked it over. He sat back, stiff-armed, unblinking.

"The questionnaire," Lymon said, another piece falling into place. "Christal wondered what they were screening for."

"Excuse me?" O'Grady asked as he scribbled furiously in his notebook. "What questionnaire?"

"It's the Genesis Athena website," Sid filled in. "I sent a copy to Tanner down at Quantico. We're going to want to access that site and have Tanner play with it for a while."

O'Grady chewed at his lip, his dark face furrowed. "You're telling me that someone is stealing DNA from movie stars, and...what? Selling it to whom? People to have babies with? Now, I don't know that much, but doesn't having a baby mean you've got to have a sperm and an egg?" He gestured with one hand. "It's not like a piece of skin or a hair follicle can get a woman pregnant. You read?"

Sid worked his jaw back and forth. "That was then, Sean. You ought to see the things they can do now."

"But, sure, they can clone sheep and dogs and stuff. But it takes a laboratory, right?"

"Yeah," Sid agreed. "These cutting-edge labs can mix and match, and with CRISPR do just about anything with DNA. It's like ordering a car made to custom specs. You can choose everything."

"So," O'Grady asked, "where's the laboratory?"

Sheela whispered, "Find Krissy, and you'll know."

"Who?" Sid asked.

"The lunatic who's having my baby," Sheela said softly.

But beneath it, Lymon could hear the cracked-glass tone in her voice.

CHAPTER 42

Christal was contemplating her growling stomach when a low knock brought her bolt upright and out of bed. She was on her feet, prepared for anything when the door—or was it a hatch?—opened and swung back.

A young man stood just beyond the threshold. The first thing she noticed was his inquisitive brown eyes. They seemed to sparkle with anticipation. She figured him for his midthirties, with sandy-blond hair, a strong-jawed face, and a tentative smile. Two muscular men in coveralls stood behind him, darkly visaged, with close-cropped hair. They had a menacing air about them. Security, perhaps?

"Ms. Anaya?" the brown-eyed man's voice was laced with a seasoning of Scottish. He wore a white-knit sweater and brown cotton pants.

"Who wants to know?" She propped her hands on her hips, knees flexed, ready to flee or fight.

"Dr. Gregor McEwan, at your service." His smile deepened. "Hungry, perhaps?"

"Why would I be hungry?"

"It's been two days since ye've eaten. Come, then. Let's take you off to the cafeteria."

She glanced over his shoulder, and he read her concern as she eyed the guards. "Oh, don't be worrying about them, now. They're more for my protection than yours."

"Really?"

"What if it turns out that ye're not friendly? Ex-FBI? Against a marshmallow like me? You could probably pull my arms out of their sockets and twist off me head." He waved her out. "Come. Let's eat. Surely you can't plan your escape on an empty stomach." His smile mocked her, an unsettling arrogance in his sparkling eyes.

Christal considered her options. Her belly wasn't going to fill itself based on the dreams she'd been having of steak, enchiladas, and cheeseburgers. Nor would she gain any understanding of her situation by staring at the walls of her prison. "Sure."

When she stepped out into a white corridor the air seemed fresher. The steel walls were lined with piping, thick wire, and welded braces, all covered with a heavy coat of paint.

"This way, then." McEwan started off, motioning her to walk at his side. The corridor was just wide enough for the two of them.

"So, where am I?"

"Aboard ship. Her name's the *ZoeGen*."

"And just where are we, exactly?"

"I can't say...exactly. Navigation's not my thing. Somewhere in the middle of the Atlantic. Well, maybe a couple of hundred miles off the Maine coast, actually."

She gave him a skeptical look. "How long was I unconscious?"

"Aboot twenty-four hours. Maybe a tad longer."

"Why did you kidnap me?"

He gave her a sheepish sidelong look. "I'm afraid some of our people panicked."

"Panicked? Do you know what you just unleashed? People are going to miss me. That means federal as well as local police involvement. Hank and his little band of friends are going to be at the center of a hurricane."

They stepped through a bulkhead and took a right into a wider passageway. She glanced over her shoulder, aware of the lurking presence of the guards. They watched her with flat brown eyes, faces expressionless.

"Nothing we can't make amends for," he said hopefully. "I really do apologize. We'll see what happens, and it's currently under discussion, but I'm sure we can reach some agreement that will be mutually acceptable."

Was he a lunatic? Or just plain nuts? "Gregor, you can't kidnap a person, drug her, transport her across state lines—hell, out of the country—and not expect a whole ration of shit to rain down."

"Oh, I don't know. They took me in the beginning. Bagged me right in front o' me own house. It was only after I understood the potentials and the money to be made that I took over running the program for the Sheik. And a good choice it was. I'm now in charge of research and laboratory operations."

"Wait. You mean you changed sides—in spite of what they did to you?"

"Ach, what? Hold a little kidnap against them when I could be in charge of the most advanced genetics laboratory in the world? What others do in theory, we do in practice. Lass, I don't even have to write a grant proposal here."

He chuckled at that and pushed open a large double door. Inside Christal found a rather mundane-looking cafeteria—perhaps thirty by forty—packed with tables, plastic chairs, and a food line of steam tables staffed by four women, also Arab, if she was any judge of such things. She counted fifteen people—still more Arabs given their looks and the sibilant tongue they spoke—who sat at the tables, eating. They were dressed in lab wear: green smocks, pants, and the women all had loose hijabs that could be draped over the face. Females, she noted, sat strictly to themselves at a back table and cast curious glances her way.

"Help yourself," he instructed as he led her to the line, picked a tray out of a rack, and added silverware, napkin, and a plate from their various stacks and holders.

She was famished, no doubt of it. No doubt, too, that she needed to keep her strength up. The fare was mostly European in nature: roast beef, lamb, potatoes, gravy, steamed cabbage, bread, and cheese—but couscous, hummus, falafel, and other dishes smacked of different appetites by the other diners. She opted for Coke while he took juice from the machine at the end of the line.

She followed Gregor to a chair, settling herself across from him. The table was a Formica-topped ubiquitous model that might have been found in any institutional lunchroom in the world. Neither of the guards had taken a tray. Instead, they discreetly seated themselves far enough away for privacy, close enough to be there in case Christal lunged for McEwan's throat. Her days with LBA had heightened her sense of awareness about these things.

"Who are the Arabs?" She inclined her head toward the others and attacked her plate.

"Geneticists. Lab techs. They're the muscle and bone of Genesis Athena." That flare of arrogance betrayed itself again. "Most of them, I trained. So they're the best in the business."

As she wolfed her food, she asked, "I don't get it. Why steal celebrity DNA?"

McEwan studied her thoughtfully as he neatly cut roast beef into cubes, skewered them with his fork, and chewed. "We want to be the first."

"To steal DNA?"

"Not to steal it, to *use* it, Ms. Anaya."

"You can't *use* someone's DNA. It's...well, it's *personal*!"

He laughed at that, genuinely delighted. "Do you know that no law, in any country, protects a person's exclusive right to their own DNA? Not even in your dearly provincial USA."

"Bullshit!"

"Oddly, bullshit is protected. You can't walk off with a wheelbarrow of manure from someone's bull paddock. That's theft. But once your DNA is out of your body, it belongs to anyone who can lay hold of it." He spread his fingers wide. "Poof! Gone. It's no longer yours."

"I don't believe that."

"Well, I can't affect yer beliefs, lass, but when you do go home again, you may be well advised to check the statutes. Take a hard look at the Myriad genetics ruling.

See if you find 'naturally occurring DNA' listed anywhere in the definitions of personal property. Meantime, however, let's just say I'm right, hmm?"

"What? I can tell you that as a graduate of—"

"How often have you had a blood test? Oh, say for cholesterol? Perhaps for a blood chemistry board? You know, to measure lipids, bilirubin, hematocrit, things like that."

"A few, why?"

"What happened to the extra blood?"

"What do you mean?"

"I mean, they may have needed a tenth of a milliliter—that's less than a drop, eh? But they took a syringe full. That's an extra three or four whole milliliters of blood. What did they do with it?"

"Threw it out?"

"Hardly! They sold it! Some they distilled for plasma, some for insulin, some for albumin—lots of things. Right! So let's take the insulin, for example. Your body produced it, eh? It was part of you. Does anyone think once it's drawn that it still belongs to you?"

"DNA is different. I mean, as I understand it, I'm still using my DNA. Cells are synthesizing proteins, dividing, things like that."

"And all that insulin and plasma? You weren't using that as well?"

Christal struggled for words and ended up gaping.

He chuckled as he spooned up mashed potatoes. "Sorry, lass. No one cares. Laboratories all over the world are taking DNA samples from patients. And, sure as to be, the very second they're coded, they're fair game. Some come from folk with resistance to diseases, others from people with a tolerance for certain environments, some even from athletes who show certain kinds of muscle tissue. It's a mad scramble, lass, to see who can get what. A gold rush like in the Wild West. Companies are falling all over themselves to make money on anything they can sell. And, just like those long-ago miners, no one knows which genes are going to be the mother lode."

Stunned, the food half-chewed in her mouth, she swallowed and managed to say, "It's illegal to..." *What?*

McGregor stabbed another square of meat. "No, lass. Most governments around the world have only passed laws banning *cloning*. You know, the artificial *reproduction* of another human being. They've said nothing aboot the DNA. In fact, by taking the stance that you c'not reproduce yer own DNA, they have told you ipso facto that the state has more right to regulate your DNA than you do."

"I don't follow."

"Indeed?" He took a drink of juice from his tumbler. "Think of it this way: You're of the opinion that yer DNA belongs to you and you alone. In the Myriad decision, the government says it belongs to nature. A natural phenomenon. But what's a clone? A copy of yourself. It's your own DNA that you're copying. Not mine, not the president's, but yours. Now, if that was really the case, could the government regulate it?"

"But that's not the same!"

"Isn't it? Fact is, you have the right to believe in whatever god ye want, read whatever book ye want, join any political party—but not to control yer own DNA. If you want privacy, stick to your beliefs, but don't look to your body, lass." The twinkle was back in his eye.

"But laws against cloning—"

"Are laws that regulate your use of your own personal DNA. In your opinion, you think you should have the say over yer own DNA. I understand that. Most people—bless their simple souls—think they do. What the masses don't understand is that through fear that someone might clone himself, they've given that control over to the government, business, and, most onerous of all, *investors*."

"How did that happen?"

"Sheer unadulterated fear, lass. That, and the social conservatives, of course. God bless the Christian religious right, wherever they live. They've given Genesis Athena a monopoly."

Christal's mind stumbled over the implications.

"You see," McEwan continued, "all these technologies, going way back." He gestured with his knife. "Take insulin, again. No one objected to processing insulin from human blood that was going to be thrown away anyhow. And no one complained about making the genome for SARS-COVID public so the entire world could work on it. Doing so was in the best interest of society. Even Insulin used to be a touchy thing. You couldn't mix sheep with human with artificial and not have a reaction. The sources had to be pure. Millions of diabetics benefited and still do. It was the precedent, you see. DNA just got folded into the same blanket, if you get my drift."

She glared at him. "Why did you have to break the law if this whole operation is legal?"

He chuckled. "Aye, the grandstanding. Why, advertising, of course. Buyers *know* we've got the product. Oh, to be sure, we'll be sending little apologies and even checks in the mail as things begin to fall into place. Admitting to our stunts, as it were, and offering reparation. Legal division's already been hard at work over that."

"Legal division? You've lost me again."

McEwan waved his greasy knife. "It's all going to come out in the next year or so. The clients can't be expected to keep their silence. What's the point of having a little Talia Roberts running around the kitchen if you can't brag aboot her t'yer friends, eh? When it does break, it's going to be huge. Thing is, we don't want to look like simple criminals, so we'll make restitution to the aggrieved parties." His expression sobered. "It's just the right thing to do. Image, and all that."

"Wait a minute. You stole all these people's DNA, you're going to sell it, and then send them some sort of pittance to make it right?"

"Aye."

"Why not just stick a check in the mail now? It's cheaper if they don't have time to think about how they've been ripped off."

"Because the less they know now, the easier it will be to get our samples. After the story breaks, things might get a wee bit trickier. People will be more careful —not that it will do 'em much good, mind you. The common folk in the streets have no idea how much DNA they leave around in restaurants, hotels, their clothes, cars, even when they lick an envelope."

Christal shook her head. "I'm still not understanding how this works. You take the DNA, and then what?"

"Sell it, of course."

"To whom?"

"Anyone who will pay for it."

"Give me an example."

McEwan leaned back, pushing his empty plate away. "Well, take Princess Diana. Dead all these years. Our marketing research determined her to be one of the most beloved women of all time. Getting the sample was the riskiest operation we ever undertook. I'm sure you heard of it."

She jerked a quick nod. "The lab in Paris where her forensic samples were curated."

"We had a huge list of applicants just waiting for us to succeed. We've done brilliantly. The first embryos have been implanted in the clients. We've already got a list of close to two hundred candidates for implantation. We've banked over two million in deposits alone."

"Embryos?" Christal asked, fork halfway to her mouth. "Damn it, it just sank in. You meant it when you said 'a little Talia Roberts' earlier."

"Aye," McEwan said, reading her confusion. "Ye see, Ms. Anaya, we're not just selling the DNA in a bottle or anything like that. When we sell it, it's alive and ready to be implanted into the host mother."

CHAPTER 43

Hank tried to put the last forty-eight hours into perspective. Genesis Athena, he'd discovered, was nothing if not organized. He'd been surprised to find his luggage unloaded from the cargo hold of the aircraft that had carried them to Teterboro, New Jersey. April assured him his room charge at the Hilton had been taken care of. A physician had met their flight, checked on Christal's condition, inserted an IV drip, and given her another sedative. The helicopter flight to the marina at Eastham, on Cape Cod, had been both quick and efficient. He and Neal had carried Christal's somnolent body aboard a sleek cigarette boat, and an hour later, they had watched her lifted aboard the *ZoeGen* by capable crewmen. Hank had scrambled up the lowered ladder and into a hatch that opened in the cruise ship's side.

April had led him to her cabin, a snug room with wooden paneling, a plush bed, and most of the amenities. Sex had given way to sleep that had led to more sex, and so forth.

Now, showered, shaved, and rested as he hadn't been in months, Hank found himself sitting across from April. They were in her cabin, eating breakfast from a room service cart a steward had brought. He wore a white terry cloth robe belted at the waist. Pale midday light glowed through the single porthole.

"Happy?" April asked as she lifted a forkful of scrambled eggs from her plate and balanced them. Her robe hung open far enough that he could see the soft curve of her breast.

Hank washed a mouth full of bacon down with a shot of black coffee and wiped his lips. "I think I've fallen through the looking glass." He opened his arms wide to take in the surroundings.

April scraped up the last of her eggs, used her napkin, and asked, "Want to see the rest of the ship?"

He gave her a thoughtful look. "Beyond the infamous bulkhead?"

"First, I have to know. Are you in? All the way?"

He chewed his lip, gave a curt nod, and stood. "Yeah, I'm in."

"Why?" she demanded. "You used to be a federal agent. Sometimes, working for Genesis Athena, you'll have to skirt the law. Why would you sell your soul? Just for a payback?"

"Nah, I'm smarter than that." He gestured around at the plush quarters. "I like the way you do business. Charter aircraft, your own ship, and capable personnel? I could be an asset to you. And I'm assuming you weren't blowing smoke about the salary."

"No smoke."

"Things went so fast the other night. I mean, we kidnapped Christal. It's a felony, April. Whatever it was that we did, we can't go back. Can't rethink it and change it."

"You feeling trapped?" she asked as she stood and slipped her robe off.

He stopped short. A dancer had a body like that, toned and agile. She stepped to her dresser, pulled the top drawer open, and fished out a bra and panties. One long tanned leg after the other slid through the openings.

She glanced at him as she snapped her bra and slipped her arms through the straps. The question hung between them. Trapped? Hell, how did he answer that?

"Sure. But I knew what I was doing, setting Christal up. When we packed her out of that place, I had a momentary hesitation. I was doing everything I'd ever been trained to prevent, but you know, I haven't lost any sleep over it."

She laughed as she pulled gray cotton slacks on. "I keep telling you, we're not doing anything illegal. People may disagree with our methods, but there are no laws—"

"Kidnapping—"

"Shit!" she snapped. "Cut it out, Hank. Remember? I asked her. She said she'd go if we answered her questions. You heard her."

"She was drugged! A good DA would—"

April walked up to him, slipped her hands inside his robe, and pressed her palms against his chest. They were cool on his warm skin. "We'll make it right with her. She won't press charges when we're through. Genesis Athena has the resources to fix almost anything. We're here for the long term—with a product no one else is going to be able to provide." A smile curled her lips. "Trust me."

He hesitated, staring into those marvelous eyes. What the hell. "Yeah, like I said, I'm in." He gave her a sly grin. "And I could get real used to the lifestyle."

"Come on," she added impishly. "Get dressed. Let me show you why you've made the best decision of your life. You're in on the ground floor of the biggest industry of the twenty-first century."

Moments later, they rolled the cart with their demolished breakfast out into the narrow passageway for the staff to pick up, and April led him through one of the hatches and into a major corridor.

"As you've no doubt guessed, *ZoeGen* is an old cruise ship. Greek, originally, and perfect for our needs. She provides us with accommodations for fifteen hundred clients at a time. Currently we have over three hundred staff and crew on board. They berth in the lower decks. We do everything from genetic scans, genetic engineering, gene replacement and therapy, molecular engineering, all the way to providing complete reproductive services for any client, male or female."

"What do you mean, male? How does a man reproduce himself?"

"Our geneticists retrieve one of his germ cells from the testes before it divides into sperm. They remove the nucleus and insert it into a host woman's denucleated egg. Once it's implanted in her womb, she carries the fetus to term, delivers it, and after we're sure the child is healthy, it's given to the father."

"You have women who will do this?"

"It's a big world out there, and you'd be surprised

what an incentive a couple thousand US can be in a place like Bangkok. None of this comes cheaply, but what some people will pay for an exact genetic copy of themselves would amaze you. It's the ultimate narcissism on a mobile platform we can take anywhere in the world."

"As long as you stay in international waters."

"That's right. That's our ace in the hole." She had pulled her reddish hair into a ponytail that bobbed as she nodded. "We have a full legal team, but sometimes even they can't keep up with the laws in individual countries. The high seas are open territory for Genesis Athena."

She stopped at a hatch, pressed a series of numbers into a keypad, and opened the sealed door.

Hank stepped through into what had once been a two-story room, perhaps fifty feet across and sixty long. The balcony where he stood was now glassed, providing a view of the floor a story below.

"This used to be the ballroom," April said, taking a position on the railing before the glass. "You're looking down onto one of the G Deck labs."

Hank could see white-clad people seated at counters around what was clearly a laboratory. Racks of test tubes, beakers, tubing, and trays were everywhere. He could identify the microscopes, of course, but the rest of the equipment baffled him. "The last time I took science was in college. I was in the criminal justice program, not biology. What is all this stuff?"

April shrugged. "I haven't the slightest idea. What you're seeing is where the real heart of Genesis Athena lies. Those people down there are the brains that make it all possible."

"Okay, enough of the melodrama. What am I seeing?"

She gave him a sidelong glance as she said, "You would call it cloning, Hank. Pure and simple. The world market for molecular biology, gene therapy, infertility, and genetic engineering is huge. Billions huge, and I'm talking dollars, euros, pounds, what have you."

"So, what was Christal doing that hacked you off?"

"She was nosing her way onto my particular turf."

"And that is?"

"Obtaining DNA."

Hank frowned. "Whose DNA?"

"My biggest single acquisition was Elvis Presley."

"Get off it! The guy's dead."

Her laughter sounded musical. "His body, yes. We used a truck-mounted drill to bore a hole through his tomb. Center-punched his casket and inserted a probe into the corpse. By employing the correct procedures, our techs can recover intact nuclear DNA despite the mortuary preservative."

"How come I didn't hear about it? Drilling a hole in Presley's grave, I mean."

"Because Graceland covered it up. They didn't want the publicity. Put yourself in their place. Would you want the whole world to know that someone had violated your security, drilled a hole in your hero, and walked off with a piece of him? It might tarnish the myth, or worse, encourage someone else to try."

"You drilled a hole..." He shook his head, baffled.

April stared down pensively. "Since then, we've changed our methodology. Now we don't leave any doubt about the validity of our samples. As to Elvis, it's okay. You remember that eBay auction of Elvis's hair a couple of years back? We've got rock-solid provenance and can cross-compare the DNA from that to our Graceland sample. We've got a waiting list of clients scheduled for implantation for the foreseeable future."

"For tubes of dead Elvis DNA?" He was looking out at the laboratory, thinking of how much money people spent for things like Elvis's guitar.

"Tubes of...hardly! You still don't get it, do you?"

"Get what?"

She teased him with her eyes. "Do you remember the line in the movie *Men in Black*? The one where they're driving on the roof of the tunnel?"

"Yeah, Tommy Lee Jones says that Elvis isn't dead, he's just gone home."

April gave him a bewitching smile. "Our first Elvis clone was born last week. The host mother is a rich widow from Indianapolis. So, you see, the movie was right. He went home—but now he's back."

"This is a joke, right?"

"Do you remember the Tasmanian wolves a few years back? One of our people pioneered that process. DNA is only a molecule, a code. It doesn't die along with the body. If it's preserved, the code can be reactivated."

He stared, open-mouthed.

April's eyes seemed to enlarge as she shook her head. "Now, Hank, are you beginning to understand the power behind Genesis Athena and why people will pay millions for DNA that we control the patents to?"

CHAPTER 44

After a night of unrelenting nightmares, Sheela sat on her poolside recliner. In the cool protection of the shade, she watched turquoise water lap at the white cement walls. "The cement pond," the Beverly Hillbillies had called it. How appropriate for a Saskatchewan girl's final retreat. The only standing water she had known for her first fourteen years had been the clear water in the dugouts where the horses and cattle drank.

How did I get here? Looking back through the kaleidoscope of her tumultuous life, she might have been carried off by a tornado. Batted this way and that by the winds of opportunity, fortune, and plain dumb luck, she had come out on top.

How much of myself did I sell on the way?

She pursed her lips, shifting her gaze to the fountain in the flower bed where water bubbled and danced in a delighted spray beneath the Sacagawea statue.

Not as much as most do, she decided.

Truly talented people always wrestled with the green-eyed demon of insecurity. She too was constantly plagued as the beast hung its scaled head over her shoulder to whisper that she wasn't any good anymore, that she could never conjure an Oscar-worthy character like Cassie Evens in *Blood Rage* again. That *Jagged Cat* was going to be released to howls of derision. It would land at the box office stillborn, the dissection of its carcass celebrated by the wags in *Time, Newsweek, Daily Variety,* and *The Hollywood Reporter*.

"Washed up!" the headlines would decry.

How did I let Christal down? She rubbed her right thumb across the smooth back of her left hand, feeling the skin, bone, and tendons slipping beneath. *If I had taken the meeting Rex wanted me to, would it have been different?*

Had it been the gods staring down from their aeries on high? Had they seen her desperation to change her life? To save herself? Her belief in the capriciousness of fate was tragically Greek in nature. For any good thing, some terrible price ultimately had to be paid.

"Sheela?" Felix's soft voice interrupted.

She glanced over her shoulder as he came walking out in an expensive silk suit that rippled like a rainbow trapped inside gray. "Hello, Felix. Come, sit."

She watched his lean body as he bent, fingered the fabric-upholstered pad to ensure that no lotions, oils, or other liquids could soil his suit, and seated himself.

An image of her father flashed in the back of her mind: He was bent behind a cow in the squeeze chute; his arms buried up to his elbows in her rear; blood, amniotic fluid, urine, and manure dripping down his brown-duck Carhartts. She could see the expression on his face as he struggled to turn a breeched calf to free a stuck leg.

The image came from light-years beyond Felix Baylor and his immaculately tailored ten-thousand-dollar suits.

What kind of men have we bred in this business? Aloud, she asked, "What have you found out?"

Felix straightened his white cuffs where they protruded from his suit coat. "Genesis Athena is quite an organization." His brown eyes were thoughtful. "You asked me to contact them, see what kind of information they had on Sheela Marks. Well, it appears to be substantial. They forwarded a fairly complete biography of you and your achievements. The document we received would have done Dot proud."

"Flattering or derogatory?"

"Most flattering." His expression left little doubt about that. "Sheela, you asked me to contact them on behalf of the name Jennifer Weaver. May I ask why?"

"A hunch, Felix." She gave him a weary appraisal, then asked, "Who are you?"

"What?"

"I asked who you are, Felix. Really, deep down inside your bones and soul, who are you?"

"I..." He shrugged, perplexed. "I'm an attorney. Your attorney. Um, the father of three. Some of my cases—"

"Yes, yes, but do you *know* yourself? If I stripped all that away, dropped you on a deserted island like Tom Hanks in *Castaway,* would you know yourself? Would you still have that kernel of 'self on the inside' to cling to? Or are you a paste-up of your various images? A collection of events and actions stuck together with no discernible order to become this rendition of Felix Baylor?"

"What the hell are you talking about?"

She studied his wary expression, reading complete bafflement in his brown eyes. "I'm talking about *being*, Felix. Not just, What am I? Or, What do I do? But what I *am* inside, at the heart, the soul, in the marrow of the bones."

He blinked, expression thinning. "Oh, I get it. You're doing some sort of preparation for a role. Rex wanted me to talk to you about—"

"Fuck him. Fuck you, too." She closed her eyes, rubbing them. "Felix, I'll tell you this once. I'm tired. Exhausted. I've done three films a year for the last ten years. Through all of that, I've clung to something deep down inside. It was a piece of me." She tapped her breastbone. "Way down in here. Deep. Do you understand?"

He just listened with no change of expression.

"A couple of days ago, I asked Christal Anaya if she, too, depended on me. And do you know what?" She didn't wait for his blank look. "She honestly told me no. Finally, one person had the balls to tell me no. But more than that, that same woman told me that if I wanted, I could depend on her. And she really meant it. Now, isn't that a switch?"

"But she's the one who's missing."

"No shit!" Sheela narrowed her eyes. "I'm at a real rocky place in my life right now. I checked the accounts. You and your firm have made a little more than three and a half million off my production companies and me. That doesn't count the additional work that my reputation has brought to your firm."

"But that—"

"I'm *not* complaining. You earned every cent that you didn't get by padding the billing." She gave him a wry smile. "And you'll be paid for your time now."

"And that is to do what? This Jennifer Weaver thing?"

Sheela nodded. "Pay attention. Here is what you need to know: Jennifer Weaver is thirty-four, single. With the sale of her deceased father's cattle ranch, she has a portfolio worth a little more than seven million. She lives in LA and has been fascinated with Sheela Marks for years. She has seen all of my movies at least ten times. She attends every venue she can, hoping to get a glimpse of me. She wants to know if Genesis Athena can get her close to Sheela Marks."

Felix looked confused again. "But...I don't get it."

"That's your assignment. Make it happen, Felix. I don't care what you have to do. Build an identity for Jennifer Weaver. Driver's license, passport, address, billing history, whatever it takes. You can make it happen."

"What's the point?" He spread his arms. "Genesis Athena is a big company; we've checked their stats. Financially, they're huge, but they're not players. If someone wanted to get close—"

"They're players, Felix." She narrowed her eyes, using all of her skill to hide her fragile and wounded soul. "They've stolen part of me. Part of that core knowledge of who and what I am. They've stolen part of my essence, my being, if you will."

"Sheela, this sounds nuts! Maybe you should talk this over with a friend of mine. She's a psychologist. A real one from Stanford. Not one of these astro-babble psychotherapists, but the genuine—"

"You are not to discuss this with anyone. Period. Every shred of attorney-client privilege is now in effect. If you so much as breathe a word, even to Rex, I'll have your balls."

He made a pained expression. "So what am I going to do?"

"You're going to make it so that I can find them. Genesis Athena is doing something with DNA. *My* DNA. Genetics, cloning, whatever. You're going to set it up so that Jennifer Weaver can buy whatever kind of piece of Sheela Marks that they're selling."

She watched him finally glom onto the realization that whatever happened, legal action was looming at the end of it. He said, "Let's say they take the Jennifer Weaver bait."

"Then you set up an appointment for Ms. Weaver."

"Sheela, you're one of the most recognizable—"

"I'm also an actor. Just in case you've forgotten. And, in spite of what some of the critics say, a damn brilliant one. I'm going after them. Then, when I find out everything, you can have them." She gave him a predatory smile. "If they're as well fixed as your research indicates, you could clean up a tidy bundle— and add to your reputation by making some interesting new law in the process."

"It could be dangerous."

"The key to this game is deception. And no matter what your objections, or the counseling you're going to feel obliged to give regarding my safety and ethics on top of all the other bullshit, I'm doing this."

"Sheela—"

"Dammit! Don't you understand?" She felt a tear in her soul. "If I don't, *I'm going to lose what little is left of me!*"

CHAPTER 45

The knock was louder this time, more demanding. Christal sat up on her bunk and called, "Come on in! It's only locked from the outside."

She wasn't terribly surprised when the portal swung open and Hank Abrams stepped in. He was dressed in a dark-blue blazer, light-blue button-down shirt, Dockers, and white running shoes. His hair looked slightly mussed, as if he'd been standing out in the sea wind. A faint flush lingered on his cheeks, and his eyes gleamed as he studied her.

"Hey, Christal. How's it going?"

She balled her fists, gauging the distance, wondering if she could stand, swing her leg back, and land a kick in his crotch hard enough to blast his testicles up past his ears.

He read her expression and stepped back with enough haste that she decided her opportunity had vanished.

"Look," he said softly, hands out, "I'm sorry. You had some people worried."

"Yeah, well, perhaps you've forgotten the things you used to know in your old job, Hank. Like the statutes on abduction...legal curiosities like the Mann Act, reckless endangerment, breaking and entering, assault, and a whole list of fractured or broken legal codes I'm only beginning to get hints of."

"I told them that they'd be wasting their time."

"Who's wasting their time?" She narrowed an eye. "Copperhead?"

"Who?"

"The redheaded bitch that accompanied you to my apartment."

"Ah, April."

"She your latest, Hank? Wow! After Marsha, you've fallen to new lows."

A faint quiver of his lips betrayed him. "I wouldn't bring up the women I've fucked. You might be surprised at who we'd discover was right up front in that list."

Christal let it go, watching him, struggling to see inside his skin. "I don't get it. Did I really read you that wrong? This whole time were you really just a shit? Or did you cover it so well that no one guessed? I mean, damn, it's not just that you fooled me, but the whole Bureau: Wirthing, Harness, even the folks in the academy who are trained to spot bad apples."

"You know, I was just as dedicated as anyone else." His eyes hardened. "And I was doing a damn fine job until I ran into you. You wrecked my life, Anaya. I tell you, it was goddamn biblical! You're the damned anti-

Christ. One minute I was on top of the world. Then you fucked me blind that night in the van. When I could finally see again, I'd lost everything. My wife, my career, my self-esteem. Everything." He made an explosive gesture with his hand. "Slam-bam! Gone."

"Gee, Hank, I'm going all weepy for you. I remember that night in the van really well, but my hearing must have been bad, 'cause I don't remember you crying 'no' over and over as you ran your hands up under my bra, or when you unsnapped my pants. I don't remember you battling mightily against my wiles as you slipped your dick inside. And, come to think of it, even afterwards, you lay there until I reminded you we didn't want to make a mess on Ben's pad. As I recall, we spent another two hours talking about how good it had been. Remember that? You were half of the postcoital conversation—you, with that idiotic happy expression on your face."

"You bitch!"

She waved it away. "Forget it. Gonzales won. You landed on your feet, flush in your new career as a big-league felon. You know, I'm going to have the time of my life when I finally bring you down."

He crossed his arms. "Christal, they don't want a fight with you. They want to come to some sort of settlement."

"What? Bribe me? It was a bad choice, sending you down here to negotiate."

He sighed in mock despair. "You know that we're in the middle of the fucking ocean, don't you? You've got a lot of time to think about it. I'm going to say this one more time: No one wants any trouble."

"They got it the first time your sweet April slugged

me in the gut. They got more of it when mousy Gretchen shot at me. And, on top of that, I'm not inclined to forget that some bastard stuck a needle into my neck and carted me off to...where the hell are we? The Atlantic?"

"They just want a little more time, that's all. They'll pay you for the insult done to you, for your inconvenience, and, it seems, for the privilege of sampling your DNA."

"You don't get it, do you?"

"Get what?" He spread his arms. "Christal, Genesis Athena is the coming thing! I've seen their lab. Jesus! It's amazing some of the things they can do."

"Yeah, cloning the dead? Your pal the Sheik just backhanded Dr. Frankenstein right across the chops. Talk about one-upmanship."

"Christal, it's not just that." He was grinning at her now in the old way that used to excite her. This time it only incited fury. "The technology is the thing. It's about who actually has the technology to control DNA. Genesis—"

"Bullshit! It's about money. The right to control DNA? They stole Sheela's. Snatched it right off her tampon! They're involved in theft. Grand larceny. You're a bunch of fucking witches."

"Huh?"

"Soul stealers. Predators of the body and heart. Raising the dead for unsavory purposes, just like in the old stories. You're purveyors of the ancient evil. Grandmother's old-time Pueblo witches, but you're wearing modern clothes, doing it with twenty-first-century technology."

"Oh, shit! Here we go again. Not good old Grandma

and her quaint Mexican ways. I heard enough of that crap to last me a lifetime."

"But this is different," Christal continued stubbornly. "It used to be superstition, metaphysical tales told to raise the hackles on dark winter nights. No, you're right uptown now. Santa Monica Boulevard, doing it for real." She narrowed her eyes. "Why, Hank? Why are you on the other side now?"

He stared at her floor for a moment, shrugged, and said, "Because, as you no doubt recall, I've got nothing else. Not only that, but as I came to find out so recently, it's inevitable. The Raelians and Clonaid, with their little publicity stunt, were just the harbingers of the future. Genesis Athena—or some other company like it—is the coming thing. Big, funded, multinational, they'll be to molecular genetics what Microsoft is to computers."

"You really believe that?"

"The technology is here. It will be used. You can't stop it. So just accept it."

"What? Without even thinking about what it means to people?" She tried to see past his calm. "Something else is driving you, Hank. What? Pissed because you got your hand slapped? Is that it? You got caught with your pecker dripping, and now you'll pay back the whole world?"

"Fuck you!"

She paused. "That's right, isn't it? In your whole life, you've never been knocked down before. Never took a fall. You were a golden-haired boy who never had to learn what it was to lose, to fail and have to live with it."

"God! You, of all people, have a hell of a lot of nerve to analyze *my* life. Why don't you go straight to fucking hell?"

"Or is it just the money? Huh? You sold out for bucks?"

"We're not breaking any laws. Look, we're in international waters. You're riding in a legally registered vessel flying the Yemeni flag. Genesis Athena has a second lab—bigger and better—in Yemen, where this is all legal. They have corporate offices in Doha, Qatar, where there are also no laws against it."

"Seems to me I recall Genesis Athena operating on American soil, where we've got laws. As a federal agent, you damn well know it."

He chuckled. "Look, there's no winning an argument. Not with you. As to the ethics, I don't know. If someone wants to buy one of Sheela Mark's clones, why should I care? What's DNA anyway? It's a molecule. Like water, or benzene, or a polymer. You blast thousands of DNA molecules out every time you sneeze. That night in the van, I filled you full of eight million little copies of my DNA. But for a matter of timing—and your IUD—your DNA and mine might have wrapped around each other and made someone new. It's what life's all about, right?"

"Go to hell, Hank."

"I already did. And it was you who took me there. Believe me, I've paid through the nose for it." He slapped the wall absently, looking around her small cabin. "Think about what it would take to settle with Genesis Athena. They want to make things right. Find an amicable solution. They'll be reasonable if you will."

He turned to the door. "The one thing you've got plenty of right now is time."

And with that, he was gone.

In anger, she threw her pillow, watching it bounce harmlessly off the cold steel.

CHAPTER 46

Rex sat at the Formosa bar, elbows propped, his butt on a red leather stool. Across from him, he caught his partial reflection through the bottles shelved in front of the back bar mirror. His broken reflection displayed a man with a sour disposition. A glass of Macallan, neat, and a water back stood before him. He toyed with the scotch glass, rocking the amber fluid back and forth.

For this meeting Rex had chosen a dark-blue Armani sport coat over a light-blue pinstripe shirt. Gray flannel slacks were snugged with an ostrich-hide belt.

He was making faces into the partially obscured mirror, trying to understand what had jerked the rug out from under him when Tony Zell came striding through the door, slowed to look around, and met Rex's eye.

Zell's golden jewelry, shining from his neck, wrists, and watch, caught the light. White leather loafers contrasted with the wood as he walked across the parquet floor. A white sports coat over a blousy black shirt accented his faded jeans.

"What's up, Rex? Sorry I'm late. Had a thing with a client, you know?" He smiled, white teeth flashing in his perfectly tanned face.

Tony slid onto the barstool to Rex's left. "Got your message. Bruckheimer's bummed. He's going with Scarlet Johansson. Can you imagine? It's like, wham! Out of the blue, Sheela just craters. It's not like her." He turned, waving to the bartender. "Hey! Got a Remy XO?"

"Yes, sir," the man called, turning to reach for a high bottle.

Rex spread his fingers wide, seeing the contrast between his skin and the bar wood. "She's falling apart. It's a lot of things, I guess. A big one in particular."

"Anything I can do?" Tony was watching him, wide-eyed as if expecting some truth to come tumbling out like wisdom from the Buddha.

"Can you walk up behind Lymon fucking Bridges, slit his throat, and dump his guts on the ground in a pile?"

"Lymon, huh? What's he got your rice steamed over?"

"I think he's porking Sheela on the side."

"No shit?" Tony paused, thinking about it. "So? Why should we care who greases Sheela's snatch?"

"He's playing out of bounds. He's the hired help, for God's sake!"

"Uh-huh," Tony agreed solicitously as the bartender placed a brandy snifter on a napkin before him.

"My tab," Rex told the man, who nodded and

walked back to the end of the bar. "Hell, it's more than that. It's bad enough that he's screwing her. Worse, he's trying to wrap his damned wings around her. I'm starting to feel like I need Lymon's permission if I want to see my client."

"That's what went sour on the Bruckheimer deal?"

"Yeah. Part of it, at least. I know for a fact he was telling her not to do it." Rex balled a fist. "We just watched the bodyguard tell Sheela to kiss off a twenty-five million-dollar deal."

Tony frowned down at his drink, picked up the snifter, and scented the aroma before he took a swallow. "You're sure about this? About Lymon, I mean? You're sure it's not just the publicity? The thing with her tampon and all the shit that came down after that?"

"Stuff like that happens in this business. The nuts are everywhere. Sheela's been through shit like this before. Maybe not so personal, but, you know, times she and her lovers were splashed on the front pages. She never folded then."

"What's the deal about Christal's disappearance?"

"Sheela's taking it pretty hard. Did you know that Lymon and Sheela saw it happen? They were out flitting around on Lymon's bike. What's he doing running her around town in the middle of the night? And on a motorcycle, for God's sake? His job is to protect her, not get her killed."

Tony straightened. "They *saw* Christal's abduction?"

"Yeah, and that's another thing: What were they doing there? Huh? I mean, what's Lymon doing taking her to one of his employee's hotel rooms?"

"You're sure they saw it?" Tony was watching him with a sudden curiosity.

"Yeah. In fact, they got an ID on one of the muggers. Get a load of this: It was such a fuckup on Lymon's part that a paparazzo followed him and Sheela on their little ride. The guy had an IR camera...got photos. They got a facial shot of an ex-FBI guy. One of Christal's old boyfriends, or some such thing."

Tony pursed his lips, eyes gone unfocused. "No shit?"

"No shit. Look, I wanted to get together and let you know the score. I'm at the end of my rope. Bridges is butting into Sheela's business. We just lost a major film."

"They looking for this guy? The FBI guy?"

"I assume. Tony, are you listening? We've got trouble brewing here. Sheela's at the top of her trajectory. She can't take time off—if she does, she loses leverage. Leverage means money in our pockets, mine and yours. You getting this? So, what does she have on tap? How many options with how many producers?"

Tony frowned, lifted his cognac, and sipped. "For the time being, she can pretty much write her own ticket."

"For how long?"

Tony considered. "To keep her current contract, she's got a couple of months before her value starts to slip. That's depending on what happens with the release of *Jagged Cat*. If they market it right, position it right in the schedule, if they can cover for Manny's breakdown, if the post production and editing work..." He shrugged. "You know the variables. A film's a crap-shoot, Rex. With lots of different people throwing dice.

If any one of them makes a bad cast, they can scuttle it."

"So, you're telling me that Sheela's career rests on this picture's box office?"

"That's the film biz." Tony sniffed, rubbed his nose, and gave Rex a serious look. "I saw some of the dailies. Sheela was brilliant. My impression is that Bernard's got chops as director. Now it's up to the editors, but my gut tells me that Sheela's performance is going to keep the thing afloat."

"But your gut could be wrong."

After a long and pensive silence, Tony asked, "You thinking about bailing, Rex?"

He lifted his scotch, tossing back a full swallow. The amber god warmed his throat with its sweet burn. "If I told Sheela she had to pick between me and Lymon, what would she do?"

"Hell, I don't know." A pause. "Is the guy really that big a problem?"

"Yeah."

"You sure this is all professional?" Tony lifted an eyebrow. "Like...maybe there's some jealousy here? You know, the old bull is walking stiff-legged because a younger bull is mounting the lead cow?"

"Fuck you."

"Okay, so now that we've got that figured out, what do you want me to do?"

"Put pressure on Sheela. Let her know that she's flushing her career. I want her back on track, Tony. She's got another ten years, fifteen at the most before she's a has-been."

Tony smiled, amused. "Yeah, I get it. Not only is she getting fucked under your nose, but your own mortality is chewing at the edges of your well-being. Greed, jealousy, and desperation. You're a sad case, Rex." He paused. "So, what's my incentive to convince her to ditch Lymon?"

"About ten million if we can keep her working for another ten years." As Rex stared into his scotch, he could feel Tony's probing eyes, and asked, "What?"

"Last time I saw Sheela, she looked pretty ragged. I've seen 'em crash before, Rex. They go down in flames and explode when they hit the ground. You can squeeze only so much out of a person. Some take it better than others. As to Sheela, you sure this is the time to press?"

"At twenty million a picture, you tell me."

"What if she has a breakdown? What if she snaps? You know, you can kill a goose by forcing it to lay too many golden eggs."

"There are ways to handle stress."

Tony chuckled. "Yeah, pills, drugs, booze. It's the old Hollywood dance. Wring 'em dry before they burn out." He slapped the bar. "Damn, Rex, you're the only man in this town who's shittier than I am."

"You going to tell her?"

Tony lifted his snifter, clinking the rim on Rex's scotch glass. "To partners."

CHAPTER 47

Christal made a fierce face and ignored her burning muscles as she finished her last reps. She pulled her knees up, gasping after her seventy-five sit-ups.

Falling back, she pulled strands of sweaty hair to one side, rolled over, and began her battery of push-ups. Outside of staring at the whitewashed steel walls, there wasn't much else to do, so she had determined to shape up. And, who knew, it might be her ticket off this ship of fools.

All she needed was an opportunity.

Her shoulders bunched as she pushed herself up, lowered, pushed herself up, and stopped as a hesitant rapping sounded on her door.

She jumped to her feet, clawed her long black hair back out of the way, and said, "Yeah? What's up?"

The lock clicked, and a fit-looking young man glanced uncertainly around before stepping into her cabin. "You alone?" he asked quickly in a voice literally dripping with Australian.

"Nobody here but us mice. Who are you?"

"Brian Everly." He closed the door behind him, leaving it ajar. He stopped short, staring at her as if he'd never seen a sweaty, panting, and disheveled human female before.

She used the moment to take his measure. Tall, square-shouldered, he had longish sandy-blond hair, weathered skin that betrayed faded freckles, and the most fascinating pale-blue eyes. A sheepish smile teased the lips of a decidedly masculine mouth. His red-checked flannel shirt couldn't hide the deep chest that tapered to a thin waist where it was tucked into faded Levis. Buff leather shoes with crepe souls shod his feet.

"God," he whispered. "You're..."

"Yes?" She wiped at the perspiration that trickled down the fine hairs at her temple.

He seemed to catch himself on the verge of doing something foolish, and was that a hint of embarrassment that crossed his pale eyes? "Sorry, but you look a little, well, flushed."

"You caught me exercising." She arched a brow. "Uh, you got a reason for barging in? Or were you just in the neighborhood checking out the latest kidnap victims?"

He smiled, shifting from foot to foot as if nervous. "Oh, yes, sorry for that." He seemed genuinely contrite. "I'm one of the fellow inmates here, actually." He glanced back at the door. "I'm not supposed to be here. Talking to you, I mean."

"Really?" She crossed her arms, feeling the heat from her exertion through her damp clothing. Having nothing but the tiny sink to wash it in, she was suddenly aware of a warm odor rising from the fabric.

"Yes, you see, I've been working on your DNA. That's how I found out you were aboard. Um, your name is Christal, right?"

"Yeah. Christal Anaya."

"Beautiful name." He seemed to mean it.

"Thank you," she said dryly, tilting her head in a questioning manner.

He took a step forward, hands spread in supplication. "Look, I just need information. You came from the United States, right?"

"Uh-huh."

"Did you hear anything about a woman, Nancy Hartlee? She would have swam ashore off New York about a week and a half ago."

Christal stared at him. The name rang a bell, but where had she...Sid. On the phone. "Nancy Hartlee? A young woman? Geneticist?"

He nodded, hope in his eyes.

"She drowned."

She watched the hope in his eyes crumble to despair. He looked away, shoulders dropping. "Damn."

"She was a friend of yours?"

He nodded faintly. "What...what did you hear?"

"A friend of mine, an FBI agent, went to New York. He's working on missing geneticists. She was on his list. When the medical examiner's office in New York alerted the Bureau as to a possible ID, he went up to verify it."

Grief had mixed with hope when Brian looked up. "You're part of the investigation? Is that why you're here? They're looking for the *ZoeGen*?"

"Not that I know of. If they are, my source didn't mention it to me."

His intent stare left her uneasy. "You're in a great deal of danger."

She kept trying to see past his concern. Real? Or faked? "Why should you care? For that matter, who are you? What are you doing here? Why shouldn't I throw you out of here like I should have done with Hank?"

He gave her a fond look. "Good point. I'm a geneticist. Like Nancy was...and the others of us here. Like you, I can't leave. They need my skills, at least for the time being. You, on the other hand, are entirely dispensable. We've got our sample."

"Then, why am I here?"

"They're waiting for the Sheik. As I understand it, he wants to see you."

She felt a cold flush down deep in her guts. "Does he?"

She hesitated, seeing the worry in his eyes. "You can tell me, Brian. I gave up on fairy tales a long time ago. What's the rest? I'm supposed to take my place in his seraglio? Is that it? A little rape before they throw me to the sharks like your friend Nancy?"

"Oh, no. Not like that. First off, Nancy dove overboard on her own. She was a brilliant swimmer, right? In high school. She thought she might make it to shore, tell the authorities what was going on out here. Perhaps save us all."

"And the Sheik?"

Brian averted his eyes. "You're not a virgin, are you?"

Christal glared. "What kind of question is that?"

"If you're not a virgin, he's not interested."

She just stared at him, hands clenched at her sides. Fear pumped adrenal unease through every vein.

Brian added, "It's something to do with his cultural upbringing, I believe. He won't take anything but a virgin to his bed. Before he'll have intercourse, she must be pure. His alone." He made a dismissive gesture. "The stories are that he can't stand the idea of lying where another man has...well, you know."

"Then, what does he want with me? I haven't been a virgin since I was sixteen."

"He wants to see exactly what you look like. I mean, how you will look when you finally go to his bed."

"Whoa!" She raised her hands. "You lost me there."

Brian wearily rubbed the back of his neck. "Look, Christal, you're going to be hearing a lot of shocking things, but the fact is, the Sheik has no interested in you now, but in how your duplicate will look when she comes to his bed in another fifteen years or so."

He managed to look everywhere in the small cabin except into her eyes.

Her voice cracked as she asked, "You seem like a decent guy. How can you be part of this?"

He swallowed hard and stepped to the porthole, where he looked out at the rolling ocean. "In the beginning, we were just afraid. We looked at our work as a way to buy time, to wait for an opportunity to escape. Back then we didn't understand the amount of influence that Genesis Athena could wield. We always believed that the world would catch on. That the Royal Marines would land on the deck, and we'd be turned loose to expose this whole asinine mess. Time passes; things change."

"Your friend McEwan doesn't seem to share your sentiments."

In his profile, she could see disgust. "Yes, well, Gregor would have been a shit no matter where he worked or who he worked for. Most of us, the Westerners, have been replaced over the years with the Sheik's people. They came, studied the procedures, and have taken over the lab." A grim smile played. "Smart lad, Gregor. He's cut his security risk down to just me."

"Smart? He seems to be one of them."

"He is. He went right over to them when we figured out the potentials."

"Why?"

"For a share of the profits. Do you realize the potential this industry has? Genesis Athena controls the modern science of genetics. We can reproduce any organism that has ever lived if the DNA's intact; cure most of the genetic diseases. Technology developed here has been licensed to labs around the world. We're talking in terms of tens of billions of dollars from that alone. Not to mention people who have lost children and want them back, or those who have lost a spouse. People will pay incredible sums for a second chance. They'll pawn their souls to cure a dying loved one."

"And the celebrity DNA? Gregor mentioned Princess Diana."

"That's what we call the luxury market. People like our dear Sheik. By the time he's done, his collection of the world's most beautiful women will be unmatched."

"But they have to grow up first, right?"

Brian shrugged. "The Sheik is a very rich and powerful man who also happens to be young. He's smarter than so many of his peers in the Arab world. Most Arab leaders want to make life the way it was in the glory days of the twentieth century and they're doomed to failure. With fuel cell technology, petroleum will eventually fade. The Gulf States that have lived off oil profits will have nothing to offer. The Sheik, however, wants to create the future. He expects to be one of the most powerful men in the world. If you ask me, it's as if he's challenging the Prophet himself."

"These are *human beings* we're talking about. Not cattle."

"Is there any greater power, Christal, than the ability to control people? We're talking the ability to create, modify, utilize, and dispose of them. To own them, body and soul. That is the ultimate power, matched with unlimited money. The Sheik holds the future of humanity in his hands."

Christal sank onto her bunk, trying to comprehend the immensity of Genesis Athena. Finally, she asked, "How do they keep you? I mean, can't you jump overboard when the ship docks?"

"Docks where?" he asked. *"ZoeGen* puts in at select ports: Aden, Doha, Karachi, Bandar-e-Abbas, Tripoli. These places raise any flags? You'd be surprised how tight security can be."

"Doesn't anything ever break? Don't they need parts? Something?"

"The machine shop is downstairs and aft. Out of bounds for us. Just like the Royal Australian Navy, we're supplied at sea by a tender. Food, water, fuel-—it's all piped aboard, right?"

He gestured around. "You have no idea what a

perfect prison a ship can make. You're currently in the old crew section. It's completely sealed from the rest of the ship. There's one access in and out, and it's locked and guarded twenty-four hours a day. The other hatches are welded. The ventilation system is barred with titanium grating, but you'll trigger the pressure sensors under the ductwork before you get that far."

"What about the cafeteria staff? How do they get in and out?"

He crossed his arms as he turned her way. "They're implanted with small subcutaneous chips. They don't make it past the controlled entry unless they provide a fingerprint, retinal scan, and the chip reads correctly." The corners of his lips curled. "We thought about taking a sample and cloning one to get the fingerprint and retina, but the chip would still elude us."

"I'm surprised you're not all nuts."

"Oh, they take pretty good care of us. We get the latest movies, supervised access to the Internet, time off to read or study. The latter is encouraged, by the way. And we teach."

"Teach?"

"Members of the Sheik's extended family, mostly. Them, and some other young people from around the Persian Gulf who are likely prospects."

"What do you mean, likely prospects?"

"As I said, the Sheik knows that petroleum is only a temporary means of wealth. The world will find alternative sources of energy. When it does, the elite families in the Gulf will collapse like a house of cards. The Sheik's family and friends will be right there when it happens, but instead of oil, their monopoly will be molecular biology. If you want a cure for cancer, you'll be coming to the Sheik."

"This is a nightmare."

"Wasn't there a song? 'Welcome to my Nightmare'?"

CHAPTER 48

At the sound of his doorbell, Lymon padded down the hallway, crossed his living room, and looked through the small window in his front door. Movement had already activated his porch light; he could see Sheela standing there, expression pinched, her hair shining like a flame in the light.

"Sheela?" Lymon asked as he opened the door. "What's wrong? What are you doing here?"

She stepped in, glanced around, and walked into his arms after he closed the door. "I needed to see you."

He stood, holding her close, feeling her cool body against his. "You could have called. I would have—"

"No. I wanted out, Lymon. The dreams...god, nightmares, I mean." She shook her head where it was buried against his shoulder.

He had just tightened his grip when Sid stepped around the corner, caught a glimpse, and spun on his heel to beat a quick retreat.

Lymon called, "It's all right, Sid. You don't have to go."

When Sheela glanced up, startled, he could see that an unwanted third person was the last thing she'd counted on.

Sid hesitated, and Sheela turned, waving, "Go away, Sid. Lymon is attempting to protect himself."

"Huh?" Sid was poised on one foot.

"From me," Sheela added, stepping away, her voice dropping. "He's doing his damnedest to maintain his professional distance, and it's driving me berserk!"

Sid was canny enough that he promptly fled back down the hallway for the guest bedroom. Sheela met Lymon's eyes, a glittering desperation there. "We've got to talk."

"What happened?"

She took another step and turned. "Remember *Joy's Girl?* I was told after I played Jennifer Weaver that men would be masturbating to that scene. Did I ever tell you about that? About how the image of them plays over and over in my mind? About how creepy it is?"

He sighed, nodded, and walked over, placing an arm over her shoulder. "Yeah, I know. Can I get you a drink? Scotch? Orange juice? Coffee?"

"No, thanks. I was trying to sleep. But the images, Lymon. You wouldn't believe what my mind can create when it's half turned off, free to conjure."

He glanced across at the clock. "It's three in the morning. That's when the world looks the bleakest."

She placed her hands on his chest as she looked into his eyes. "I could live with the knowledge that men watched that film and masturbated. I mean, I know enough about biology to understand about males being visually stimulated. I sell my sexual image for a lot of money. I play sexual roles. It's part of the bargain, part of what I'm paid for."

"So what did your imagination come up with that was different this time?"

She searched his face, as if willing him to understand. "Genesis Athena took my DNA to make little clones of me. I was thinking about why, Lymon. I was conjuring all of the ramifications. Why would someone want a little copy of me? Or of Nicole Kidman, or Sandra Bullock? What would they *do* with them?"

"Sheela—"

She took an agonized breath. "They're breeding copies of *me,* Lymon. Selling them to people like Krissy. She said she was going to have my baby, right? How could she not have known about Genesis Athena? It was right there, tied to my website."

"We'll deal with it, I promise."

Sheela made an anxious step, her fingers locked in her hair. "I keep imagining what Krissy will do to that little girl. It's like Pandora's box when you start to think about it. People who want my clone...god, that's a terrible word. This is a child. This is me. My hand, my body, my brain, and heart." She placed a hand to her breast. "A breathing, feeling being. A being who's what? Going to be made into a little sexual experiment? Is Krissy going to cut that little baby into pieces to show her how much she loves her?"

"Sheela, you don't know—"

"*Bullshit!* Think about it, Lymon. Do normal people go out to buy a Sheela Marks clone? No, they want their *own* babies. They want a product of their DNA and their spouse's. A child conceived in love as part of a relationship!"

"Sheela, settle down." He disentangled her hand from her hair and held it. "We'll deal with it."

In a small voice, she asked, "How, Lymon? We don't even know where they are. What if we can't stop it? What if I have to live the rest of my life knowing that because of what I did on screen, some pervert is tormenting an innocent little girl? Can you imagine?"

"Yeah, I know what happens to pretty little girls when psychosexually ill people get a hold of them."

"They won't understand that I am a product of my own history. They won't understand all the things that made me who I am. The mess I got into in Saskatoon. Finding my father's body..."

Tears began to trickle down her perfect face. "What's a clone, Lymon? Is it like an identical twin, just one that's delayed for a while? Or is it different? Does the soul make an imprint on a person's DNA? Some essence that's passed down?"

"I don't know."

"Neither do I, and it's driving me insane."

CHAPTER 49

An unfamiliar pillow pressed against her cheek as Sheela blinked awake in confusion. Horrifying images spun away as the last of her irrational dreams faded into shreds. In that last instant, she had seen her father as she had that last day —seen him hanging in midair as if frozen in an aerial dance. His head cocked at an unnatural angle, his tongue protruding as if to blow a raspberry at the entire world, his eyes bugged out but the pupils gray. He hung there, a broken puppet tied to the barn beam with a red length of plastic baling twine.

I let you down, Daddy. I'm so sorry.

She turned, pulling her legs up into her belly, and looked around in relief. Lymon's bedroom was Spartan, male, and neat. She could see his clothes in the open closet, and turning her head, could draw in his rich scent from the bedding.

She blinked hard, struggling to shove the memory of that long-ago day in the barn back into the recesses of her mind.

Lymon. Concentrate on Lymon.

He had led her here, holding her in a spooned posi-tion as she cried. Now, in the morning light, she lay like a gutted fish, limp, with nothing left inside the arched cathedral of her ribs.

Did she have any tears left? Or had she cried enough for all of them? How many? One? Ten? A hundred? Or would there eventually be thousands of little Sheelas being implanted in strange women?

Are they mirrors?

Would they see reflections of her life? Would they know that terrible day when she had walked into the barn to find her father's body?

How much of me is really in my genes?

She had no idea. For the first time, she wasn't even sure what it was to be alive. The notion of personhood had been irrevocably changed, mutated, and taken into another dimension.

She pushed the sheet back and looked down at her body. She was wearing the blouse she'd donned in such a rush last night and the white cotton pants she'd bought at Jones New York. She stood, walked to the full-length mirror on the closet door, and inspected herself.

"What do they see?" She traced her fingers up her thighs, around the curve of her hips. She followed the narrowing of her waist and raised her hands to support her breasts. Her nipples raised the thin fabric of her shirt.

Why is a body like this worth anything?

She tried to comprehend the notion that people would pay to reproduce this flesh—her flesh. They would sacrifice so much to grow it inside their own bodies. Releasing her breasts, she ran her slim fingers along her face, following the indentation of her cheeks, along the bony sides of her eyes, and pulled back her thick mass of red-blond hair. She leaned close, trying to see into the depths of her blue eyes, to scry what really lurked there in the blackness of the pupils, and found nothing. Only the familiarity she'd seen in mirrors ever since she could remember.

What do I do next? Where do I go from here?

In defeat, she turned, staring at Lymon's bed, remembering his body against hers. That was twice now that she'd had him in a bed. The first time, she'd been too ridden with fatigue. This time, it had been the horror of her nightmare that had come between them.

"What's it going to take, Lymon?" She walked into his adjoining bathroom. She squatted and relieved herself in his toilet. At the sink, she washed her face, dried on his towel, and used his comb to make order of her ratty hair.

She did a final check in the mirror, wished for a toothbrush, but declined the use of his. Some things just remained inviolately personal.

Her shoes waited at the side of his bed where she'd left them. Steeling herself, she walked out into the hallway. Male voices could be heard from the kitchen.

As she approached the arch that separated the kitchen from dining room, she hesitated. Yes, that was Rex's faulty alto. He was saying, "...I don't care. It's got to stop."

Sheela stepped through the arch and asked, "What does, Rex?"

Both men looked up: Rex with distaste, Lymon with

worry. Sid was apparently—and probably most wisely —elsewhere.

She passed the stove and counters to where Lymon and Rex sat across from each other at a small table, two cups of coffee between them. Lymon's was half-empty, Rex's still full.

"You and Lymon." Rex gestured with his hands. "I know it's your life, Sheela, but it's going to get out."

"What is?" She crossed her arms, leaning back against the counter.

"I repeat: You and Lymon."

"What about us."

"Do I have to spell it out? You're an adult, sure. You ought to be able to have sex with anyone you want."

The explosion came from deep in her wounded soul. In a leap, she was on him, bending over him, finger jabbing at his face. "We're *not* having sex, Rex! I wish to God we were, *but we're not!* You got that?"

Rex swallowed hard, trying to back away. "Then... what are you doing here?"

From the corner of her eye, she caught the amused expression poorly hidden on Lymon's face but centered her hot gaze on Rex's half-panicked visage. "I'm here because I needed to talk to someone I could trust."

She could see the incomprehension in his eyes, and that, more than anything, defused her. "You just don't get it, do you?"

"Get what?" he almost squeaked.

She took a deep breath and backed away, met Lymon's neutral eyes, and shook her head. Turning, she walked to the cabinets and started rummaging from door to door.

"What are you looking for?" Lymon asked.

"Coffee cups."

"Third from the left."

She found a cup, walked over to Lymon's Capresso machine, and pushed the green button until all the lights were flashing. As the machine ground, hissed, and filled her cup, she let herself fume.

When she turned back, Rex had a slightly chastened look on his face. Sheela stalked across, pulled out a third chair, and seated herself. She gave Rex a frosty glance. "What if Lymon and I decide to take our relationship to the next level?"

Rex looked uneasily back and forth. "Sheela, I don't want to—"

"Just answer the question. What? You'd quit? Out of what? Jealousy? Is that what we're talking about here? Or would it be insecurity?" She slapped the table. "Damn! Don't tell me you're in love with me! Is that it? You couldn't stand to think of Lymon and me together?"

Rex made a wounded face. "No."

"Then, what?"

He sighed, lifted his coffee, and sipped. Buying time, no doubt. "Look, you do whatever you want with whomever you want, all right. I'll keep my nose out of it"

"Then what's your problem?"

"Are you going back to work?" Rex said it so hopefully.

Sheela chuckled dryly. "Oh, god, is that it? You're seeing your cash cow stumble?"

"Look, we've had this conversation."

"I'll call Felix. Have him nullify our contract. You're free, Rex. No penalties. I won't make a fuss."

Rex stopped short, sputtered, and seemed to have suddenly discovered an upset in his stomach. "Wait a minute, Sheela, I'm not saying I want out."

"Then why are you here, and why are we having this conversation?"

Rex closed his eyes, reopened them to glance uneasily at Lymon, and asked, "Do we have to talk about this now?"

Sheela smacked her lips and said, "Yep."

Lymon was halfway to his feet. "I could—"

"You're staying." She reached out, grasping him by the wrist.

Lymon looked slightly uncomfortable as he reseated himself. She decided that she liked that. "You are the two most important men in my life right now. Here's the word: I'm not doing another movie for a while. I need some time for myself. I have things I need to see to. You are either with me or against me. Lymon, I already know is with me. Where are you, Rex?"

She knew the look she was giving him; she'd used it with great effect on screen. Apparently it worked just as well in person. Rex began to squirm.

"With you."

"Good. You're sure?"

"Yes."

"Because, Rex, if you're not, I'm happy to make that call to Felix."

He nodded, upset but apparently on board. "It's not necessary."

She released Lymon's arm and took a sip of coffee. "Good. I want you to call Dot and make sure that my schedule is cleared for the next month."

"Cleared for—" Rex began hotly, then caught himself. "Okay, Sheela. What about after that?"

She smiled wearily. "Then I'll do whatever picture you and Tony can come up with." That, or, given what she had in mind, who knew, she might be anything. Even dead.

But then, risks had to be taken when a woman was dedicated to slaying a monster.

And Genesis Athena was the biggest monster of them all.

A LOOK AT BOOK THREE:
ATHENA'S WRATH

With *Athena's Wrath, New York Times* **bestselling author W. Michael Gear brings the multilayered and provocative Athena Trilogy to an unsettling and stunning conclusion.**

Determined to rescue Christal Anaya, Sheela Marks plays the role of a lifetime as she adopts her Oscar-nominated character of "Jennifer Weaver" in order to infiltrate the shadowy organization known as Genesis Athena. When she's ferried to the mysterious *ZoeGen*—a converted cruise ship hovering off the Eastern seaboard—her forbidden love, bodyguard Lymon Bridges, barely manages to catch up.

Meanwhile, locked away in her cabin aboard *ZoeGen*, Christal discovers the ship has been converted into a sinister genetics laboratory and hospital. She must risk everything in a desperate bid to escape. If she fails, the only thing waiting for her is a watery grave.

In the end, Sheela must gamble her life and soul. But win, lose, or draw, the price will be more than she can conceive. Genesis Athena has pulled its dark and perverse web around her and the man she loves—and there is no hope of escape.

Compelling and insidiously realistic, Athena's Wrath is at once unsettling, addictive...and terrifyingly predictive.

AVAILABLE MARCH 2024

Acknowledgments

We hope you have enjoyed *Genesis Athena,* part two of the Athena Trilogy.

Sheela, Christal, and Lymon's story continues in *Athena's Wrath*, part three of the Athena Trilogy!

Sheela Marks hatches a bold plan to rescue Christal and bring Genesis Athena to its knees. To do so, she will have to enter Abdulla's lair. And in the end, victory might very well come at the cost of both her body and soul. But what if the ultimate price is too much to pay?

About the Author

W. Michael Gear is a *New York Times, USA Today,* and international bestselling author of sixty novels. With close to eighteen million copies of his books in print worldwide, his work has been translated into twenty-nine languages.

Gear has been inducted into the Western Writers Hall of Fame and the Colorado Authors' Hall of Fame—as well as won the Owen Wister Award, the Golden Spur Award, and the International Book Award for both Science Fiction and Action Suspense Fiction. He is also the recipient of the Frank Waters Award for lifetime contributions to Western writing.

Gear's work, inspired by anthropology and archaeology, is multilayered and has been called compelling, insidiously realistic, and masterful. Currently, he lives in northwestern Wyoming with his award-winning wife and co-author, Kathleen O'Neal Gear, and a charming sheltie named, Jake.

Made in United States
Troutdale, OR
02/20/2024

17807333R00181